THE LOST HIGHLANDER

*Kit Scarlett Mysteries
Book Four*

Adele Jordan

Also in the Kit Scarlett Series
The Gentlewoman Spy
The Royal Assassin
A Spy at Hampton Court
The Traitor Queen

THE LOST HIGHLANDER

Published by Sapere Books.

24 Trafalgar Road, Ilkley, LS29 8HH

saperebooks.com

Copyright © Adele Jordan, 2023

Adele Jordan has asserted her right to be identified as the author of this work.
All rights reserved.

No part of this publication may be reproduced, stored in any retrieval system, or transmitted, in any form, or by any means, electronic, mechanical, photocopying, recording, or otherwise, without the prior written permission of the publishers.
This book is a work of fiction. Names, characters, businesses, organisations, places and events, other than those clearly in the public domain, are either the product of the author's imagination, or are used fictitiously.
Any resemblances to actual persons, living or dead, events or locales are purely coincidental.

ISBN: 978-1-80055-909-7

CHAPTER 1

Greenwich, 1586

"Where is she?"

"There! Ahead. Are you blind, lad? What lady could stand out more in this crowd than the one held up by eight men in a chair clothed with gold curtains?"

Kit Scarlett ignored all the hollers and cries around her, of each man and woman looking past other heads in an effort to glimpse the queen. Her eyes were on the crowd, not the monarch. Necks craned, and eyes darted over cloth hats and pheasant feathers that had been thrust into cotton rims, as people strained to see but a shimmer of the queen's cream gown. Ladies tilted back coifs from their temples, turning their chins upward and elbowing competing ladies out of their way, ignoring the shrieks of pain that rang forth like chickens that had been stepped on.

"She's here! There. Oh, Gloriana!" Some of the cheers were so loud that Kit winced. She tipped back her own cloth hat and pushed the short locks away from her eyes, threading them behind her ears as she looked across the crowd, searching for anything strange. The cobblestones beneath her feet were sharp, poking into the arches of her feet. They were still damp, even though the rain had stopped before sunrise, for the winter air was too cold to dry anything.

The press of bodies made it difficult for Kit to see much in the crowd. One face looked much like another, with eager eyes, like that of a hawk on the hunt. Hands grasped frantically, each one pushing past another's shoulders for a better view.

"This is madness," Kit muttered to herself as she walked along the side of the crowd. As an intelligencer and protector of the queen, she was one of the few allowed to walk down the main body of the road. She and the other guards had been organised by Sir Francis Walsingham — the royal spymaster and Kit's employer.

Most people were tucked away, standing under the eaves of buildings or along the bank beside the River Thames. Glancing over her shoulder, Kit saw that the queen was held aloft in her palanquin by many men, each one dressed more elaborately than the last, with deep crimson velvet cloaks. The queen bestowed a gentle smile on the crowd, but her beady eyes never lingered long before they moved on.

Kit turned forward, her eyes flitting between the tall timber buildings on one side and the river on the other. By the water, she sought out the guards that had been arranged to watch the docks. Yet there was only the riverbank staring back at her.

Kit's feet faltered as she observed the empty space in the crowd where a guard should have been. Beside her, the crowd called out for the queen's attention.

"She looked at me. She did! She looked at me."

"Oh, for one touch of that gown. Do you think it's true what they say? Can her touch heal?"

The people continued to gush, as if God himself was walking amongst them. Kit ignored it all and crossed the road, slipping between the workmen that were shovelling horse manure out of the cobblestoned road ahead of the parade. As she reached the other side, twisting her head back and forth on the riverbank, she reached for her weapons belt. She looped her thumbs through the thin brown leather, knowing that something was amiss.

"He's gone," she murmured. She jerked back and forth, checking the markers she had been told to look for by Walsingham.

"Between the old oak tree on the riverbank, the one with bark like bound ropes, and the docks, a guard will be standing there," he'd told her.

There were no guards. There was only empty earth and drabs from the crowd who were trying to get closer to the queen. There wasn't even a man carrying a rapier, or a pistol in his belt. Many men carried staffs, their permitted weapon, but no trained guard or soldier was amongst them.

"God's blood." Kit moved off from the riverbank, turning her attention to the cobblestone road.

The parade was growing. Queen Elizabeth was not only flanked by the multitude of gentlemen who carried her, but also by several ladies, each one draped in a fine gown and with such an abundance of jewellery that they glittered in the winter sun. Kit stepped amongst the ladies, trying to reach the centre of the parade. Scents of orange flowers and cinnamon shot into her nose, making it tingle.

"Walsingham? Walsingham!" Kit called out as she moved closer to the back of the palanquin chair that carried the queen. She struggled to make herself heard over the calls of the people, all desperate to be noticed by the queen.

Walsingham soon appeared, walking at the rear of the parade with other members of the privy council. Lord Burghley was on his other side, holding a cane so thin and feeble-looking that it seemed a miracle it kept the man straight at all. The inlaid stick and the silver edging suggested it was more a statement of fashion rather than utility.

"Walsingham!" Kit called. She moved closer, momentarily masked as one of the ladies dancing past her wrapped a gossamer-thin scarf around her face. Kit brushed it off, almost knocking the lady over before she reached Walsingham's side.

"Tell your pet to be quiet," Lord Burghley snapped as she reached their side. "We have no time for tattlers today."

Kit slowed her pace to walk alongside Walsingham. The two ageing men ambled beside each other, their black clothes stark against the sea of effusive colours dancing around them, like a rainbow that had dropped to earth.

"Tattler?" Kit repeated, her eyes shooting straight to Walsingham.

He shook his head, his gaunt face shaking off the insult as his eyes widened, warning her against risking the wrath of a man like Lord Burghley.

"Walsingham, your guard has gone," she said.

This not only captured Walsingham's attention, but Lord Burghley's too. His cane nearly slipped from under him, until the silver tip jammed between two cobbles. Walsingham turned his pointed chin in Kit's direction, his eyes darkening. His lips quivered.

"I saw to the guards myself this morning. Each soldier was in his place, Kit."

"Well, one is missing now." She lifted a hand from her weapons belt and pointed to the riverbank. The sleeve of her jerkin billowed in the wind, the same way the ladies' skirts and farthingales were dragged forward around her.

"Pah! That's a reason for suspicion, is it?" Lord Burghley laughed and turned his attention forward, his eyes on the queen alone. "Guards are known to steal a drink or three, especially at times of celebration. Do not take a wager against me, tattler. He'll be caught drinking down on the dockyard."

Kit swallowed, holding back her retort. Once more, her eyes landed on Walsingham, who shook his head in warning.

"See if you can find him, Kit," Walsingham said in a quiet voice. "Come back to me when you do."

Kit walked off. The parade had grown thicker. The boundary between the parading ladies and gentlemen of the queen's court was almost indistinguishable from the line of her countrymen and women that bordered the street. Each lady that danced caused a young boy or girl to hurry forward, wanting to be a part of the scene. Pipers led the way, followed by lute players, some wearing pointed shoes, others wearing heeled boots, clicking as loudly on the cobbles as their string instruments were plucked.

It was a cacophony of sound, a carnival of excitement. Kit pushed past them all, angered by the happiness. More than once her elbow was caught by a smiling lady, who would swing her round, encouraging her to join the dance. When one larger lady seized her, it was not so easy to escape. Kit's hands were captured and she was spun round in a circle, forced to listen to the lady's cackle.

"Release me!" Kit demanded, but her words were not heard. Looking away from the lady, someone in the crowd caught her eye. It was a tall man, with a figure so familiar to Kit that she dropped the lady's hand. "It cannot be."

"Ah!" The lady nearly fell over from the momentum of spinning, so that Kit had to reach out and grab her under the arms.

"Oomph!" The sheer weight of the lady along with the gown, corset and farthingale nearly dragged Kit over. She winced as she heaved the lady to her feet, who then danced off. Judging by the stench of liquor that followed her, there was a good reason for her disorientation.

Kit looked to the figure in the crowd, standing completely still. For a second, she could have sworn she saw a familiar cloak and dark hair, as well as the outline of a long nose and bearded jaw that she had not seen for a year.

Yet the man was no longer there. Gossamer and silk scarfs whipped past Kit's face, ladies shrieked like parakeets in her ears, and paupers swayed back and forth to the music in their rags.

"I'm seeing things," Kit muttered, walking away from the parade. She stopped speaking as she returned to her place on the riverbank, searching for any sign of the missing guards.

The crowd around her waved handkerchiefs — specially dyed for the occasion — hoping to catch the queen's attention. Kit ducked round their flapping hands, almost being clonked on the head more than once, as she hastened toward the dock that stretched out into the Thames.

It was impossible to hear the sloshing of the river because of the music, though she could see the green water bubbling and lapping around the few small boats that were tied up with rope. She searched every boat, looking for a guard or a spent bottle of sack that could explain the guard's absence.

A voice met Kit's ears on the wind. "You all right there, laddie?"

She turned to see there was an older gentleman at the edge of the dock, reaching down to where a young man was prostrate on the wood. Kit darted to his side, bending to see that the man was awake, though bleary-eyed, thanks to a strike across his brow, from which blood beaded.

"What happened to him?" Kit asked the older man beside her.

"I don't know. Found him here, like this. Poor lad can't string two words together."

Kit reached inside her jerkin to pull out a cloth, then pressed it to the young man's head, trying to stem the bleeding. "Can you see straight, boy?" she asked, aware that the lad was much younger than her, barely an adult at all.

He stirred at her words. "Just about."

She sighed with relief when the boy spoke. His eyelids fluttered closed for a second, then opened again.

"Man ... struck." The boy gestured to his temple. "Then he…" An errant hand waved down at his belt. Kit grimaced when she realised what the boy was trying to tell her. Here was the guard she had been searching for, only his weapons had been stolen.

"I understand." She took the boy's hand and pressed it over the cloth on his head. "Your wound is a small one, but you'll be stunned. Hold this until the bleeding stops." She turned to the man beside her. "Would you watch over him?"

"Yes, lad, I mean ... lass." His eyes widened when he saw her face.

Kit offered him a small smile before she stood and crossed the dock, heading back to the riverbank. At the edge of the crowd, that strange figure emerged again, the one who had caught her interest before.

"It's not him," Kit murmured, though there was something familiar about the man. She realised soon enough what that was. The height was similar to that of the person she was thinking of, as were the features, but the hair was not dark enough. "It is not Iomhar." Kit hoped that if she uttered the words aloud, she would be persuaded. Her spy partner and friend, Iomhar Blackwood, had left to undertake a mission the year before. Much to Kit's dismay, she hadn't heard from him for a while, and Walsingham refused to reveal where he had been sent. The stranger in the crowd looked more like Iomhar's brother, Niall. As she tried to track him, he disappeared into the parade, his figure devoured by the ladies' farthingale skirts and waving scarfs.

Brushing off the sighting, Kit returned to the matter at hand. She searched the riverbank, where the guard should have stood. Turning her head back and forth, she saw only excited faces, beards that had been trimmed and clean linens that had been brought out for the majestic event. Everyone was standing as close to the road as they could, except one.

On the edge of her vision, dancing like a fly, someone's dark cloak whipped around the oak tree that watched over the river dock. Kit shifted her focus to the tree. As Walsingham had described, the trunk was gnarled and knotted like a rope. The branches were bare at this time of year, and the twigs were rimmed with frost. Between these branches was an arrowhead, the iron bolt barely discernable against the branches.

Kit reached for her weapons belt, gripping the hilt of her dagger. She then crept around the tree, not needing to move quietly thanks to the raucous crowd.

Slowly, a man came into view. He was hiding his body against the tree trunk and resting a crossbow on a branch. With one hand, he was slowly twitching back the string, preparing the bolt for its release. The crossbow clicked in his hands, and he smiled, his lips curling back from his teeth like a dog's snarl.

Kit held her breath the closer she moved, not wanting to alert him to the fact she was there. She could see his belt was stuffed with weapons, betraying that he was the one who had taken the injured guard's store. A club that hung loose from his belt glistened with blood, as one bead dripped onto the roots of the oak tree.

Kit's eyes flicked from the man to the crossbow. The man shifted the bolt and closed one eye, resting his chin on the tiller so that the skin of his jaw wrinkled as he took aim. Kit stepped behind him, looking for his target.

Soon, the palanquin moved into view, and Queen Elizabeth appeared.

CHAPTER 2

"Step back from the crossbow." Kit raised the dagger in her hand and pointed the blade at the back of the man's neck. His head froze. When the man didn't move, Kit pressed the dagger against his skin. "I said, step back," she ordered, this time pausing for good measure.

Slowly, the man began to move. His boots inched back on the oak roots, and the crossbow hung loose in his arms. Kit stepped to the side, moving around him and reaching for the crossbow. When his eyes found hers, she could see the surprise in his face. His dark blue gaze narrowed and his lips curled, as if he were tempted to laugh.

"Now, now, girlie, you wouldn't want to get yourself into trouble, would you?" He tightened his hold on the crossbow, clearly intending to take aim again.

"I'm used to it by now," she said quickly. Drawing back the dagger, she tilted it and struck the man in the back of his head with the hilt. It was enough to stun him. Buckling forward, he yelped, releasing the crossbow so that both of his hands could clutch the base of his skull, cradling his injury and leaving the crossbow on a branch.

Kit shoved him away. As he stumbled on the roots, in danger of tipping over, she stepped up to the branches and grabbed the crossbow, flicking the string so that it was made safe in its notch on the tree.

The sound of a blade rubbing against leather made her release the crossbow and turn round. The stranger was standing straight once again, though his smile was gone. In its place was a glower that roved over Kit.

With one lunge, he lifted a sword. Wider in girth than a rapier, it held more weight and danger. Kit dodged the first blow then brought down the dagger over his outstretched arm, cutting his exposed knuckles.

"Argh!" His cry alerted some of the crowd. Heads twisted their way, and soon there were jeers and gestures in their direction.

"Fight! There's a fight!"

"Lads arguing over liquor, no doubt."

Kit watched as the man shook his injured knuckles and tossed the sword to his left hand, evidently skilled at using either arm. This time when he lunged forward, Kit's jump away was not so effective. One of her boots slipped between two roots of the oak tree, holding her in place. She snatched up her second dagger and crossed the two of them together, creating a barricade in front of her face. They scarcely held his sword back, halting it from coming down upon her head.

She shoved him away with her full strength. He stumbled, the earth beneath them uneven and treacherous. One of his feet became stuck between two roots as Kit released her own. With him distracted, she turned to the crossbow and snatched it up, not wanting to give him the chance to use it on the queen.

"You polled knave!" the man spat in her direction. When he advanced toward her this time, she lifted the crossbow, pulled back the string, and aimed it straight at his chest. Yet, she didn't release the bolt. The threat was enough.

The man fell still, with his sword raised in the air. His eyes shot down to the crossbow in her hands, and his arm shook with the effort of holding the heavy blade aloft.

"Take another step and…" Kit had no need to finish the sentence, for the man backed up. She was about to lower the crossbow when he took off.

"Stop him!" someone from the crowd shouted, having watched the scene unfold.

The man pushed people away, tipping over ladies so that they fell in bundles of skirts, and sending gentlemen on top of them so that they cried out.

Kit lowered the crossbow and ran after the assassin. Following the path that he had already carved through the crowd, she stayed on his heels. They whipped past paupers dressed in rags and smocks, then pushed past the finer ladies that twirled their farthingales.

When the man reached the parade, Kit ran faster, sensing the danger. The dancing ladies shrieked and squealed, running back with hands held to faces, reaching for their friends beside them.

"He has a sword!" one lady cried, as the man ran, brandishing his weapon.

Kit could see where he was heading. His head was turned in one direction, toward the queen in her lofted chair and the gentlemen that surrounded her.

As the crowd grew more panicked, more and more people bumped together, sending others flying. Soon, Kit was separated from the man, caught behind ladies that had fallen. Tripping on their farthingales, she tumbled over, with her knees scraping against damp cobblestones and her dagger crushed beneath her. The crossbow was only saved from the same fate as she held it up, away from the ground.

"Save the queen!" Cries went up, each one more deafening than the last.

Kit shoved a lady's farthingale off her. The lady that had landed on top of her shrieked and rolled away, displaying more of her legs to others than she would have wished to. Kit moved to her knees, lifting her gaze to see where the man was now.

Some of the gentlemen that surrounded the queen had scarpered, each one preferring to save his own life. Others held their ground, reaching for the rapiers they carried in their belts, though they would do little good against the finer and broader weapon that was meant for battle. The queen was scurrying off the back of her chair, with her ladies-in-waiting reaching up toward her.

The assassin was close, too close, his sword mere inches away from the men that guarded the queen. When he reached for another weapon in his belt, Kit realised how futile those guards could be.

The man had a pistol. It had to have been preloaded, for he held it aloft and took aim, straight at the queen. The hilt glistened in the cold sun, and the barrel barely wavered in the wind. Screams and shouts echoed around the street as people grew sure they were about to see blood.

Kit looked down at the crossbow in her hands and lifted it high, not hesitating as she set her sights on the back of the assassin. At first she aimed for the centre of his back, then she shifted her aim to his shoulder. Her finger closed over the trigger and the bolt shot out of the crossbow.

It whipped through the air, like a leather flog cracking against a stone wall.

The assassin's bellow of pain silenced the crowds. Ladies no longer rolled across the cobbles, bound by their skirts and loose sleeves, and gentlemen froze, eyes peering straight over their billowing ruffs.

Kit lowered the crossbow, breathing heavily as she saw exactly where her bolt had landed. It had struck the assassin in the shoulder perfectly — enough to send him sprawling forward, dropping the pistol and his other weapons. Kit scrambled to her feet and hurried toward the assassin along with other guards.

The man's weapons were collected, and his arms were thrust up behind his back, where his hands were tied with rope. He continued to scream, with tears rolling down his cheeks as blood seeped out of the arrow in his shoulder. Kit gulped and looked away, placing the crossbow into the hands of one of the guards beside her.

"It was his," she said. The guard nodded and added it to the hoard of other weapons being taken off him.

A courtier leading the pageant attempted to take control of the parade, pleading with the crowds to be calm, but his words were almost impossible to hear thanks to the sudden questions and flurry of gossiping. Kit walked past them all, heading toward the chair that had been placed on the ground. The queen sat there, still half in and half out of her palanquin. Her breathing was uneven, her fear palpable, though she attempted to smile and right herself as she looked at the people, trying to play the part of a fearless monarch.

"Miss Scarlett," she said as Kit appeared at her side. "You have a habit of making yourself useful."

"Your Majesty." Kit curtsied as she had been taught to do by Walsingham. One quick glance to her side showed that Walsingham and Lord Burghley were approaching. Walsingham was issuing orders to his guards for the assassin to be taken to the Tower of London, and Lord Burghley's dark eyes rested on Kit, as if in disbelief. "Might I suggest the pageant is at an end for today?" Kit said, wary of Lord Burghley's reaction.

"Who are you to make such a decision?" he spluttered, his cheeks turning purple before he shifted his attention to the queen. "Are you uninjured, Your Majesty?"

"How curious. That was the second question you uttered, Burghley," the queen said with a trace of humour, though the smile didn't last long. Her eyes were flicking over the crowd, evidently wary of more assassins. "I am well. As for Miss Scarlett's advice, I will choose to listen to it."

"But she is —"

"I am what?" Kit asked, standing tall and turning to Lord Burghley. Within seconds, Walsingham was at her side. He took her shoulder, silently instructing her not to say any more to goad the baron.

"Your Majesty, I must second my intelligencer's advice," he said quickly. "If one assassin has hidden in this crowd, then there may be more that have crept past our guards."

"You should do a better job of appointing your guards, Walsingham." The queen waved her hand, indicating that despite her censure she intended to follow the advice.

Kit glanced Walsingham's way, tempted to ask why one of his guards was just a boy, not a man who would be capable of holding himself in a fight.

"Let us leave," the queen commanded to her ladies in waiting beside her. She turned to take the hand of Lady Hunsdon, one of her closest friends. Kit saw her knuckles turn white. "Oh, Miss Scarlett?"

Kit froze, tilting her head higher to show she was listening.

"Come to see me in two days' time at the palace. There is something I must speak to you about."

"Of course, Your Majesty." Kit curtsied, waiting for the queen to depart before she stood straight and looked back to Walsingham, certain that the anger in her face was evident. "What happened here should not have happened."

"I agree." He nodded and took her arm, jerking her far away from Lord Burghley. They stepped into the crowd, where those who had fallen over were being pulled to their feet and others were dispersing. "I must investigate. Did you find the guard?"

"Yes. He is on the dock, with a nasty gash on his head."

"Then I shall see to him myself. Kit, go home. You have done well today." Walsingham stepped away, but it was not enough. Something curdled in Kit's gut, knowing how close they had come to disaster that morning.

"He is just a boy, Walsingham." Her words made Walsingham freeze. He looked back to her, flanked by those that had made merry before and were now wandering off, holding bruised body parts from where they had fallen on the cobbles. "Since when do you send boys into danger?"

"You seem to have a habit of questioning my aptitude for this job at the moment. I wonder where you learned that from?" Walsingham's question made Kit lift her chin higher. Neither of them were prepared to utter her spy partner's name, not after it had been so long since either of them had done so. "You did well, Kit. Go home. I will clean up the mess here."

CHAPTER 3

The winter sun slipped down past the tiled and thatched roofs, casting white and burnt orange streaks across the street. Kit looked between those beams, her eyes darting over the faces of those that wandered to and fro. Each person seemed to have left the queen's pageant with questions.

"Who do you think he was? The man with the gun?" one young lady asked the man beside her as they walked arm in arm. Dressed in a coif, woollen stays and an apron, she was clearly a serving woman. Her companion seemed to be walking rather hastily, glancing over his shoulder, as if afraid that the danger they had witnessed would follow them.

"A madman? A supporter of the Scottish whore? Who knows?" The man's tart reply made Kit slow her pace. Her eyes hovered on the couple for a minute, before they hurried off, far ahead of her. "He came rather close to the queen today, though, did he not?"

"Too near indeed," the lady agreed.

Kit's steps slowed even more, before she came to a stop, letting the couple disappear ahead of her. This street was smaller than that where the pageant had been held. There was mud beneath her boots and divots where the ground had been churned up by horses' hooves and carriages, as if the earth had been mangled by a giant running his fingers through it. Kit stared down at the ground. She couldn't shake the feeling that there should have been more footprints alongside her own, but there were none. She stood alone in the street. There was no one for her to talk to and bemoan how close the queen of England had come to death that day.

Night was quickly falling, and the bells of the churches rang out, announcing that the watchmen would soon be out to guard the streets, looking for any late walkers. The sound hurried Kit forward.

She passed the street where her attic room was located, but she did not turn down it, nor did she even glance that way. She walked on through the streets and down narrow lanes, heading for another part of London altogether. The more she walked, the more she heard people prattling.

Even those that hadn't attended the parade seemed to have heard of what had happened. Printing shop boys skulked in doorways, whispering to one another, and apprentices loped down the street singing ditties, before they would break off and ask their friends if they'd heard about the attempted assassination. With each scrap of conversation Kit overheard, the tale grew in exaggeration.

"I heard there were three men, each one pointing a pistol at the queen."

"I heard there were four," another apprentice declared. "They were only stopped by one of Walsingham's men. He fired four bolts with his crossbow and killed them all in seconds."

Kit could have laughed at the outrageousness of it all. She turned to repeat the story to someone at her side, but still that space was empty. Only the bitter wind moved alongside her.

Turning one last corner, Kit came to a halt, looking ahead at the place she came back to every night. Iomhar's house stood tall, pressed between two other grand buildings. His was hardly the largest in the street, bordered by timber, made with wattle and daub, but it had certainly taken money to construct it, with glass windows and a tiled roof.

Reaching into her doublet, Kit took the key out from a secret pocket and pressed it into the lock of the oak door, twisting it so that it clunked loudly, before she pushed it open.

The dimness of the dusk met her inside. Her eyes flitted across the corridor, searching for any discarded bags, maybe even mud from freshly soiled boots or spent candles on the side. Yet there was nothing, only the empty floorboards and the dark air. Kit sighed as she stepped in, knowing it was becoming foolish to hold onto any hope. It didn't seem to matter how many times she walked back into the house, calling herself a fool. She always searched the corridor, looking for any sign that Iomhar had reappeared, but she never found anything.

"It has been a year," Kit mumbled to herself. "Perhaps he is not coming back." She turned and closed the door behind her. As she advanced further into the house, Kit heard footsteps. "Who's there?" she demanded.

Turning on the spot, she grabbed a tinder box from the windowsill, pressed between the lead lining and the stone frame. With quick hands, she lit a candle and thrust it forward.

"Oh! My heart." The cook's dulcet tones rang out.

Kit's shoulders slumped as she eyed Elspeth. The older woman wafted a hand in front of her face, making her loose grey tendrils quiver at the edges of her coif.

"You frightened the life out of me."

"My apologies," Kit said, trying not to sigh. The candlelight streaked across the corridor. To one side was the painting of Iomhar when he was a boy, alongside his family. On the other side were the hooks where her own loose jerkins had been thrown. "It seems we both keep looking at this door in the hope that someone else will step through."

"One of these days, aye, one of these days." Elspeth nodded then waved her hands at Kit. "Come, off with that jerkin. You are carrying a smell in with you."

"I am?" Kit wrinkled her nose, unable to tell. Placing the candle down on the nearest table, she turned, allowing Elspeth to take the jerkin off her shoulders.

"Aye, the master was much the same. Too busy doing his work to remember to care for himself. There are clean linens upstairs for you, and dinner will be ready soon."

"Thank you, Elspeth." Kit offered a smile that did not last long. As Elspeth turned, ready to hurry off down the corridor, she hesitated. "Is something wrong?" Kit asked.

"I was just wondering." Elspeth paused and made a point of looking down at the jerkin, playing with the dark red folds and the errant loose threads. "Have you heard anything from the master?"

"No. I have not." Kit's answer came quickly. She was tired of being asked. "After his first letter, no other came."

Elspeth nodded and offered a sad smile. "That dinner will be ready soon."

"Thank you."

Kit hastened for the stairs. She was so eager to be in the bedchamber Iomhar had given to her that she took the steps two at a time, carrying the candle in front of her. She found the clean linens laid out on the bed and dressed hastily. She knew by now that the longer she was still, the more her thoughts dwelled on why she was in Iomhar's home, and why he was not here too.

She let her shirt hang loose and took off her cap, ruffling out the short tendrils of her hair. They sprung up wildly about her ears, no matter how much she tried to flatten them. Preparing to leave the room, she hesitated when the floorboards creaked.

Kit reached for the door handle and cocked her head to the side, listening for the sound again. Turning away from the door, she held her breath, still waiting, but no sound followed.

She was the only one in the chamber. Vastly different to her own attic rooms, it was the chamber Iomhar had often given her to stay in before he had disappeared. With dark wooden furniture and small windows, it was not the lightest of spaces, but there were so many coffers and chairs that the space was comfortable, though a little lonely at times.

"No one is there." Kit told herself that the sound had been a rat beneath the floorboards, nothing more. It would explain the odd scent that was in the room that day, as if something that had touched the dead had carried the stench across the wood.

Flinging open the door, she hurried out of the room and down the stairs, taking her candle with her. At the bottom of the stairs, she hovered beside the painting of young Iomhar and his family. Her eyes had often darted across their faces in the past year, their expressions all far happier than she felt. Finding she was irked by this, her fingers clenched around the iron candle holder as she turned down the corridor and headed to the dining room.

Pushing the oak door wide, she found the space was already lit with three candles spread across the table, which was set for two people.

"Elspeth?" Kit looked around. Through the doorway on the other side of the chamber, Elspeth returned, pushing her coif back with one hand and proffering a jug of small beer with the other.

"Aye?" she said, her eyes shooting straight to Kit.

"The table. It's set for two again. Does that mean you will join me?"

"No. I told you. I don't join the master and his guests."

"The master is not here," Kit reminded her, gripping the back of her chair.

"I've eaten already. Aye, you enjoy your food. I'll take my early night." Elspeth placed the jug down on the table with a light thud. "Goodnight."

"Sleep well, Elspeth."

Kit waited for Elspeth to leave before she turned her eyes down to the table settings. The two pewter trenchers were bare, on either side of the dark oak table. In the middle was a bowl of stew, not too full tonight. The scent of pigeon meat and honey hovered beneath her nose, though there were few vegetables. Pulling out the high-backed chair Kit sat quickly, with her eyes on the empty space opposite her.

A light tap on the door showed she wasn't alone quite yet.

"Yes?" she called, urging Elspeth to come back in.

"Sorry for intruding on you. You're tired, I can see it in the darkness under your eyes."

"Yes, I am tired, but it is no matter." Kit served herself some stew, waiting for Elspeth to go on.

"I forgot to tell you about something odd that happened earlier today."

"What was that?"

"A man was watching the house."

Kit stopped with the spoon mid-air. Drips of stew slipped back into the bowl as she moved her eyes to Elspeth. The cook shrugged, as if uncertain what to make of it all. The wrinkles on her face were dappled orange in the candlelight, and it was bright enough for Kit to see that Elspeth was truly worried.

"What exactly did you see, Elspeth?" Kit asked, putting down her spoon. Sitting back in the chair, she unconsciously reached down for her weapons belt, until she noted its absence. It was upstairs, in her chamber.

"I returned from the market to see his eyes on the house. Odd man, he was!"

"Odd? How so?"

"Skulking in shadows, like a young lad hiding from his mother, he was. Looked like he needed a good clip around the ears to me. No good comes from strangers watching a house like this."

"Hiding?" Kit held back her smile at the cook's urge to beat the man like a boy. "Whereabouts?"

"Under the eaves of the house across the street. You know, that one with the pillars, and the mistress so loud and argumentative she'll have any other lass's coif off her head."

"I know the one," said Kit. It was a good place to hide, and one she would have chosen herself. So many people would have been looking at the noisy mistress as she stood in her doorway, shouting at passers-by. Few would notice a silent man hidden under the eaves. "This man, what did he look like?"

"Had a hat so low over his face his eyes might as well have been tassels off it." Elspeth shook a hand in front of her face. "No, I didn't get a good look at him. Tall though, aye, tall as a horse."

"A man who stands out in a crowd, then." Kit shifted forward in her seat, uncertain what to make of such an event. "You are certain he was staring at this house, Elspeth? Nothing and no one else?"

"I may be old, but my eyes haven't failed me yet." She laughed and shook her head, reaching for the door behind her. "He was staring at this house for most of the day. Mark my warning. He had business here, I am certain of it."

"No knock came to the door? No peddler pushing wares?"

"No. He kept standing there. All day." Elspeth opened the door wide again, stepping out into the dimmer light. "I kept going to a window to watch him. This afternoon he caught me staring at him. That sent him scarpering. He did not come back again."

"Good. Well, thank you for telling me, Elspeth. Don't let this bother you. Get some rest."

"Aye, thank you." Elspeth smiled before hurrying out of the room.

Kit picked up the spoon, ready to delve into her stew, but she couldn't settle. What Elspeth had seen made something burn in her gut.

"Who would come here?" she whispered. As she pushed back her chair, it scraped loudly. The sound reminded her of the creak she had heard upstairs. Any hesitation she may have felt left her, as she hastened out of the room.

She started with the sitting room. Feeling around the edges of the windows, she checked everything was in place, and there was no crack in the glass, nor an opening, before she searched under the furniture. Each chair she turned over, she righted again, before hurrying out of the room. Striding across the corridor, she explored the rooms downstairs. Some chambers were practically empty, for Iomhar had found no real use for them. Kit even went as far as the kitchen, from which Elspeth had retired. The scents of the stew still hovered, and the fire on the hearth had burnt down to embers, filling the air with soft black smoke, but there was no sign of an intruder. No windows were cracked and the door that led out of the back of the house was firmly locked and bolted. Kit checked it twice to be sure.

"No one here." Her mutterings did nothing to soothe her restlessness.

She hurried up the stairs. On the landing, she heard another creak. Freezing, she looked down, certain her boots were not the source of that sound.

When no noise followed, she reached for her chamber, pushing the door wide and stepping in, looking back and forth. She crossed the room, walking on the balls of her feet. With one swift bend, she searched under the bed, then moved onto the coffers, looking for anywhere an intruder could hide, but still, there was no sign.

Reaching the landing again, she was ready to believe it was her imagination playing tricks on her, when she heard the creak for the third time. Now she knew for certain. Such a creak could not be caused by a rat scurrying beneath boards. The creak came from a heavy foot.

Kit's eyes darted down the corridor, looking to a chamber she had never been inside. It was Iomhar's chamber.

Hastening into her room, she picked up her weapons belt and snatched one of the daggers out of the leather. Hiding the blade against her forearm, she stepped back into the corridor, where she left her candle on a nook in the wall. With the flame casting light down the long hallway, she inched forward.

At the door to Iomhar's chamber, she pressed an ear to the wood, listening. When there was another creak from within the room, she grabbed the handle and flung the door open.

In what little light filtered in from the candle, she could see the chamber window was ajar. There were clear signs of an intruder, illuminated by the moonlight that reflected off the glass. On the windowsill were scuff marks, as if someone had clambered into the house with dirty boots.

A silhouetted figure moved. It tried to hide in the corner of the room, yet more floorboards creaked beneath its feet, and it slipped on something. The figure fell to the floor so heavily that Kit could have sworn the timber walls shook.

"Do not move," she warned. She rounded the bed, heading for the corner where the figure had fallen, then leaned down, with the dagger outstretched.

The figure turned over and a sword struck up, dwarfing the blade of the dagger.

CHAPTER 4

The long blade clashed against Kit's dagger, forcing her backward. The shadow scrambled to its feet, its sword the only thing visible, and advanced toward Kit.

Reaching behind her, she grasped the curtains that were draped around the four-poster bed, tore one down and tossed it through the air at the intruder. It covered their face and half of the sword, making the blade thud dully as they lashed out. Rearing backward, Kit lifted a knee and kicked, landing the blow straight in the middle of the intruder's chest.

"Oomph!" The intruder was clearly winded.

Kit jumped forward and stood over the curtain, driving her foot into the arm that held the sword.

"Argh! Och, ye trying to take off my arm?"

Kit froze. Feeling beneath her boot, she could make out a wrist, and a hand that dropped the sword. Bending down, she reached under the curtain and snapped the blade away, before dragging the curtain off the man's face.

"Well, I'll be damned, ye are different to the last time I saw ye."

"I do not believe it." Kit stood back and dragged the curtain away with her. Her shadow no longer blocked the window, and moonlight fell on the intruder's face.

The brown hair was familiar, as was the long nose and the whiskered jaw, for they were so like Iomhar's, and she had seen them before.

"Niall?" Kit's voice was sharp as the man began to move. Scrambling to his knees, he moved like a rat, wriggling from side to side then grasping at his wrist. Kit abruptly realised where else she had seen him. He had been at the parade, and he was the figure she had at first mistaken for Iomhar.

"In the name of the wee man above and all his angels, Kit. Did ye have to stomp down on me hand so hard? Ye could have broken the bones." He shook his head, his eyes darting between his hand and her.

"Why did you have to break in?" Kit waved the sword at the open window before sighing. "God's wounds, Niall, I could have run you through!"

"I noticed." He nodded at the sword she now had in her hand. "Rather good at taking that, were ye not?"

"I am trained. Did Iomhar never warn you?"

"Aye, he said ye are better than any of the soldiers under my command, but they are partial to a whisky." Niall struggled to his feet and leaned against the wall, still rubbing his wrist. "Be lighter next time."

"You pulled a sword!"

"I did not know it was ye."

"I could say the same thing." Kit tossed the sword onto the bed beside them and motioned to the window. "Couldn't you have knocked on the door like any other visitor?"

"I did not know it was ye living here. When I saw someone was here, I thought someone had taken Iomhar's house. I had to see who ye were."

"And give me the fright of my life." Kit rubbed a hand across her chest and turned away, panting as her heartbeat calmed down.

"Aye. Ye gave me a fright too. Feel like me bones have jumped out of me skin." Niall shook out his arm.

Kit paused, staring at Iomhar's brother as he turned his wrist back and forth. "Is it broken?"

"Och, sympathy at last! I thought it was not coming," Niall said wryly and stood off the wall.

"Do you need me to point out that you broke in again?" Kit moved to the window and peered through the glass, seeing exactly how Niall had managed to climb up. He had to have used an adjoining wall on the house next door, as it was just high enough for him to climb and then vault from there to the chamber window. "Why are you not in Scotland?"

"Why are ye in Iomhar's lodgings, Kit?" Niall asked, his eyebrows raised. Kit stepped away from the window, slowly moving toward him with narrowed eyes. "Aye, it's good to see ye too, Kit." Niall laughed then, snapping the tension in the room. "Last I saw ye, ye'd tripped on a horse stirrup."

"I remember." Kit could recall it well. She had met Niall in Northumberland when she and Iomhar had been tracking a Jesuit spy. Niall had just revealed that he and Iomhar were the sons of an earl. The shock had been enough to make Kit slip in the saddle, and land on her back.

She saw that Niall was slipping down the wall and offered a hand to him. "Here, let me see."

"I'm nervous to come near ye now. Skittish, like a horse."

"Very well, suffer as you like."

"Aye, aye, I'm coming." Niall stepped forward. Kit took his forearm and turned it over, analysing the bruising in the moonlight. She then tilted his wrist.

"Bruised, that is all. Nothing is broken." As she released his wrist, a rumble echoed in the air. Kit smirked as Niall laid his injured hand on his stomach. "Hungry?"

"A wee bit."

"Well, going to a parade and then standing outside a house and watching it all day without something to eat will do that. I take it you are the one who I saw at the parade, and you came here to give poor Elspeth a fright earlier today?" Kit beckoned him to follow her as she headed for the door.

"Aye. That would be me." Niall hurried behind her and down the main staircase. "I had to see the parade. A chance to see the queen of England? Aye, too much temptation to refuse. After that, I wanted to see who would come to this house. Plain as the sun on a bright day that Iomhar is not here anymore."

Kit stumbled to a stop at the bottom of the stairs, then turned to face Niall.

"What?" he said, halting.

"You do not know where he is?" Kit asked slowly. "You spoke as if you thought he might be here."

"I hoped he might be. Why else do ye think I've come all this way? Just to wish ye good day?" Niall scoffed. "As charming as ye are, Kit, Iomhar is more likely to go that far to see ye, not I."

Kit chose not to rise to his mischief. Instead, she walked on, beckoning Niall to follow her. She led the way to the dining room and sat down at her place, gesturing for Niall to do the same in the other seat.

"It looks like ye knew I was coming."

"No. Elspeth sets the table for Iomhar every night. It stays empty." Kit dished up some more stew then offered the spoon to Niall, who gladly took it. She lit more candles on the table, looking at Niall through the orange light. He was staring back at her just as curiously, bending his injured wrist back and forth.

"I have questions."

"As do I." Kit nodded at Niall. "You can begin."

Niall shovelled a big spoonful of stew into his mouth, before levelling his gaze at her. "Why are ye living here? Last I heard, this was very much Iomhar's house, and ye two are not wed. At least, I was never told ye were."

Kit choked on the stew. A small chunk of turnip shot down her throat and she coughed, spluttering for a few seconds until it was clear.

"Surprised ye, did I?" Niall asked and poured out some ale for her from the jug. "Drink that."

"No more teasing, Niall," Kit warned with a raised finger as she took the cup.

"I cannot agree to that."

"You will." Kit pushed the jug back toward him. "About a week after Iomhar left, he sent me a letter. He told me to come here and use it as my own house, and that Elspeth expected me to come."

"Did he say why?"

"No." Kit shook her head and turned her focus to the stew. The situation felt very strange, having Niall sitting where his brother used to be.

"Aye, I can guess well enough." Niall busied himself with his stew. "Knowing Iomhar, he would not want ye to be alone in that attic of yours."

"He told you about my attic rooms?"

"Aye. Said they were easier to break into than a coaching inn stable."

"That sounds like him."

"I just mean that he would want to see ye cared for. Makes sense he would want ye to come here."

"What does that mean?" Kit asked, her spoon hovering. "Iomhar was not my carer."

"I did not say he was." Yet there was a small smile on Niall's face as he uttered the words. "I cannot say any more if ye wish me to keep my promise about not making comments concerning ye and me brother." The words made Kit shift in her seat, abruptly uncomfortable.

"Just eat your stew." Kit pushed the main stew bowl toward him, prompting him to serve himself another portion. "Now it is your turn to answer questions. Why are you here, Niall? You are a long way from home."

"Aye, I know. London seems to be at the end of the world, I travelled that far. I had a horse nearly fall asleep under me, lubberwort of an animal." Niall grunted and paused with his stew, lifting his eyes to meet Kit's again. "When Iomhar left last year, he came to see us."

"He said he would go to see his family." Kit remembered Iomhar's words before he had parted from her in Walsingham's house.

"He did. Stayed with us a few days, but it was all so strange. He was not himself. Quiet, much quieter than usual, saying odd things too. Next thing we know, he's gone, and he's left things behind."

"Things? What things?"

"Things he always carries with him. His rapier marked with our father's emblem, a leather purse our mother bought for him. Aye, much was left behind. After that…" Niall paused, with his spoon set firmly in the stew. "Nothing. We have not heard a word from him since."

Kit swallowed around a sudden lump in her throat. Every day she had looked to the door, hoping Iomhar would walk back through it, but she hadn't truly considered what it meant for his family. She had assumed he would see them, and she had certainly thought it possible he was still with them. "Then, he truly is missing?" she whispered. Niall nodded. For a minute, the only sounds in the room were the drops of stew that fell off Kit's spoon. Slowly, she lowered the spoon to the bowl, deciding she'd had enough. "You have not heard from him since? Not once?"

"Nay." Niall shook his head. "I also wrote to ye, to see if ye had heard from him. But I wrote to your attic room. I now know why I did not receive an answer. I was beginning to think the worst. I take it ye have not heard from him either?"

"Not since just after he left." Kit thought back to the day Iomhar had parted from her. He had kissed her hand, a much more intimate gesture than they usually shared, before saying goodbye and slipping quickly out of the house in Seething Lane.

"Aye, this is great," Niall muttered wryly as he sat back in his chair and rubbed his hands over his face. "I do not understand. Iomhar would not just disappear like this. There has to be a reason."

"There is a reason." Kit's words caught Niall's attention, and he looked up. "Walsingham gave him a job to do. What it is, I do not know, but it was plainly something of interest. He insisted Iomhar was the one for the task."

"He's doing work for Walsingham?" Niall sat forward in his seat so quickly that the chair creaked dangerously beneath him. "Nay. Nay, that is not good news." He continued to shake his head, gripping the edge of the table until his knuckles turned white. "Are ye not going to ask me why it is not good news, Kit?"

"I can take a guess at what you are thinking." Kit reached forward and topped up her ale, desperately needing to quench a sudden dryness in her throat. "It is not possible."

"How do ye know?" Niall hissed with barely restrained anger. "He risked his life last year in Hampton Court for ye and Walsingham, did he not?"

Kit spilled a little ale, reminded of that day. She could still see Iomhar in her mind's eyes, stepping in front of her, taking the thrust of the blade that was meant for her.

"He did not die that day."

"Who's to say he is not dead now?"

Kit slowly lifted the cup to her lips, hoping the tremble that had threatened to overtake her body was hidden. "He cannot be dead."

"He's been gone for a year, Kit. A year! Nay word to ye, and nay word to us." Niall thrust a hand against his chest. "He has disappeared doing a task for your spymaster, and all ye can say is, 'he cannot be dead.'" Niall mimicked her English accent. It was so poor that she glared at him over the rim of her cup.

"Your accent needs work."

"I thought it was not half bad. But I am not here to improve my accent." Niall sat back in his chair. "I want to talk about this, Kit."

"He cannot be dead." Kit stood, wanting to flee the conversation. She downed what was left of her ale before she poured herself some more.

"Ye look as if ye need something stronger."

"This will do." She moved away from the table, gulping from her cup. "He sent me a letter, Niall. A week after he was gone, he wrote to me." She reached the window and looked out. It had grown late, and all she could see were the watchmen doing their rounds with their lanterns swinging back and forth. "He wrote. Therefore, he is alive."

"He wrote to ye when he was still with us." Niall's words made her turn sharply. "He was with us for nearly a week before he disappeared. He has not written to ye since, has he?"

Kit downed what was left in her cup. She didn't want to believe it. Iomhar couldn't be dead. Any day now, he would come through that door. He would say he'd heard tales from Walsingham of how impulsive she had been since he had been gone, and when she mimicked his Scottish accent, he would find flaws in her performance.

"If he was dead, would your family not have heard of it?" Kit asked Niall.

"Remember what I said, Kit. He left things behind at our house. The sword bearing our family emblem, and the leather purse etched with his initials."

"Oh ... anything identifiable, he left behind." Kit cursed and moved to the table, pouring out another cup. When Niall slid his cup forward, she topped it up. They both needed it in that moment. "I am not ready to believe he is dead. If he was, Walsingham would have told me."

"Ye think a spymaster would tell ye that?"

"Walsingham would." Kit found the words fell sharply from her. Walsingham may have been keeping secrets from her. He may even have done things at times that she did not understand, but he was still the man who'd raised her. He was the one who watched over her and told her to go home and rest up at the end of a long day. "He would tell me if he knew."

"Then maybe he does not know. The question is, where did he send Iomhar?"

Kit paused with the cup halfway to her lips. A memory flashed in her mind of something she had seen the day Iomhar had left. "A unicorn..."

"What?" Niall said, leaning forward. "It's like talking to a child. Is it my turn to name a mythical animal?"

"The day Iomhar left London, just after he had seen Walsingham, papers were burnt."

"Papers? What kind of papers?"

"Walsingham had some in his office. He was burning them, directly after his meeting with Iomhar. One had the emblem of the unicorn at the top. It was the same as that tattoo we keep seeing." She rubbed a hand across the top of her neck. She had now seen that mark on so many people.

"The old Queen of Scots' supporters," Niall murmured, with venom in his tone. "If Walsingham had a letter with that emblem, then it was surely sent by one of them."

"It is possible." Kit nodded slowly. "What will you do now? Now you know Iomhar is not here?"

"I will go home and tell my mother." Niall grimaced and ran a hand through his hair, apparently not relishing the task. "Then I'll run for the hills before she can react. I'm going to keep looking. I'm not giving up yet."

"Where, though? You do not know where to look."

"I know." Niall gestured to the jug. "Pour me another. It will have to do when ye have nay whisky."

Kit slowly poured out the ale as an idea occurred to her. "Perhaps there is a way to find out where you should look for Iomhar."

"Ye have an idea, Kit?"

"Well, someone knows where Iomhar went. The challenge is to make Walsingham tell me."

CHAPTER 5

"Kit? Kit? Are you listening?"

Kit snapped up her head from where she had been staring at the hearth. The fire in Walsingham's study was burning brightly, and each flame was as lithe as a dancer, bending around its partner. Beside the hearth stood Walsingham, his body slightly bent thanks to the latest pains in his back, with parchments clutched in his hands.

"You are not here today, Kit. I can see it." Walsingham gestured between his eyes and hers with a goose feather quill. "You have a touch of melancholia about you."

"I am perfectly well." Kit spoke quickly and folded her arms across her body, staring at Walsingham without explanation.

Walsingham was not convinced. His eyes darted down her, taking in her defensive stance, before returning to her face. "I was trying to tell you about the assassin that you caught at the parade."

"What of him? Is he refusing to speak?"

"Oh, he was happy to confess." Walsingham marched in front of the fireplace, clicking his bones and basking in the warmth. "We didn't even have to make him talk, nor even threaten to. He was more than happy to tell his tale."

"Which was?" Kit asked distractedly, glancing down at the flames. She could remember all too easily how the parchment bearing the unicorn had curled into a black ball, then faded to ash.

"He was paid to do it. Former army man, and assassin by trade. Well, supposed assassin. From what I can gather, he is some sort of hireling or mercenary, paid to do the things other people do not want to do."

"Paid by who?"

"That is the question. He claims he does not know. I'm inclined to believe him. Especially when he so willingly handed over this." Walsingham fished into the papers he was carrying and pulled out a single sheath, which he passed over to Kit. "This came wrapped around his first payment for the deed."

The paper bore the unicorn symbol. This one was more elegant than the one Kit could remember being burnt.

"Ruskin? Or the last Queen of Scots herself?" Kit asked, passing the paper back to Walsingham.

"Or any number of the group that support her." Walsingham shrugged and stepped away from the fire. "We might never know who on this occasion."

"The last time I saw that shape…" Kit began slowly.

"Hmm?" Walsingham urged her on, but he was distracted, making his way to his desk and setting the papers down amongst a number of others.

"It was last year. In this very room."

"Here? Are you certain of that?" Walsingham didn't even look up from where he was rearranging the papers.

Kit turned away from the fireplace, shifting her focus to Walsingham. Niall had left Iomhar's house that morning for Scotland, and on his parting, she had promised to find out where Walsingham had sent Iomhar.

"I saw it in this room, and you were burning a letter. It was the day you sent Iomhar away."

Her words caught Walsingham's attention. He dropped the papers to the desk and turned his gaze on her, his long face tense, and his dark eyes narrowed. "I thought we had ended this conversation."

"Ended? You merely wish to keep brushing this matter under a rug." Kit motioned toward the fireplace another time. "What letter did you burn? Did it relate to where you sent Iomhar? It bore the same mark. The unicorn. It must have come from one of her supporters."

"If you are going to become irate and wild, I cannot deal with you." Walsingham motioned toward the door. "You can return when you are calm."

"Why? I deal with you when you are not calm." Kit's words made Walsingham move away. He reached for the chair behind his desk and sat heavily, with the wood creaking noisily beneath him. "I wish to know where you sent Iomhar."

"It is not your business to know, Kit. It serves no purpose."

"Then it can hardly hurt for me to know."

"Of course it can hurt!" Walsingham barked, his voice so loud that it echoed off the lofted ceilings.

"Now who is not calm?" Kit said, her wry tone only earning another glare from Walsingham.

"He was doing a task for me. He accepted the risk. When he returns, he will tell you the same thing."

"*If* he returns."

Walsingham shifted in his seat. He reached forward, shuffling the papers and lifting the quill, ready to write some notes.

"Have you heard from him? Since he left?" Kit pressed.

Walsingham's quill hovered for a few seconds, with the nib not quite touching the paper. Ink dripped off the end and blotted the parchment. "I have not."

His answer made Kit turn away. She reached for the mantelpiece above the fire and leaned upon it with her elbow, resting her head in her hand. "Then I beg of you, Walsingham. Please. Do me this single kindness. Tell me where you sent him." Lifting her gaze from the fire, she eyed Walsingham again.

"Kindness?" Walsingham repeated the word with the corner of his lips flickering into the smallest of smiles. "Recently, I have wondered if you thought me capable of such a thing."

"What does that mean?"

"It means you have changed. You question my orders." Walsingham moved to his feet. "You second-guess everything. By God's blood, you even thought I may have betrayed our queen last year —"

"I never said as much."

"Yet you thought it." He tapped his temple, moving out from behind the table and crossing the room toward her. "You thought it was possible. God's wounds, you even think I am lying to you about where you came from."

"I know you are."

Kit's quiet words made Walsingham stumble. He too reached out, clinging to the mantelpiece, before he stepped forward. "You want kindness, Kit? Then I will give you kindness." He took her shoulder. That single touch made Kit slump, and she leaned on the mantelpiece a little more. "To tell you where Iomhar has gone would only be putting you in danger. With one intelligencer not returning, do you truly think I would place another in the same peril?"

Kit blinked, turned numb by the question. Silence lingered between them as Walsingham stared at her. He was looking older now, ageing by the day. His already grey hair was white in places, and the top of his scalp was balding. A scent hung around him too, of something metallic that reminded Kit of the medicines he was constantly gulping, and the red wine. That scent was more prominent these days.

"That is a kindness, Kit, is it not?" he asked.

Kit wanted to resent Walsingham for keeping secrets from her. She knew without a doubt after challenging him last year that he was not telling her everything about where she had come from, but she could not blame him for keeping a secret now if he thought it would protect her.

"Yes. It is," she murmured reluctantly, knowing she would probably say the same thing had their positions been reversed. Still, it did not help her. She had to find a way to discover where Walsingham had sent Iomhar.

Her eyes flicked away from Walsingham to the back of his study. Shelves upon shelves were nailed to the wall, some as deep as her arm, holding scrolls and loosely bound books with various messages, letters and notes hidden inside. If Walsingham had any surviving note on Iomhar's whereabouts, that was where she would find it.

"Master! Master?" A mad call went up through the house.

Walsingham lowered his hand from Kit's shoulder as they both turned to face the door. Beyond it, someone was hurrying up the stairs, evidently desperate to see him.

"Master?" The voice was high-pitched and belonged to Doris, Walsingham's housekeeper. She knocked on the door.

"Yes, yes, come, Doris." Walsingham waved a hand at the door. It opened and Doris fell through, with her white coif askew and her cheeks red as newly grown raspberries. "What is it now?"

"Oh! She has done it again, Master. She has done it again." Doris flicked her eyes to Kit, and her manner softened momentarily. "Kitty, when did you arrive?"

"Just a few minutes ago. I would ask how you are, Doris, but I can see —"

"Oh, I am ill, very ill indeed, and she is the one who is doing it to me." Doris flung her arm backward and pointed down the stairs. "This maid you have taken on, Master, she will not do. I cannot stand for it."

"Pray, what has she done now?" Walsingham asked, adopting a more patient tone than that he had taken with Kit.

Kit turned away and hid her smile. This last year since the new maid had been hired, Kit had seen repeatedly how she had upset Doris's rather particular way of running the house. No matter what Doris did, it seemed the maid did things differently. Kit rather suspected the maid had little interest in really learning how to care for the house.

"She has dropped the coal scuttle, sent it all over the floor, and now she has vanished. The door to your secretaries' room is open too."

Walsingham did not need to hear more. He was out of the room with his black cloak billowing behind him, nearly whipping Kit across the arms.

"She is a wild child, Master!" Doris called, hurrying down the stairs after Walsingham. "Far too curious for her own good, and not enough of a hard worker…" Her words began to fade as the two of them disappeared down the steps, their heavy tread masking Doris's shrill voice.

Kit waited until she heard a door close far beneath her, then she shifted her eyes to the shelves.

"Well, when else will I have such a good chance?" Kit murmured, then hurried to the back of the room. A quick peer at some of the scrolls showed they were organised. There were matters relating to the privy council and Walsingham's work as private secretary, though the taller shelves lacked any labels at all.

Grabbing the creaking chair from behind Walsingham's desk, Kit moved it to the shelves and stood on top, the better to reach these higher shelves. At first, she found nothing that was obvious. There were a series of letters that had been coded, some with translations attached, and others that had nothing with them at all.

Soon enough, voices were moving about downstairs again. The young maid had plainly been reprimanded for her curiosity and her clumsiness, and Walsingham and Doris were returning this way. Kit's movements became frantic. She picked up letters haphazardly, barely opening them in her effort to catch a glimpse of anything promising inside.

The bottom step creaked under someone's foot as she found a letter bearing something she recognised. The words were encoded, yet in the corner was another unicorn. Like the one she could remember being burnt, it was drawn rather scruffily.

Kit folded the parchment and stuffed it deep in her doublet, before jumping down from the chair and returning it to its place behind the desk. By now, the footsteps on the stairs were getting closer. Kit didn't have a chance to return to her place by the fire, so she moved to the window instead and sat on the sill, pretending she had been interested in observing the activities beyond.

"That girl. Nothing between her ears but wool, I swear," Walsingham snorted as he stepped into the room once again.

"Doris would be glad if you hired someone new," Kit said, attempting a nonchalant tone as she glanced at the letters on the shelves, praying she had not spoiled their organisation enough for him to notice her intrusion.

"She will do for now. She only needs training." Walsingham shrugged and moved to his desk, sitting down in his chair. He grimaced and reached beneath him, pulling pieces of grit from his seat.

Kit glanced down at her boots, seeing where the grit had come from. She then uncrossed her legs and flattened the soles of her shoes to the floor, praying Walsingham would not realise.

"Is our conversation from before at an end, Kit?" Walsingham asked.

"You know I will not stop asking where he has gone."

"Yes, I had guessed that." Walsingham dropped the grit to the floor and sat back with a deep sigh. "Perhaps it is best I put you with a new partner, someone else to think about for a while."

"Not yet." Kit's words came so fast that Walsingham lifted his head off the back of his chair, eyeing her curiously. "He might return yet."

"Hmm." Walsingham's noncommittal sound made Kit shift on the windowsill.

"He is not dead," Kit whispered.

Walsingham did not seem to hear her. He picked up his quill and dipped it in a brass inkwell beside him, intending to return to his notes. "Let us talk of the matter at hand." Walsingham scrawled quick notes across the paper. "This assassin in our tower. He may have been working alone, but someone paid him."

"I can think of a few people." Kit's mind shot to Lord Ruskin, the Scottish lord who had set traps in Hampton Court the year before, trying to see the end of Queen Elizabeth.

"I do not need guesses. We can all make those. I need proof," Walsingham croaked. "I have some intelligencers on the trail of where this assassin picked up his money."

"What do you wish me to do?"

"I wish you to keep your appointment with Her Majesty." Walsingham's words reminded Kit of the promise she had made to the queen. "She asked to see you. Tomorrow, was it not?"

"Yes. Do you know why she wishes to speak with me?" Kit stood, ready to depart, conscious of the way the parchment crinkled inside her doublet as she moved. She scuffed her boots on the floorboards, being careful to cover up the sound.

"No. That's what worries me." Walsingham paused and tilted his quill, so that the grey and white strands of the feather brushed his beard. "She likes you, Kit. Ever since what happened at the palace, she has an *affection* for you."

"An affection? Yes, I suppose I am like one of her dogs. She clicks her fingers, and I come running," Kit said with an amused smile.

"Is it that?" Walsingham asked, peering at Kit as she moved toward the door. "She likes you. I'm beginning to think she tells you things that she doesn't tell me."

Kit smiled, remembering what had passed between her and the queen at Hampton Court Palace. When facing death and finding herself alone with Kit, the queen had trusted her to retrieve a ring emblazoned with an image of herself in a small locket, along with a painting of her mother, the once ruined queen, Anne Boleyn.

"Perhaps some things," Kit admitted with a slow nod.

"What? What does she tell you?" Walsingham asked tersely, his hand gripping the quill so tightly that he was in danger of snapping it.

"Now, that would be betraying her trust." Kit reached for the door. "I could not do that. If you are worried about what she has to say to me, then you should come to the meeting too."

"I intend to." Walsingham's tone was firm. Kit opened the door, curious at his need to be there, but before she could step through and hurry away with the parchment hidden in her doublet, Walsingham spoke again. "Are you still staying at his house?"

Kit paused in the doorway and looked back at Walsingham. Neither of them needed to say Iomhar's name to know they were speaking of him. "He asked me to, until he returns."

"Well, at least it is better than the attic rooms." Walsingham nodded with an approving smile. "Go home, Kit. Rest up before your meeting with the queen tomorrow."

Kit stepped out of the door and down the staircase. When she reached the bottom, she tapped the place in her doublet where the parchment was hidden, checking it was there. She had no intention of resting when she returned home. She would decipher the code in the letter.

Kit waited until Elspeth had retired for the night. Sitting in the corner of the front room of Iomhar's house, she tapped the pewter goblet in her hand restlessly. She was tapping out the rhythm of the tune she had used to call to Iomhar in a crowd. It was a ditty they'd once heard, 'Leave Lightie Love', and he had sometimes whistled it back to her.

It had been a long day, but Kit had not felt prepared to examine what was in the letter she had taken from Walsingham's study until she was alone. As the oak door thudded into place and Elspeth's footsteps receded, Kit's tapping on the goblet stopped. When she heard another door close, she moved at last.

She hurried to place her goblet on the nearest table and then knelt by the fireplace, pulling out the folded-up parchment from her doublet. Using the light from the flames, she laid the parchment out flat, peering at the scrawl across the surface.

The unicorn was scruffy indeed, as if drawn in haste, or by someone who was ill adept at drawing anything. The writing was just as messy, with each letter replaced by a number.

"A common cipher," Kit whispered.

Jumping to her feet, she crossed the room as quickly as she could and retrieved a fresh sheet of parchment from a bureau, along with a quill and a half-full inkwell. Returning to her place by the fire, she leaned on the stone hearth and stared at the letter.

"I need a key." She huffed, not seeing a way into the code. If she made it a pure guessing exercise, then she could be by the fire for hours, even days. She needed to be quicker than that.

Something caught her eye. Twisting her head, she looked to the chair where she had so often seen Iomhar settled. She could remember him sitting close beside her, another time she had cracked a code. He had waited patiently, with eyes trained on the fire.

Kit growled at the silence of the room now and turned her focus back down to the parchment. When she snatched it up, she held it a little too tightly. It made the unicorn in the corner of the letter crinkle, with the ink standing up at strange angles. Something was odd about the makeup of the emblem.

Turning the paper round, Kit looked at it upside down, then lifted the parchment closer to her face. Tucked away in the corner of the unicorn's head, what was supposed to be shading to reveal the eye was actually tiny letters.

"*E. 12*," Kit read.

She hurried to write down the first transcription on her blank sheet, then she looked to the unicorn again. Shifting it around, she found another clue, buried in one of the unicorn's hooves that were lifted high: *S. 8*.

There were no more clues. It may have been little to go on, but it was a key, and enough to get Kit started.

She hurried to write out an exact transcription of the coded letter on her new sheet, then wrote the corresponding letters above all the twelves and eights. Gradually, other possible words became apparent. *Taurus* and *the* grew easy to guess, and with more and more letters, she decoded the missing numbers until she had a complete translation. There was a blank number too. *11* stood for nothing, a common 'null' symbol to try to confuse a decoder, but it was something Kit had been told to look for at an early stage in coding. What was plain to see was that though the code took time to crack, it was not complicated. Whoever had put together the cipher had a basic knowledge of codes, but they were not especially skilled.

At the bottom of the letter, Kit was left with only one phrase she could not understand, for the numbers seemed to correspond to a codename: *God's friend.*

Kit scrunched her nose, turning her focus away from the codename and reading the letter:

Taurus,

I received your response to my first letter, and I will be at The White Hart, Inverness, as planned at the end of the month with the turn of the moon.

Know this. If your man does not come with his pardon, then our deal is worthless. You will not learn all I have to tell of Ruskin's plans, nor of Queen Mary's aims. This agreement will be at an end.

Hold true to your bargain, Taurus, and I will hold true to mine.

May God be with your man.

God's friend.

Kit lowered the paper to the hearth, wrinkling her brow. The dates at the top of the letter fitted perfectly with Iomhar's departure from London, and the mention of Scotland made it even more likely. After all, she now knew for certain that Iomhar had gone to see his family, before he went on to complete his task. It was possible the sender's first letter suggesting such a meeting was the one Kit had seen burned in the grate by Walsingham. This second one had perhaps been kept as proof that the deal had been made.

"Someone changed sides." Kit's summary made her linger on the codename, wondering exactly who it could be. "God's friend…" Brushing a finger across the original letter, she jumped to her feet, leaving the parchments by the fire as she hastened from the room. She had a burning feeling in her gut that she had read the codename somewhere before.

Across the corridor, she found a chamber that Iomhar had used as a storeroom. Inside, coffers were stacked side by side, their lids difficult to open and close. Kit managed to shift one, tipping it back so that dust filled the air. She held her breath through the cloud and bent down, reaching into the depths of the coffer.

There were discarded scrolls and a few loosely bound books, as well as old pamphlets. Squashed between two pamphlets were some coded letters, ones that she and Iomhar had deemed too important to be burned. Hidden between these sheets, they were difficult to locate, but she knew where to look.

One letter stood out amongst the others. The code was unreadable to her now, for she had not left any of the coded letters with their keys. Dropping the other documents into the box, she raised the letter higher.

Through the door she'd left ajar, there was enough orange light filtering into the room for Kit to read the message. She could remember looking at it with Walsingham, shortly before she and Iomhar had left for Northumberland, well over a year ago.

"He is ready for you," Walsingham had said, pressing the letter into her hands as proof. "My man will meet you at Hadrian's Wall and give you a place to stay in the county."

Kit's eyes danced over the sheet, resting on the bottom where the codename was written. The letters were as scruffy as they were in his other message: *God's friend*.

Kit could remember exactly who had met them at Hadrian's Wall, only a couple of weeks before he had run with Lord Ruskin from Holy Island, defecting to Mary Stuart's side.

"By God's blood," she muttered. "Iomhar went to meet Oswyn."

CHAPTER 6

"It is rather different to Hampton Court." Kit looked over the palace before her. There were white turrets reaching to the sky, pure as lambs' coats, adorned with golden struts and the occasional redbrick chimney.

"I think that was rather the idea," Walsingham said from beside her as he waved a hand, urging her on.

Rather than heading for the main door of the house that stood towering over them, twice the height of an average man, Walsingham led Kit around the palace, circling the turreted building.

"Does the queen no longer return to Hampton Court?" Kit asked.

Walsingham scoffed. "Would you desire to live there?"

Kit grimaced, the only answer she needed to give.

"Just so. Any normal man or woman would stay away from that place after what happened last year, but for someone as superstitious as Her Majesty? The idea of staying was impossible. That old fool, John Dee, fed her delusion. He claims the palace has a curse upon it, and that it sits under unlucky stars."

Kit followed Walsingham, aware that as they hurried forth, more than one guard turned to look in their direction. When they recognised Walsingham hobbling, they looked away, as accustomed to his presence as they were to the queen's own.

"I thought we were seeing the queen?" Kit motioned to the palace they were now turning away from, as Walsingham took a path through the garden.

"We are. She is not fond of meeting people inside the palace at the moment. She says there are few doors through which to escape." The words made Kit pull her doublet tighter, suddenly aware of the chill in the air. It seemed the threat against the queen's life had made her a very nervous sort.

As they walked along the white-gravel path, Kit slipped more than once on the ice. Her eyes searched past empty flower borders and frost-mottled earth to see that people were gathered at the far end.

The queen was sitting on a raised bench, wearing a gown and vast cloak to keep her warm. She took up a large amount of space, equivalent to three men of great girth sitting side by side. One of her maids fussed over the voluminous skirt, before the queen waved an ivory hand in the lady's direction, prompting her to step back. When Kit's eyes met the queen's, the elder lady sat forward with clear interest, making the high collar of her gown rise up behind her head.

Kit and Walsingham grew closer, and she became aware of his harried movements.

"What has you so worried?" she whispered as they rounded the last flower border.

"My worries may be unfounded yet. We shall see." Walsingham shook a hand in her direction, urging her not to speak again.

As they reached the queen, Kit dropped a curtsy, and Walsingham bowed. The ladies beside the queen all turned their gazes in Kit's direction. She could feel the power of those stares, remembering them all too well. Some looked at her with suspicion, others with curiosity.

"She's back," one of the ladies whispered. "The draggle-tail dressed as a man." Kit tilted her chin upward, hardly caring if it was improper at this time. She found the young lady who had spoken with a harsh stare, revealing that she had heard her. The laughter that had followed the lady's comment abruptly died.

"A powerful look, Miss Scarlett." The queen smiled, then glanced at the lady who had made the comment. "You would be wise not to fall on her ill side. She is known for leaving damage in her wake."

Kit was curious at this comment and nearly stood straight, but Walsingham reached out and grabbed her arm, keeping her firmly bent in her curtsy. The queen allowed them both to stand at last with a flick of a long bony finger, then she gazed around at her ladies.

"Leave us." The words were firm. Not one lady questioned the order, though Lady Hunsdon hovered for a second by the queen's side, only sent away by a firm glare from her mistress.

Kit watched as the ladies wandered off through the garden in their ostentatious gowns, each one buffeting against the other as they fought for room on the slim path.

"Your Majesty, may I enquire as to the purpose of this meeting?" Walsingham asked. His voice was calm, though Kit knew him well enough to sense it was deeper than the tone he usually used.

"You may, though it was your intelligencer I wished to speak to more than you." The queen turned her eyes on Kit, a small smile curling her thin lips. "How do you fare, Miss Scarlett? You offered quite the performance the other day at our parade. Already your exploits with that assassin have been whispered by my ladies so many times, they have quite forgotten the original details." She waved a dismissive hand in her ladies' direction.

"I do not believe they are the only ones, Your Majesty." Kit remembered hearing in the street how the tale had been mishandled.

"Astute of you." The queen nodded slightly at Kit. They held each other's gaze for a minute in silence, with nothing but the caw of jackdaws in nearby trees to disturb them. Kit felt like a sparrow being eyed by a cat.

"Your Majesty…" Walsingham began.

"You do not allow enough time for silence, Walsingham." The queen sighed at him, as if he had disturbed some great pleasure or intrigue. "There is goodness in silence; it allows space for thought."

"And what thoughts lurk now?"

"Impatient!" The queen tutted, then laughed under her breath. "I have a task that needs doing. One that is a little delicate." She glanced over her shoulder, apparently wary of her ladies being close enough to hear her. Judging that they were far enough away, she returned her focus to Kit, her dark eyes unblinking. "I need someone to complete a task whose word and secrecy I can depend upon. Who better than an intelligencer for such a task?"

"Yet you are choosing me, Your Majesty. I must presume you have more cause than that alone to pick me." Kit made the point with raised eyebrows.

"Perceptive, though I am keen to see what makes you think so."

"Some of Walsingham's friends like to avoid me." Kit shrugged. "Though I cannot think why," she jested, then straightened her doublet in emphasis.

The queen smiled with genuine humour. "You will find you will draw much censure over the years, Miss Scarlett, and as much interest. Rather like some performance at a theatre." She cocked her head to the side, the movement so abrupt that the jewels placed upon her red hair shifted, in danger of falling out. "You ask why else I pick you? Very well, I will tell you. I believe you, of all of the intelligencers I have seen, will understand what I am about to ask of you."

Kit's interest was caught, but not as much as Walsingham's. He stood so straight she could have sworn his back cracked like an eggshell.

"What is it you ask of her?" Walsingham asked impatiently.

The queen's eyes darted to Walsingham, then she looked to Kit again. "I wish you to deliver a letter, Miss Scarlett, to my cousin. Mary Stuart."

"Your Majesty!" Walsingham stepped forward, though Kit did not move.

"Shouting my name will not make me respond to it any more than if you had whispered it." The queen glared at her spymaster, before looking back to Kit. "That is my request. What do you make of it, Miss Scarlett?"

"I —" Kit did not manage to utter any more sounds.

"This is beyond the pale, Your Majesty." Walsingham stepped forward. He dropped to his knees in front of the queen. "I implore you, do not do this." His jowls shook as he held his hat close to his breast, as if covering his heart.

"Say your speech, Walsingham. We both know you wish to." The queen waved a hand at him. "Once you are done, you can satisfy yourself that you have given me your advice." Kit chewed the inside of her mouth, attempting to stop herself from laughing. When a small sound still escaped her, the queen turned to look in her direction. "I have amused your pet, Walsingham."

"Your Majesty, this will be an error in judgement." Walsingham's words came rapidly. "All communication with your cousin must be overseen by the privy council. We must ensure that the message is sound."

"Do you imply I write madness?" The queen stood up and Kit eyed her. She was not the tallest of women, yet the breadth of her gown, the height of her collar, and her elaborate hairstyle — which looked like red serpents writhing on her temple — made her presence seem all the greater.

"You know that is not what I meant." Walsingham's words were solemn. He did not move from his place down on one knee in front of her. "We have systems for these sorts of communications. Letters must be countersigned, overseen by Lord Burghley and myself. If we cannot ensure what is said in the letter, how will we know what Mary Stuart is to make of it?"

"I will know what to make of it, which is rather the point." The queen stared down at the spymaster.

"I advise not to make this error."

"Your advice has been heard and will not to be followed." The queen moved around Walsingham, buffeting him with her skirts and farthingale as if he were a dog to be brushed aside. Walsingham nearly fell from his knees, scattering gravel as he began to stand.

Kit held her ground, alarmed as the queen moved toward her. She had been poisoned the year before, and when she was this close Kit could still see the damage it had done. The white makeup was particularly heavy under the queen's eyes, suggesting that dark shadows were hidden beneath. There was also a paleness to her lips that Kit remembered observing as the queen had lain in her bed, clinging to life.

"There was a time when my cousin and I were not as we are now. No, indeed, we wrote to each other, without the watchful eye of the privy council." She waved a hand in Walsingham's direction. "I even have gifts from her." The queen allowed herself a small smile. "She has always excelled at embroidery and when we were younger, she sent me the most beautiful pieces. A kindness, they were. A gift." Then her expression changed, and she looked rather sickened. "Though it was long ago, I struggle to believe that woman is lost for good. I wish to speak to her as I once did, without any threat between us. One letter, not seen by the privy council, is all I wish for. Miss Scarlett, I need you to deliver it. Do you accept the task?" She said this with such insistence that her voice shook.

"Kit, hold your answer." Walsingham's order made the queen flinch. Slowly, she turned to her spymaster, with a redness in her cheeks that bled through the pale makeup.

Kit stayed perfectly still, uncertain whose orders she should be following.

"Please, Your Majesty, before you send Kit on this mission, I must know more." Walsingham stepped forward, gravel crunching beneath him. "Tell me why you wish to do this. Is it simply to recapture the days of your youth with Mary Stuart?"

"Do not belittle me." The queen pushed her skirts to the side and stood tall, meeting Walsingham's gaze. "Every letter you have me send to Mary Stuart does not say what I wish it to say. It says what *you* and Burghley wish it to say. Now is no longer a time for propriety, decorum or excessive formality. Your diplomacy is like an ant walking on sand — ineffective, without leaving a footprint." The queen waved a hand dismissively. "There was yet another attempt on my life two days ago."

"I have vowed to you that we will keep you safe. I intend to keep that promise." Walsingham's dark eyes flicked to Kit, clearly willing her to second the statement.

"We will," Kit said at last. She earned a quick look from the queen.

"Your intelligencer has gone far for my benefit, last year and this year." The queen nodded approvingly in her direction. "Yet what happens the day Miss Scarlett takes ill and is not at my side when an attempt is made?"

"Another intelligencer will be there."

"Perhaps. And when they are taken ill?"

"I have many intelligencers."

"Are they all as good as the ones that came before them? Are they as good as Miss Scarlett here?"

It was a compliment, but Kit did not feel pleased in that moment. She felt trapped between the glowers of the queen and Walsingham.

"Sooner or later, luck ends, skill fades, and danger… Well, it prevails." With these words, the queen clasped her hands. Kit watched as she laid her thumb over a ring on one of her fingers. Kit knew at once she had seen that ring before. It was the very one she had retrieved for the queen when she was dying, bearing the image of her mother inside. "I do not want the threat of my cousin hanging over me forever." The queen's voice deepened so that her words were difficult to discern, with the wind picking up and the blackbirds chirping. "It must come to an end."

"I agree." Walsingham nodded. "Then let us use the diplomatic channels to bring her threat to an end. I have intelligencers watching her."

"She is under house arrest and yet people conspire to put her on the throne anyway. No, watching her is plainly not enough." Once more, the queen turned. She brushed the skirt of her gown to the side and pinned her gaze on Kit. "I need to ask my cousin to abandon any claim she has to the throne. She must declare it, quite openly. Only then will I be safe."

"That is the letter you wish me to take to her?" Kit asked slowly, beginning to understand.

"It says something to that effect." The queen reached into the billowing sleeve of her gown and retrieved a letter, folded up so small that it fitted snugly in the palm of her hand. As she passed it to Kit, the plain red wax seal brushed her skin. With no royal emblem, the letter could have been sent from anyone.

"No," Walsingham whispered. "Your Majesty, you know as I do that Mary Stuart is not a woman to be reasoned with. She will merely try to use such a letter against you."

"Should she try, then I can deny all knowledge of it, can I not?" the queen asked, with a triumphant smile. "After all, why would a queen have a letter delivered not by an envoy, but by a woman travelling quite alone?"

Kit froze, meeting the queen's gaze and understanding exactly what her purpose was. "It is to be a complete secret."

"Just so." The queen nodded. "No one can know of it — only the three of us. Consider this my olive branch to my cousin. If she accepts, then maybe there is a way out of the world we find ourselves in." The corner of her thin, pale lips quirked a little. "I hope it is possible." She turned and stepped away, returning to the raised bench.

"If she refuses your olive branch, Your Majesty? What then?" Kit still held the letter in her palm, not pocketing it quite yet.

"Then I know where I stand with her." The queen slowly reclined on her bench, turning to Walsingham. "Do you have any further complaints?"

"It is a risk. An unnecessary one." Walsingham was breathing heavily.

"On the contrary, it is quite necessary." The queen motioned toward Kit. "You will go to Mary Stuart. She is not expecting a visitor and I do not intend to tell her keepers in advance that you are coming, for this letter, as we say, must not be revealed to anyone. You will have to find your own way into Chartley Castle."

"I can do that." Kit moved to put the letter in her doublet, and Walsingham hurried to her side.

"Try to read that letter, Walsingham, and you will find yourself dismissed from your position." The threat hung in the air, forcing Walsingham to fall still. "That is how much I need this to happen."

For a few seconds, nothing was said, then Walsingham nodded, the movement so slight that it was almost imperceptible.

"Good," said the queen. "Miss Scarlett, I do not want anyone to know where you have gone, so I hardly expect you to hurry there. Take your time about it if you must, and carve a path across the country that would make it impossible for anyone to follow you. Go to Cornwall first, for all it means to us, or the islands of Ireland. Either way, you must guarantee that no one sees you going to that castle."

"You have my word, Your Majesty." Kit glanced at Walsingham, but he made no objection to the idea of being without her services for so long.

"That will be all." The queen raised her chin, showing the meeting was at an end.

Kit curtsied. This time, she was the one to grab Walsingham's arm and urge him to bow, for he was so dumbfounded that he was not himself. The queen called to her ladies. As they hurried forward, their skirts fluttering, Kit took a firmer hold of Walsingham's arm and dragged him away, far down the garden path.

"It is not to be borne," Walsingham began to mutter to himself. "It is madness. Turmoil could ensue. Mary Stuart will hold up that letter as a sign of the queen's weakness."

They turned at the end of the garden path, heading back out to the front drive and past the yeomen guards that kept watch over the queen.

"Walsingham?"

"What has happened to her? I do not understand it." Walsingham's manner had become wilder. He thrust his hat on his head, so firmly that the rim came down past his eyebrows. "This is unwise. I fear this moment, Kit, more than I can say. With reason, Her Majesty must acknowledge that this is an error not to be made."

Kit took hold of Walsingham's arm, pulling him to a jerky stop. Ahead of them, a cart waited for Walsingham, and a horse stood beside it, with the reins in the clutches of a young guard. Kit was to take the horse back to Iomhar's house.

"We do not always act with reason, Walsingham."

"What does that mean?" he asked distractedly, his eyes dancing over her.

Kit lowered her voice, glancing at the guard and the driver of the cart before she continued. "It means that when we are warped by fear, we do things we once thought ourselves incapable of doing." Kit could remember such moments. She thought of hurrying up the hill in Newcastle, with a man running after her, determined to see her blood. "The queen has nearly met her death many times now — enough to change the way she thinks. Maybe that is what has sparked this?" She tapped her doublet.

"Is that supposed to comfort me?"

"It comforts me." Kit shrugged and moved toward her horse. "Make of it what you will."

"We must talk more of this, Kit." Walsingham followed her to the horse. "If this must be done, then I want to make sure it is done right. That what she asks for is followed completely, and no one discovers where you have been."

Kit paused with a gloved hand on the saddle, looking to Walsingham as the guard hurried off, leaving them alone. "I intend to follow her wishes."

"With no planning? No thought?" Walsingham laughed without humour as Kit pulled herself up into the stirrups. The mare beneath her whinnied softly, eager to go. "You cannot leave at this moment."

Kit turned her eyes to the open driveway of Richmond Palace, tempted to do just that. Then she remembered something the queen had said. "She does not wish me to be followed. If I journeyed elsewhere, created a path across this country that was too difficult to follow, that could work." Kit didn't look at Walsingham, for her mind was elsewhere.

The queen had suggested she could go to the far reaches of Cornwall, or even Ireland, but what if Kit went somewhere else altogether? What if she went to Scotland first? She needed to tell Niall what she had discovered in Oswyn's letter, and if what she had found there was true, then that was where the trail began in search of Iomhar. *Scotland*.

"It's a start, but more must be done in order to conceal you." Walsingham was quite frantic, rubbing his hands together as Kit shifted her focus to him. His eyes kept lingering on the pocket in Kit's doublet.

"I must follow her orders." Kit made the words slow and clear. "She does not want you to see what is in the letter."

"I know." Walsingham's eyes darted away. "Come to me tomorrow, Kit. We may discuss how this mad plan is to happen." With these words he stepped back and clicked his fingers at the driver of his cart, urging him to action. As Walsingham climbed up into the rear, the cart was already pulling away, leaving Kit to wait behind for a minute, with her mare snorting restlessly.

"It could work," Kit whispered as Walsingham and his cart disappeared down the drive. "Perhaps I can look for him now."

CHAPTER 7

"You are certain of this?" Elspeth's voice trembled as Kit began to pack. She thrust one item of clothing after another into the saddlebag, half aware that as quickly as she packed something, it was pulled back out by Elspeth. She folded each doublet and shirt neatly, then returned them to the bag.

"I am." Kit's voice was strangely calm as she marched past a coffer, on top of which balanced a single candle. The flame flickered with the movement. It was the only light they had, as darkness had come early that day. Reaching into another coffer, Kit pulled out more doublets, and brought them back to the two saddlebags she was taking with her. "If anyone should ask where I have gone, tell them I am travelling."

"Travelling where?"

"Do not tell them where." Kit shook her head.

Elspeth chewed her lip and struggled to fold one of the shirts she had taken out of the saddlebag. "Do you think that this is wise? The master is *gone*." Her words made Kit abruptly draw away from the bags and reach under the bed, looking for some boots. "If you follow him, what if you too…" Elspeth trailed off.

Slowly, Kit moved to her knees and peered over the edge of the bed, watching Elspeth on the other side as she busied herself with packing more clothes. The older woman's face bore even more pronounced lines than before, her brow furrowed deep.

"Elspeth, I am not going to die," Kit whispered.

Elspeth paused. "This house keeps falling quiet." She glanced around the room, as if ghosts lingered in the shadows. "I don't like it quiet."

Kit pulled out some boots and laid them on the bed, catching Elspeth's eye. "I will return, Elspeth. I give you my word on that."

"It's a promise you cannot make freely."

The words unsettled Kit. She bent under the bed again, reaching for more boots, when she found a small box. Unable to remember what was in the box, she pulled it out and lifted the heavy wooden lid, peering inside. "Oh." Kit gasped at the sight.

"What do you have there?" Elspeth hurried round the bed. "Oh!" she echoed. "What are you doing with a little dress like that?"

"I took it. Last year."

"You stole it?"

"No." Kit stood straight and laid the small dress on the bed. It was pink satin with a beaded neckline. "I think it used to be mine, when I was very young."

"Fine lass, were you not?" Elspeth said with a giggle.

"Fine?"

"Aye, a handsome dress indeed." Elspeth laid a hand upon the dress then reached for the neckline, admiring the beading. "Fine workmanship, this. You see these stitches? Aye, not made by a seamstress you'd find in a backstreet in London."

"I suppose not." Kit picked up the gown abruptly, determined to put it back under the bed. She had found it hidden in Walsingham's house the previous year, and she had a strange memory of wearing it as a child, before she had come to live with the spymaster. Ever since she had taken it, the dress had served as a reminder that Walsingham was hiding something from her.

"Why is it hidden under your bed?" Elspeth asked.

"Because I do not know what else to do with it." Kit laid it in the box and then kicked it away, far under the bed. "Elspeth?"

"Aye?"

"Would you do me a kindness, and let us not talk of that gown again?"

Kit's question made Elspeth's frown grow deeper. "You're a strange lass. If you wish." She rounded the bed and returned to her work with the saddlebags. Kit followed her, grabbing the boots and pushing them in haphazardly. They were instantly rearranged by Elspeth. "When will you go to look for the master?"

Kit grimaced. She intended to keep her promise to the queen, and not reveal why she was really leaving London, but she hadn't felt she could leave Elspeth with no explanation at all. "Tomorrow."

"Tomorrow?" Elspeth spluttered, dropping one of the saddlebags.

Kit managed to snatch it from the air before it could reach the ground. "As the sun rises and the moon departs, I will go."

"So soon?" Elspeth began to wring her hands. "This house will be silent again when you are gone."

"Hopefully not for too long." Kit sighed and looked over all that she had so far packed. She wasn't sure how long she would be gone for, but she had no intention of hurrying to Chartley Castle. As long as she kept the letter well hidden, that particular purpose could wait for now.

"Where will you go first?" Elspeth asked as Kit buttoned up one of the saddlebags.

"To Iomhar's family home." Kit busied herself with her task. "Niall came because his family were desperate for news of Iomhar. I promised that if I discovered something, I would tell them. I intend to keep that promise."

"You will want the address, then. Aye, it is in the bureau downstairs. I will fetch it for you." Elspeth hurried out of the room. The moment she was gone, Kit gathered some other items. She started with her weapons belt, then her two daggers, and a few more items that were a little more secret.

She tucked her compass containing hidden gunpowder deep into a secret pocket in the sleeve of her doublet, then she packed a second weapons belt, this one with an opening on the inside where a message could be stored. She was still hurrying with the items when Elspeth came back, proffering a letter from Niall that bore the family's address.

"You have a long way to go."

"Scotland is a long way."

"It is not just to the border, but further still!" Elspeth blew out her cheeks. "Aye, beyond Inverness. You are going to the Highlands."

Kit banged on the hidden door to Walsingham's house so hard that her palms turned bright red. "Come on, Doris, time to wake up!" she implored.

When the bolts were eventually slid back on the other side of the door and it opened inwards, the face of a rather weary Doris was revealed. Her coif was askew on her head, and she had a shawl wrapped around her shoulders to hide the fact that she was not fully dressed, with only her linen chemise beneath.

"Kitty!" she cried. "Why are you here so early?" She blinked a few times, her eyelashes sticking together with the sleep dust.

"It cannot wait. I have to see him." Kit glanced at the horse behind her that was ready to go, with two saddlebags pinned to the leather seat.

Doris looked between Kit and the horse in the early morning light. "You better come in, then."

Kit stepped inside, listening as the door shut heavily behind her and the bolts were fastened.

"You!" Doris snapped. Kit flicked her head round, startled to hear Doris using such a firm tone. "This is not your business. Away!" She waved a hand toward the kitchen, as if she were shooing a wayward cat.

Kit craned her neck, just enough to see the young maid being dismissed. Like Doris, she was not yet dressed for the day, with her hair hanging loose about her shoulders. She hastened away, though she kept glancing back, her blue eyes settling on Kit with curiosity.

"That girl, she will not do for us." Doris shook her head and led the way down the corridor. "The master insists that as an intelligencer's daughter, she's the best for the task. That does not mean she knows how to be a maid."

"I am sorry, Doris, I would like to talk, but I —"

"I know. I can see it in your face." Doris offered a rather weary smile. "You do not have the time for such things. Off you go, up the stairs to him. He did not retire last night. I'd wager my evening's mead he has fallen asleep by the fire again."

"Thank you." Kit shared one last smile with Doris and then rushed up the steps. Before she could even knock on the door, Walsingham's voice called from within.

"I can recognise your footsteps these days," he called. "That and the way you bang on the front door."

Kit took hold of the handle and swung the door wide, to find Walsingham bathed in grey light, his face ashen. The fire behind him had burned down.

"You are leaving so soon for your task?" He beckoned her in sharply.

"The sooner the better." Kit closed the door. "We do not want anyone in London to hear of where I have gone."

"Hmm." Walsingham nodded tersely and then rubbed his eyes. "I still think this is a poor idea."

"Do you intend for me to defy her orders?" Kit asked, dragging another chair over to the fireplace. She sat down heavily as Walsingham shook his head. His chin rested in one of his hands, with his elbow propped against the arm of the chair.

"I wish I could." He sighed deeply, his eyes darting to Kit's and away from the fire. "Take a breath for a moment, Kit, before you run off."

"Why else do you think I am here?" Kit could see it was not the time to jest, for Walsingham's lips were pursed.

"The queen is sending you on a mission you may not come back from. If you are seen by any of the people that guard Mary Stuart, then they will have you arrested — on our own orders."

"So lower the guard."

"I cannot do that. To do so would be to tell them a letter is coming. What is more, if I got them to lower the gate for you…" He grimaced, turning his eyes back to the fireplace.

"Then there is no guarantee someone else wouldn't walk through that gate."

"Exactly."

Quiet descended around them for a minute, and Kit fidgeted with her gloves. "I will not be caught."

"I choose to believe that." Walsingham smiled at her rather sadly. "You haven't been caught yet, have you?"

"I think that was a compliment. A rarity from you."

"I am not in the business of giving compliments." He chuckled softly but then lapsed into silence once more. "You must make me a promise, Kit. For the sake of the queen, and this country."

"Go on." Kit waited, watching as he lifted his chin from his cupped hand.

"If you are caught, and should anyone else follow you and try to take that letter, do not let the contents be known, by any man." Walsingham held her gaze, those dark eyes unblinking. "Burn it, if you must."

"And if it is read?"

Walsingham didn't move, his meaning becoming plain.

Kit shifted in her seat. "I am no killer, Walsingham."

"I would not have you be. Yet this situation remains grave. Protect the queen, Kit, that is all I ask of you."

Kit nodded slightly. She would burn the letter if it came to it, but anything more she would not commit to aloud. "Is there anything else you wish to say before I go?" Kit prepared to stand.

"Take care." Walsingham's gentle entreaty was so unusual that she stilled. "I mean it, Kit. Take care with this one."

"I will," she promised, standing tall. Her eyes shifted toward the door. "You truly think it is possible I might not return?"

"As I said, I choose to believe you will." His voice was calm, and very quiet.

"What if I do not? What if this were the last time you and I were to see each other?"

Walsingham stood and offered his hand to her. It was an odd action, but she took it, waiting to see what he would do. He clasped hers between both of his palms and gave another one of those weary smiles.

"Then God be with you, Kit. For both of our sakes." It was an odd sort of goodbye. It left Kit bereft, empty. This was the man who had raised her, who had watched over her ever since she could remember, and these few words were supposed to be enough of a parting. He went to release her hand, but she gripped his tighter, not letting him go just yet.

"Would you answer me one question before I go?"

"What is that?"

"Tell me the truth." She held his gaze, watching as his lips pressed together. "You know what truth I am referring to. You may have avoided this conversation for a long time, but we must have it at some point. I have no memory of begging or seeing you pass me in the street. If you did not take me from the street, where did you take me from? How did I come to be here?"

Walsingham looked down at their clasped hands. He used his other palm to pat the back of her hand just once, a small comfort. "There are some truths you are better off not knowing, Kit. Now go, before you are seen leaving this house." With those words, he released her, stepped back and gestured to the door.

Kit felt dismissed, as if she were a child again and had gone scrambling out onto the rooftops when she should have been at her lessons.

"Come home, Kit," he said quietly, before taking his seat by the fire and turning his gaze on the ashes. Kit knew better than to ask him another time, for it would not produce an answer. She hurried from the room and made plain her displeasure at his secrecy by not uttering another word.

As she rushed down the steps, Kit's footsteps were easy to hear, but when she reached the ground floor, she could have sworn that there were quieter steps behind her. She angled her head, listening out for the sound, but it had faded. Presuming Doris had merely been returning to her bed, Kit crossed the corridor and peered in through the kitchen doorway.

"You are off again, are you not, Kitty?" Doris's words made Kit jump. She was sitting in the kitchen, nursing a cup of something that smelled like cinnamon and cloves. Kit looked behind her, wondering where the footsteps had come from if they had not belonged to Doris.

"I am." Kit stepped in through the door as Doris stood.

"How long will you be gone?" Doris's question was only answered by Kit's wince. "Oh, I do not know why I continue to ask such questions. You'd think I would have learned by now that I do not get answers." She laughed at herself, but it was hollow and short-lived. "Would you like something for your journey? Food, perhaps?"

"That is not necessary."

"Please, let me do something, Kitty. Last time you and Iomhar ran off, you were gone for weeks. Oh! Each day looking out of that window here, wondering when you were coming back." Doris tittered at herself and placed down her cup. "You forget, I still think of you as the girl who first walked through these doors."

Kit smiled and leaned on the doorframe, watching as Doris bustled around the kitchen, clutching her shawl with one hand and collecting things with the other. Cheese was rolled up in a muslin cloth, along with manchet bread, some fruit, and a flagon of beer. Finally, Doris reached into a tin she kept at the far end of the kitchen and waved it for Kit to see.

"Your favourite. Just a little bit."

"Thank you." Kit smiled, strangely delighted by the sight of the marchpane that was being slipped into a bag for her to take.

"There you go. Be sure not to lose it now." Doris presented her with the bag. "And promise you will come home, Kitty?"

"You never will call me Kit, will you?"

"Never." Doris shook her head. "You're Kitty to me. Now, off with you. The sooner you're gone, the sooner you're back. I hope."

CHAPTER 8

"This is taking too long," Kit said to herself as she lifted her head, peering out from beneath the brim of her hat at the trail ahead of her. She had been riding for two days and had swapped horses, rested, and rode out again. She had made good progress and travelled into the north of England, but the Scottish border was still far away.

As she lifted the brim of her hat higher, rain dripped off the edge, marring her view of the road and hills. She was on one of the main routes between Doncaster and York, a road so well-travelled by others that the chances of meeting highwaymen were slim. It didn't stop Kit looking about her furtively, watching every passer-by for any hint of suspicion.

People didn't look her way, for they were far too caught up in their own business, either making hasty repairs to carts that would not move or urging their horses on with the crack of whips. Kit moved between them all with ease, as if she couldn't be seen. Dressed as a man and on a lone horse, she was not conspicuous enough to attract any interest. So far, it had meant her journey was uninterrupted.

The road began to slope down between two hills, prompting her horse to speed up a little, moving into a trot before Kit pulled on the reins, urging the mare to save her energy. The sun was already fading in the sky, and it wouldn't be long before she had to stop for the night. The clouds were streaked purple and separated in the wind, briefly revealing the cathedral rooftop of York far ahead.

"York," Kit whispered and pulled her hat lower, hiding her face from the rain and the people around her. The city would do for a stop for the night.

Prompting the horse on, she hastened between the carts and other riders, heading toward the city. Trees and banked earthworks along the road soon fell away and were replaced by cobbled paths and timber buildings, each one slanted, with eaves hanging out over the roads and glass windows closed tightly against the weather.

Kit followed a trail of travellers that led to the inner city, where a sign swung above a coaching inn that read, *The Golden Fleece*. Along with the others, she passed under an archway and into a courtyard, handing her horse's reins to a stable boy. Not once did the stable boy look at her face. He merely accepted the coin she offered and then moved on.

Kit headed for the nearest door through the courtyard, stepping inside behind another crowd, only to find the building was somewhat busier than she had expected. The drinking rooms were full, with not a table unattended. Most had their heads bent over tankards of ale, with their noses practically balanced on the brims, and some had pies in front of them, breaking the crusts with eager fingers.

Kit froze, her eyes darting between them as she realised something odd about the inn. Not a single woman was amongst them.

Turning her head away from the revellers and drinkers, she moved toward the bar at the far end of the room. Some men in front of her paid for their rooms for the night and moved on, leaving Kit with the perfect view of the innkeeper.

The plain black clothes and the broad white collar, yellowed from use, told Kit a lot about the man before her. He had to be a puritan to wear such staunchly religious clothes. His hat rested on the bar beside him, a small cap with no brim at all. The hat of God, as Kit had sometimes heard it called.

"One coin for the night, another for something to drink. Pay, and you'll be given a key," he said in a thick Yorkshire accent. He gestured down to a book in front of him. "Name?"

"I can't write my name, but I'll leave a mark," Kit lied, knowing she wasn't prepared to write down her name anywhere.

Her voice made the puritan innkeeper hesitate. His quill hovered over his guest book before he slowly lifted his chin, revealing his bushy beard. "Wait…" He leaned forward over the bar, eyeing Kit as if she were a cat that had wandered into his inn. "Hat off."

Kit didn't take it off but nudged it up a little, revealing her face. The man's eyes went wider still, taking in the sight of her before leaning back.

"I have the coins." Kit delved a hand into her pocket, but she didn't have the chance to take out the necessary money.

"No."

"No?" Kit repeated.

"Women are not welcome in this house. It is ungodly. Women should not be drinking in such a place."

"Truly?" Kit couldn't hide her amusement at such an idea. She glanced back over her shoulder, eyeing the rest of the inn. "Drinking to extreme wasn't godly the last time I looked. Neither is gambling." She nodded at a table where some men were playing dice. The innkeeper bristled, standing taller, apparently trying to seem a little intimidating, but he was shorter than Kit, and wiry too, so his efforts failed him. "What is so wrong with permitting a person to stay the night when they are willing to pay for the use of the room?"

"You are a woman."

"And?" Kit shrugged, not understanding the objection.

"Are you travelling alone?" The thought seemed to disgust the man even more. He glanced behind her.

"You do not need to look for anyone else." Kit pulled out the two coins and rested them on the bar in front of her. "Now, will you give me a room for the night, or not?"

"No." The man took the coins and slid them back in her direction. "Some places round here might rent to an unnatural woman," he said with scorn, his dark eyes looking her up and down, "but I won't be one of them. This is a godly house."

Kit was prepared to give him another argument as the drinkers behind her became brash and loud, guffawing at some awful jest as one of them fell to the floor and squealed like a hog. "Some godly house," she scoffed and snatched the coins back, turning on her heel and preparing to leave.

"Who was that?" someone asked the puritan innkeeper behind her.

"Didn't get her name. Stay clear. We don't need her sort here."

Kit huffed, loud enough so that the man could hear her as she stood in the doorway. They exchanged another glare before Kit stepped out into the courtyard of the coaching inn.

The rain was coming down harder now, the droplets like needles. Kit brushed them away from her cheek and stepped out, heading to the stable where she had left her horse. Hovering in the stable doorway, she was calling to the stable boy to find her horse when another group of men approached.

"She's not here."

"She is here. I'm sure I saw her come this way. Aye, have patience. She'll be here."

The curious words and the one strong Scottish accent caught Kit's interest. To hear they were looking for a woman made the hairs stand up on the back of her neck. Stepping further into the stable, she lowered her hat and placed herself behind a timber pillar, listening carefully. Angling her head to the side, in the light of one lantern that was hung over the archway to the stable, she could see three shadows cast. Three men walked into the stable, each one towing a horse.

"Boy! Take these," the Scottish voice demanded of the lad. Kit jerked at the voice, certain she had heard it before, though she was unsure where. Straining to listen, she watched the shadows as they passed over their horses' reins to the stable boy.

"She will be long gone," a second voice said. This English accent belonged to the tallest in the group, who waved his hands as he spoke. "We shouldn't have stopped for the night."

"Are ye blind? She came this way. I am sure of it."

"Are you certain that was a lady?" the third and final man asked. He was much shorter than the other two, rather rounded as well, and kept fidgeting with his clothes. "Looked like a boy to me. Had the clothes of a boy. Rode alone, too. Last woman I saw riding alone was my old cousin — mad as a march hare, she was. Rode without a coif. Or any clothes at all, come to think of it."

"Enough, Temple. Nay more of your humour now." The Scottish man slapped the third around the back of the head with the words. "Ye did not see a lady, because ye do not use your eyes."

Kit raised her head to see the stable boy looking her way, curious as he tended to the horses. Kit lifted her hand and placed a finger to her lips, silently begging the boy not to say a thing. He quickly returned his focus to the horses.

"The inn's that way, sirs," the boy said, gesturing to the door behind them on the other side of the courtyard.

"Hmm," the Scottish man grunted in acknowledgment, then turned and stepped across the courtyard, followed closely by his friends.

Only once the shadows had disappeared did Kit step out from behind the pillar. The boy moved to her side, staring at her face.

"They were looking for you, weren't they?"

"That I do not know." Kit shook her head. She couldn't think who the men were, so it seemed odd they would be here, looking for her, yet how many ladies had reached York that evening dressed as a man? Something about it didn't sound right. "Would you grant me a favour?" Kit asked and proffered another coin to the boy. "If they ask if you have seen me, you haven't."

"Blind as a bat, I am." The boy smiled and took the coin, before hurrying back to fetch her horse. "Not staying the night, ma'am?"

"No. Your master didn't see it as proper to give a lady a room for the night." Kit glanced at the archway, watching as the three men shuffled toward the door of the inn.

In the fading light, she could see a little more of them. The tallest gentleman could have been a soldier, for he walked with that customary broad stance and had weapons hung from his belt. The short and round one seemed out of place. He kept trying to start a play fight with his tall friend and was only rewarded with a firm punch to the shoulder that made him wince and buckle forward. The sight would have been funny, had Kit's eyes not rested on the third and final man.

"I do not believe it," she whispered, moving to the edge of the stable archway and peering beyond.

"Our master is odd like that," the boy called to her as he hurried to prepare her horse, clearly not aware of what had really captured her attention. "He puts his beliefs first, always. He doesn't do anything he sees as ungodly."

"Including offering shelter to a lady?" Kit scoffed, her eyes resting on the third man.

He was dressed finely, his doublet a deep purplish red, with white lace cuffs and a ruff so starched that it barely moved as he turned his head back and forth. His earring glinted as he faced his friends, telling them off and revealing features Kit had seen only twice, a long time ago.

"I'm not saying the master makes sense. He just has his beliefs."

"Or his excuses," Kit muttered angrily, still distracted. The last time she had seen the man before her, they'd been fighting. He had tipped her over the wall that bordered the edge of the River Thames in London and tossed her into the watery depths. "Graham Fraser," she whispered.

"What was that?"

"Nothing." Kit brushed off her words as the boy appeared at her side, proffering her mare.

"I hope you find a place for the night, ma'am. The Shambles is your best bet. It's a street in town, has an inn at the far end. Left at the end of the road, and again, you can't miss it."

"Thank you." Kit nodded and smiled at the boy, grateful for his help.

Any doubt Kit might have had that the men were looking for her vanished. If Graham Fraser was amongst them, then he knew of her. He knew she dressed as a man, and he would have also known she was behind his brother's imprisonment a year and a half ago, not to mention the fact that she'd foiled a plan he was involved in to see Queen Elizabeth murdered. She had no wish to stay in the same city as him.

Pulling her hat down, Kit stepped out of the stable, careful to draw the horse alongside her to mask her face and body. Walking nonchalantly, she tried not to draw attention to herself, even as she peered through the vigorous rain at the three men. Graham Fraser led the way into the building, after duly admonishing his friends. The tall man followed next, then the rounded one, who couldn't resist playfully trying to swipe one of his friend's weapons. The resulting yelp Kit heard from inside the inn was enough to show he had been punished for his actions.

The moment they were out of sight, Kit hastened the mare forward. Overtired, the horse snorted, objecting, but Kit couldn't listen to her, not if she wanted to stay clear of Fraser. They passed out under the archway and into the street, where Kit tried to clamber into the saddle. She barely had a foot in one stirrup when she heard a cry from behind her.

Whipping her head back, Kit looked into the courtyard to see the tall man running back into the centre.

"Where? Where did she go?"

Graham Fraser ran after him, stumbling in his leather boots that were fastened tight with pink bootstraps. "The man said she had just left, mere seconds ago. Aye, we cannot be far…" He didn't finish his sentence as his eyes found Kit's under the archway. She prayed he couldn't see her face in the growing darkness, but what he could see was evidently enough, as beneath his preened and heavily coiffed moustache, his lips curled into a smile.

"Good evening to ye, Miss Scarlett."

CHAPTER 9

Hauling herself into the saddle, Kit set about fleeing. She didn't know why he had come looking for her, but she wasn't going to stay to discover the reason.

"Fire, Kynborough," Fraser snapped.

Kit flicked the reins of the mare as the shot of a pistol rang out. She tried to dart out of the way, diving around the edge of the building for cover, but she was not quick enough. The mad squeal of the mare confirmed that the shot caught some of its target. The horse's legs immediately went weak beneath Kit, the hooves seemed to lose their footing, and the horse began to tumble.

"For a soldier, ye do not know how to aim, do ye?" Fraser bellowed from the courtyard.

"No, no, stay up!" Kit flicked the reins, but it was useless.

The horse tipped over and took Kit with her, rolling across the cobbled ground. Kit rolled further away, planting her hands against the damp cobbles and scrambling in the effort not to be hurt by the falling horse. She lay there, winded, listening to the horse squealing in objection, before she turned to see exactly what had happened.

The mare was on her side, lashing out with one leg, as if pawing for help the way a pup might do. The rump of the mare was bleeding heavily from the shot, the blood mixing with the puddles of rain.

"No." Kit felt anger spike inside of her, hating the men for hurting the animal.

"Kynborough! Find that rope. I'll do this myself." Fraser's Scottish accent grew nearer.

Kit jumped to her feet and moved toward the horse. One quick glance showed that the animal could not be saved. Kit cursed under her breath, laying one hand on the horse's neck, a soft touch, before she unlatched the bag from the saddle and bolted.

"Nay! Stop!" Fraser ran after her.

Kit glanced back just once through the cobbled street to see that Fraser was not alone. The tall soldier, Kynborough, was keeping pace, and the rounded fool that accompanied them, Temple, lagged behind, heaving like a cow might when it tried to run.

With quick feet, Kit followed the instructions given to her by the stable boy. She took to the main street then turned two lefts, darting down the road. It was growing late, so there were few to see her run. More and more lanterns were lit, and candles were placed in windows, casting the cobbled streets in an apricot-tinged light. Each time Kit thumped a foot into the ground, the hard cobbles made twinges ricochet up her legs. She was tired, like her mare had been, and she couldn't run for long.

"Cut her off!" The barked order came from behind and made Kit glance back briefly.

The tall soldier was shoved into another lane by Fraser, who must have been guessing what path she intended to take. Uncertain of the layout of the city, Kit had no choice but to carry on.

When a lantern light fell on a sign that read 'The Shambles', she realised the boy in the stable had been talking about a road. It was a narrow lane, barely wide enough for a cart to drive down, with meat shops either side and hooks that stood out proudly from the plastered walls. Kit sprinted down this lane, travelling up the slope, having to dart around the occasional person that was still in the street.

"Watch it!"

"Runaway boy, up to no good, you mark my words."

The shouted objections reached Kit, but she didn't once slow down, aware that the tall soldier could emerge from anywhere.

Flicking her eyes forward, she found him. He appeared at the end of The Shambles, his pistol raised. With a powder flask cupped in his other palm, he was preparing to fire.

Kit reached down to her weapons belt, searching for anything she could use. Her daggers were there, her saddlebag was tossed over her back, slapping against her spine, and at her hip was her final weapon, a crossbow. Yet she couldn't load it in time, not before Kynborough would take his shot.

Without thinking, Kit snapped up the crossbow. She kept running forward, heading straight for Kynborough, and pulled the trigger. The sound it made, as if it would release a bolt, was enough to spook Kynborough. He shuffled back, nearly dropping the pistol, though no bolt fired his way.

"Ye fool!" Fraser barked from far behind Kit in the street. "Ye are a soldier, can ye not see when a crossbow is empty?"

It was too dark, Kit knew that. As Kynborough raised the pistol another time, she had reached him. Without hesitation she took one of the short daggers from her belt and brought it down over Kynborough's hand, before he could take his shot.

He gave a guttural roar of pain, like a wild boar that had been struck by an arrow, before the pistol clattered to the cobbles.

Kit ran on, not even looking back, though she could hear Fraser cursing at Kynborough, bemoaning that he hadn't been given better men to accomplish his task.

"What task?" Kit whispered to herself as she reached the edge of the road, where it split into two streets. She dived to the left, choosing the lane that was narrower, with taller buildings on either side, and therefore much darker and quieter. However, with fewer lanterns in this lane, it was difficult to see where she was going. Still, Kit did not slow her pace. She just kept putting one foot in front of the other until her lungs burned.

Behind her, footsteps had faded. She could no longer hear Fraser shouting, nor the heavy breathing of his rounded friend, or the firing of a pistol. It was just possible she had shed her chasers, but Kit didn't stop yet.

A fear had crept into her mind. The last time she had seen Fraser, he was working for Lady Ruskin — a woman who had wanted Kit's blood. What was worse, ever since Lady Ruskin's death, Lord Ruskin had wanted to kill Kit in revenge.

"No," Kit murmured, not wanting to believe that Fraser could have been sent here to complete that task.

Turning at the edge of the road down a new street, all Kit could think of was finding somewhere to hide. Glancing over her shoulder, Kit found the street empty. With that single look, unaware of where she was putting her feet, she tripped over a misaligned cobble. With her body flinging forward, Kit landed on the ground, her chin ramming against one of the cobbles so hard that the pain sparked up through her jaw.

"God's blood," Kit cursed and lifted herself slowly. Raising a single finger to her chin, she found a drop of blood.

Footsteps echoed. Kit glanced back to see the tall soldier not three steps away, apparently having taken a different street through the town. A second and third set of footsteps soon followed, and Kit looked forward to see Graham Fraser stepping out from the shadows. Beside him was Temple, breathing heavily and clutching his chest.

"Good evening, Miss Scarlett. Quite a mess ye are making of yourself." Fraser gestured to the cut on her chin.

Kit scrambled to her knees, looking between the men, searching for a way out of this situation. Her eyes briefly darted to the windows around her, but no one was looking down at them. This part of the city was quiet, and though she could see one lone candle in a window, no face peered out.

"Did ye think ye could keep running forever?" Fraser asked, squatting in front of her.

In the time that had passed since she had seen him, he had changed. More wrinkles lined his face, as if carved there by time and worry. His ruff was still in place, but as she peered above the line of that starched linen, Kit could just about see the tattoo she had once spied on his neck, the unicorn.

"I thought I might," Kit said. Her voice shook slightly as the soldier, Kynborough, walked forward, drawing level with them.

"Give it to me." Fraser held out his hand and Kynborough passed him his pistol. "Lord Ruskin says goodbye, Miss Scarlett." He lifted the gun and pointed it at Kit's temple.

In the darkness, Kit's eyes shot to the trigger of the pistol. She had no time, and time was what she needed if she was going to escape. "I'm not going to die today."

Kit's words seemed to baffle the three men before her. Fraser paused, his finger not quite squeezing the trigger. Temple laughed.

"You forgot to say she was mad. Now I understand why she's dressed the way she is," he tittered.

"Be quiet." Fraser eyed his friend, before looking back at Kit. "Ye have some magic we should know of, eh? Do bullets not hurt ye?"

"Not exactly." Kit was glad to have his attention. Slowly, she lowered her hands to her belt, slyly hooking her fingers around the hilt of one of her daggers.

"Then pray tell, how do ye plan to survive a bullet?"

"Not accurate, are they? These pistols." Kit gestured to the weapon.

Fraser stepped closer and placed the barrel flush to the middle of her temple. The metal was cold against her skin. "I'll hit ye from here."

Kit didn't give him another chance at the trigger. She brought up her dagger. Fraser must have seen her movement out of the corner of his eye, for as Kit slashed at his hand with the dagger, the gun went off, echoing loudly around the narrow street as the bullet landed somewhere in the cobbles.

"Damn ye!" Fraser roared, cupping his injured hand. Kit scrambled back, moving to stand. In the dim light, she could see that the skin across his knuckles had peeled open, and he was breathing heavily.

"Fraser! Here, let me." Temple hurried forward, wrapping a rather fine handkerchief around Fraser's hand.

"Leave me, go after her!" Fraser barked.

"Oh, yes, right you are." Temple stepped forward, his eyes flicking nervously down to Kit with the dagger in her hand. Evidently, he did not like his chances.

Kynborough went to pick up the pistol, but Kit kicked it away before he could reach it. The weapon collided with the nearest wall, and a horrid crack emanated. The gun fell to the ground in two pieces.

"Find anything to do the deed. Just kill her. Follow your orders," Fraser snapped, cradling his hand.

Temple hung back, uncertain what to do, but Kynborough wasn't so nervous. He had cut off part of his sleeve and wrapped it around the hand that Kit had wounded earlier. As he advanced on her, he snapped up a battle-axe from his belt. It was small, with the metal head as black as its wooden pole, but it was also heavy, judging by the way Kynborough carried it, with the head pointed downwards.

Kit backed up as much as she could, moving quickly across the cobbles. She knew well enough that her daggers wouldn't do much against such a weapon. One well aimed blow, and her blades would shatter into pieces. Taking up the other dagger from her belt, she clutched both, preparing herself for what would undoubtedly be a difficult fight.

Kynborough advanced first, swinging at her with the axe, but it was heavy, and his movements were laboured, so she was able to dodge the blow with ease, stepping to the side.

"No dancing now, lass," he ordered. His accent was northern, though she couldn't identify where it was from. He swung, but once again she dodged the blow easily enough, making him grunt in anger. He began to circle the axe, aiming two continuous blows in Kit's direction. Bending down, she dodged the first blow and barely escaped the second by diving to the side and rolling over, hurrying to her feet.

In this new position, on the incline of a hill, she had a good view. Further down the road, Fraser was still angry about the cut on his hand, and Temple was wrapping it up. Behind them, the lane forked into two streets. On one side, the road went down, heading further into the city with high timber walls on either side of the track. The other lane led to a high gate, with an archway made of stone and etched with depictions of creatures and saints, their faces eerie in the shadows.

The gate led out of the main body of the city. It was Kit's best chance to escape.

When Kynborough came at her, she beckoned him forward, practically taunting him. He roared as he swung the axe. She dived at a particular angle, glancing at the wall behind her at the edge of the road before she did so, knowing where his axe would have to fall.

It lodged in the plasterwork of the building. Kynborough tried to release it, tugging with both hands.

Kit moved to stand beside him, then acted quickly. With one swipe of her dagger, she cut through his weapons belt, then pulled it from his body. Kynborough released his axe, trying to grab the belt back from her. Using it as a whip, she lashed out in his direction. He backed up before she could make contact, winding himself in the back by walking into the handle of his axe and buckling to the ground.

Kit hurried back. Seeing Kynborough was no longer in a fit state to chase after her, she ran in the direction of the other men.

"Look, look!" Temple cried, hooting like an owl and pointing at her. "She's coming."

"She's not a witch, ye fool. Find me a weapon," Fraser commanded. Yet Temple had started to run, barely held back by Fraser snatching the tail of his cloak and dragging him into position. By the time Temple had fumbled to get a dagger from his own belt and passed it to Fraser, Kit was with them.

Swiping the belt through the air, she knocked the dagger from Fraser's hand. He backed up, his eyes going wide and his moustache twitching. Kit grabbed him, not hesitating, before switching their positions. Standing behind him, she held one hand firmly at his throat, bearing the dagger. Everything fell still.

Temple quivered, pointing at Kit as if he were watching some tragedy on a stage. Kynborough was staggering toward them, rubbing his back where he had injured himself. In her grasp, Fraser was breathing heavily, betraying his fear.

"Ye won't kill me," he quipped as Kit backed up with him, heading for the fork in the road.

"You do not know that." Kit's words were quiet as she glanced behind her, checking she was heading for the gate.

"Nay? Ye're an intelligencer, not an assassin. Ye will not kill me." Fraser's words grew more confident as the blade of Kit's dagger stayed firmly on his neck but didn't move.

"Do you wish to find out?" Kit's eyes darted between Kynborough and Temple, following them. "Stand back," she warned, "or…" She trailed off, just pressing the dagger a little harder against Fraser's throat. He tipped his head, making a gagging sound at the pressure.

Fraser waved a hand at his men. At once, they skulked back. Temple was the first, eager in his steps, but Kynborough hovered a little more, reaching down for his weapons belt before remembering it was no longer there. His hands fell limp at his sides.

Kit moved a little closer to the gate. She was so close now that she could see what was on the other side. The road sloped down a little bit, the cobbles soon giving way to a dirt track. On either side, the buildings opened out, before they stopped completely. A short distance away, there was a river, its surface as black as spilled ink.

"Do not follow," she warned, backing up further with Fraser. This time, Kynborough nodded. He stayed where he was, with Temple panicking at his side. Temple grabbed Kynborough's shoulder and shook him.

"She's getting away. She's going to kill him!"

"She will not kill him if we stay here."

"Ye fools," Fraser muttered, his voice croaky in Kit's grasp. She backed up further, passing under the gate so that the two of them were momentarily hidden in the shadows, before they stepped out on the other side.

The moonlight was growing, bathing the street as the clouds moved and the rain began to slow. That light was enough for Kit to see her path. It wasn't far now. She was nearly at the river. She just prayed that when she reached it, it could offer an escape route.

When enough distance was between the two of them and the others, Kit knew it was time to release Fraser. A short distance away was a bridge. If she ran fast enough, she could flee across the water.

"You will stay here, and you will not move," Kit whispered in Fraser's ear.

"Ye going to let me go?" he asked, startled. "I knew it. Ye are nay killer."

"I am not you," Kit hissed, thrusting him forward out of her hold. She turned, ready to run for the bridge when Fraser ran forward. With his hands outstretched, he headed straight for her neck.

Kit brought her dagger up again, but she was too slow. His hands found her throat. The pressure was sudden, unyielding, squeezing so tight that she couldn't take a single breath.

"Ye made a mistake," he sneered. "Only one way to fight a killer."

Kit knew her mistake. She could have taken the opportunity when he was in her hold. She could have hurt him, or worse, killed him. No matter how many times the words echoed in her mind that she was no killer, the reality came back to her. It didn't make a difference, for it all could be about to end.

Kit stopped trying to peel his fingers away from her neck. Lifting the dagger, she aimed for a sensitive spot with the hilt — straight at Fraser's breeches. He groaned, the sound barely recognisable as human, as he reeled backward. His hands fell from Kit's neck as she swiped out again with her dagger. This time, she wounded him. It sliced open the back of his doublet and he fell to the cobbles, clutching the cut on his back.

Reminded of her fight with the assassin in Newcastle, Kit stumbled back, knowing she was getting closer and closer to the edge of the wall that stood tall over the river.

"Do something, ye fools!" Fraser yelled. Kynborough and Temple were running down the road, hastening through the gate toward her.

Kit glanced between the bridge and her position, knowing she wouldn't have time to make the escape now. Her only chance was to try something else entirely. Turning to face the river, she placed the dagger in her weapons belt and moved her toes to the very edge.

"Fortune favours fools," she whispered, jumping into the water.

CHAPTER 10

Holding her breath, Kit lingered in the depths of the river for a second, the bubbles fizzing around her, then looked up. This time, she wouldn't let the fear return. Since childhood, she had been plagued by nightmares in which she was suspended underwater, with someone walking away from her, and Walsingham's hand reaching down toward her. Over the past two years, she had become sure that the dream was a memory, although Walsingham refused to talk about it, but today she did not have time to dwell on such visions.

Thrusting her head toward the surface, she broke through, breathing deeply. Flinging a hand to her chest, Kit realised what she had done. Hidden on her person was the queen's letter, which now may well be soaked, the ink blurred.

"By this light," Kit cursed, just as she heard hurried footsteps. Angling her head upward as she treaded water, three figures appeared at the edge of the wall, staring down at her.

"Do not just stare. Temple, ye go after her." Fraser looked ready to push his rounded friend into the water. Temple wobbled on the edge, waving his arms like a baby bird flapping its wings.

"I can't swim! I'm not going in there."

"We do not need to." Kynborough stepped forward. He had the two pieces of the gun Kit had broken earlier in his hand. As she bobbed, she saw she had not broken the weapon completely. Kynborough snapped the safety catch into place and reloaded the weapon from his powder flask.

In the moonlight, Kit saw Fraser smile down on her, before he waved goodbye with his injured hand. When the barrel pointed in her direction, Kit gasped, diving under the water.

It was hard work. Remembering everything Iomhar had instructed when he had taught her to swim, she thrust herself deeper, praying that in the darkness Kynborough could not see to aim properly. Iomhar's lesson burned in the back of her mind, as well as the reassurances he had offered: "Nothing will happen, I promise ye."

The memory was torn by the bullet that shot through the water. It sounded odd, a muffled whistle, followed by bubbles against Kit's eardrums. She looked behind her to see the bullet mere inches from her, with a trail of bubbles behind it. Kit swam forward, heading further and further down the river, wary of lifting her head again.

She kept swimming, as more bullets peppered the area. One landed in front of her face, forcing her backward, then another behind her. Feeling her lungs beginning to burn, Kit took a chance. Her hat was slipping from her head, falling down the back of her neck and about to bob away on the water. She grasped at it, then pushed it high, praying it would float. It hovered there for a minute, not going anywhere as she treaded water. Then it bobbed higher, caught by the current of the river.

When the hat reached the surface, more bullets followed, yet they traced the path the hat took, bobbing down the stream with the current. Kit turned under the water and swam the other way. By now, her chest was hurting, and she could feel her heart thudding hard in her chest. She swam as far as she could, before she had no choice but to break the river's surface.

Swimming quickly to the top, she broke through. Rivulets of water ran down her neck as the rain came down hard. In the distance, she could hear the shouts of Fraser and his men, but she could no longer see them. They had followed the bend of the river and were no doubt shooting her hat until nothing remained but scraps of cloth.

Kit coughed, ensuring no water was left in her lungs, then she swam upstream. Sometimes the current was too strong, and she had to pull against the wall beside her to propel her further down.

Kit didn't know for how long she swam. The clouds kept moving, and sometimes it rained. Other times, the moon came out to gaze at her, as if checking on her progress. Soon, the wall that bordered the river fell away and a riverbank appeared, showing she had left the city far behind. When reeds grew at the edge of the river, Kit took hold of the fibrous strands and heaved herself out of the water.

The air was cold, far too icy, and she began to shiver so much that she could have sworn her skin was separating from her bones.

"At least I'm alive," Kit reminded herself and flung the saddlebag down beside her.

Worried for the queen's letter, Kit reached for her weapons belt and hurried to undo it, before pulling open the very end where there was a small gap. Inside, she had hidden the letter away, in a case of its own. Carefully, she inched the holder out a little at a time, hunching her body over it to protect it from the rain. She revealed a very small silver case, engraved across the top with an ornate F and W. It had belonged to Walsingham many years ago, but he had given it to Kit when he had found her playing with it as a child when she should have been practising for her lessons.

Kit opened up the case to see that the letter remained inside. There were drips on the edge, and one or two words of the address were a little blurred, but most of the letter appeared undampened, protected by the silver case.

"Thank the Lord." Kit waved the letter in the air with the words, doing her best to dry the wet bits.

As the rain stopped, Kit sat back on her haunches. *This* was her task, to deliver the letter. Someone must have known she was going to leave London for such a task to be able to warn Lord Ruskin, and thereby Fraser too, of her departure. What made it all the more worrying was that she was on the wrong road for Mary Stuart's prison, Chartley Castle. She was heading to Scotland, yet Fraser had still managed to track her.

Kit lay down on the riverbank, hardly caring if the earth was wet, for she was already sodden to the bone, trembling. Snatching up the letter, she placed it in the silver case, then hid it in her belt, being careful to fasten it around her waist. With her eyes trained on the sky, she gazed at the stars, wondering what to do next.

She couldn't head back into York now, for fear of coming across Fraser and his men again, but the main route north that she knew of headed through York.

"I need to find another way." Kit's sigh was met with the sound of twigs snapping. Jerking to her knees, Kit looked either side of the riverbank. On the far side, fields stretched out, no doubt belonging to a farmer judging by the cows that were huddled together in a corner. Yet on her side, the riverbank was crowded with trees. Another twig broke, and leaves rustled. "Who's there?" Kit called, wary of Fraser and the others having tracked her this far.

"There's someone there, Cicely."

"You're hearing things again."

Two strong Yorkshire accents emanated from the trees, both belonging to women.

As Kit stood, the squelching of her boots in the riverbank was enough of a noise to draw attention.

"No, I definitely heard something."

"Last night you thought you heard the Lord speak to you."

"Maybe he did," the first voice insisted.

"Why would the Lord tell you to take better care of our house, Wyn? I think he concerns himself with other things."

Kit could see the women were getting closer, for a tree rustled nearby and the leaves shook. She tried to inch back, but her boots squelched again.

"There! I heard something."

"It will be a deer, or an owl. Maybe God's holy spirit has come to warn you to sweep up more."

"Cicely!"

"Calm yourself. Now, where did this noise come from?"

Before the first woman, Wyn, had time to answer, she swept some branches away.

Kit froze, staring back at the two women who gazed at her. They were both pale in the moonlight, almost as white as owl's faces.

"See? I told you I heard something," Wyn declared quite proudly.

"A highwayman, by the looks of it." The larger of the two began to retreat, almost colliding with a branch behind her.

"I'm no highwayman." Kit's words made both women freeze. She tried to shake off the excess water from her hands, but her body just began to tremble all the more.

"It's a woman!" Wyn cried and stepped forward, coming so close to Kit that she backed up, nearly ending up in the river again. The stranger saved her by clutching her wrists. Wyn was a small thing, both in width and height. She just about reached Kit's elbow, yet she had the grasp of a much broader woman. "Look at you. Gone for a swim? No time for swimming now."

"It was not intentional," Kit said, though she had jumped in.

"Wyn!" Cicely snapped from behind her. "She is not an animal you can drag in out of the cold."

"Look at her. She's shaking all over like a leaf." Wyn bestowed a rather sweet smile on Kit that left her wrongfooted. She tried to extract her hands, but it didn't do any good. The small lady held onto her tightly, peering at Kit through the loose locks of grey hair that had fallen down from her coif. "You hurt at all?"

"Just cold," Kit said hurriedly.

"Wyn? You took a hedgehog home last night. It's still wrapped up in your bed. You want to take a woman now too?" Cicely appeared to do a double-take, her dark hair flicking around her ears as she looked at Kit. "What are you wearing?"

"Clothes," Kit answered dryly. Her words made Cicely smile a little.

"She needs help. Look at her," Wyn pleaded.

"You can't take a woman home."

"Where is home?" Kit asked.

"Never you mind." Cicely shook a hand at Kit, urging her to be quiet. "Wyn, come. We shouldn't be out at this time of night anyway."

"But…" Wyn looked most disappointed, releasing Kit and taking a few steps away.

Kit picked up her saddlebag and latched it over her shoulder. The action must have drawn attention to the weapons at her belt, for Wyn dug her heels into the ground and stared. The suddenness of her movement nearly dragged her companion over.

"Oomph! Why are we stopping?"

"Look!" Wyn gestured to the belt. Cicely's eyes went wide as Kit lowered the weapons on her hips, suddenly self-conscious, aware of how strange she must seem to these country women. They were dressed in clothes that weren't particularly fine, though they certainly looked warm. Their heavy woollen dresses were pale blue and grey; they wore darker cloaks around their shoulders and coifs that didn't sit easily on their heads. The skirts of their gowns bore signs of work, and their boots were scuffed. They seemed to have a habit of continuously talking, as if Kit wasn't there at all.

"I see them," Cicely said.

"Not seen something like that before."

"The soldiers carry something like it."

"Not like that. And no soldier is a woman!" Wyn insisted, waving a hand at Kit again.

Kit sighed. This strange encounter wasn't getting her anywhere, and her body was becoming so cold that her legs hurt. "Excuse me," she said, stepping forward. "Could you point me to a road leading north, please?"

"North?" Cicely repeated, before she exchanged a worried glance with Wyn. "Are you heading somewhere on foot?"

"As you see." Kit glanced at the river, thinking of the poor mare that was left behind in York city. The suffering of the animal was another reason to despise Fraser and his friends.

"Where are you going?" Cicely asked.

"Scotland." Kit saw no point in lying.

"You cannot go all that way on foot," Wyn laughed.

"I'll try." Kit stepped forward and walked around them. At first, Cicely dragged back Wyn, as if fearful that Kit would hurt them. Kit was careful to give the ladies a wide berth, before discovering just where the ladies had come from.

A thin path led through the trees. One way led deeper into the forest, while the other seemed to lead out toward some houses in the distance. They weren't part of York, but a village close by. Kit took off toward it, soon aware that Cicely and Wyn were on her tail.

"Dear, you cannot go all the way to Scotland on foot," Wyn said again, this time adopting a familiarity that made Kit snap her gaze toward her.

"I'll do what I can. Now, I need a fire. If you would excuse me, I need to warm up." Kit strode forward, faster this time, not thinking of anything except heading for the village. As her teeth began to chatter, Wyn waved a hand madly at Cicely.

"Look at the girl! Cold to the bone. You want her to die, Cicely?"

"You already have a hedgehog in your bed. I'm not taking another animal home."

"Animal?" Kit spluttered, turning to face Cicely.

She jumped back, nearly colliding with the trees. "My sister has a habit of collecting things," Cicely hurried to explain. "Why else do you think we are out on a night like this? She likes to help the injured and the sick."

"That I do." Wyn took hold of Kit's arm. "And look, I have found someone injured and sick."

"I'm not —"

"If you don't get some dry clothes on you soon, you will be sick. Now, come." Wyn pulled Kit forward. "We have a fire at home, ale too, and a bed to warm yourself. What do you say?"

"I…" Kit struggled for words. She looked to Cicely, who seemed equally dumbstruck. "I should say thank you." Kit managed eventually. She wanted to be pushing forward to Scotland, but with her body shaking so much, she could not go on until she was warm and her saddlebag was dried out.

"You are most welcome." Wyn looked thrilled with herself. "Come on, Cicely, lead the way!" She waved a hand dramatically in front of her. Cicely began to murmur under her breath as she trudged down the path, but she made no louder complaint. "Ignore her. She is not fond of waifs and strays."

Kit looked down at herself, realising what an ominous figure she must have made. "I can hardly say I blame her."

"Will you tell me why you were in the river?" Wyn asked, still holding onto Kit's arm.

"I was running from some men." Kit wasn't sure why the truth fell from her lips; it merely seemed odd to think of lying to these ladies. After all, who were they going to tell? "The men... They wanted to kill me."

At these words, Cicely stopped ahead of them and turned back. Neither woman said anything, but they seemed to nod, as if a silent understanding passed between them.

"This way," Cicely said with sudden vigour and charged forward.

"Looks like you have a bed for the night after all, dear."

CHAPTER 11

"Here you are."

A bowl appeared in front of Kit. She looked up from where she had been staring into the fire, with her short hair beginning to dry.

"Thank you." She took the bowl that was being offered by Wyn, then shuffled closer to the fire, looking around at the room she was in.

The cottage Cicely and Wyn lived in together was small, barely two whole rooms, though it was enough for them. The moment Kit had arrived, Wyn had urged her out of her wet clothes, which were now hanging over the fire along with her saddlebag and the clothes that had been tucked away inside. Her boots sat on the floor of the stone hearth, dangerously close to the flames. Kit wore nothing but a smock that Wyn had insisted she borrowed.

"Get that down you. It will help," Wyn assured, sitting in a chair nearby. Kit hurried to eat. The stew was only made of vegetables, but it was warm, fragrant, and filling. At that moment, it was what Kit wanted. "There, you've got some colour in your cheeks already. What can we call you, dear? You have a name?"

"Kit."

"Kit?" Cicely scoffed. "Is that a woman's or a man's name?"

"It's short for Katherine, or Kitty." Kit kept her focus on her stew, not bothering to explain any more.

"Well, Kit. There is no need to worry for the night. You'll be safe here," Wyn said with a kind smile.

"Your hedgehog will be most disappointed to hear his bed has gone for the night," Cicely chuckled as she took the seat beside Wyn.

"I'd say they could share, but he might be a prickly companion." The two women laughed together.

Kit paused with her stew and stared at the women. They were easy with each other, warm, and laughed readily. It was rather nice to be around them, even with Cicely shooting suspicious glances at Kit every now and then.

"You do look like a soldier," Wyn said after some minutes.

"As you said, women can't be soldiers." Her sister dismissed the idea.

"Then who carries those sorts of weapons?" Wyn gestured to where Kit's weapons were discarded on a nearby table, before they both looked at her, evidently wanting an answer.

"I cannot say what I do," Kit said between mouthfuls.

"Can you tell us who is hunting you?" Cicely asked nervously, shooting a glance at the door. It was locked tight, but she had drawn a table in front of it, apparently nervous of who would follow Kit.

"They want me dead," Kit whispered as she poked at the food. "That's all that really needs to be said." She lowered the spoon to the bowl and lifted her hand to her neck, where Fraser's fingers had pressed against her. She could feel a swelling, suggesting she would soon have bruises.

"Well, don't you worry, dear. You can stay here tonight," Wyn declared. Her sister tutted, discomforted, yet she didn't refute the idea. "You want to tip her outside?"

"No," Cicely conceded. "I won't send a girl to her death."

"Thank you," Kit said again. This time, Cicely offered her a small smile, though it didn't last long. In the firelight, Kit could see the wrinkles in Cicely's face. They were more pronounced than her sister's.

"You said you were travelling to Scotland?"

"Yes."

"Why?" Cicely angled her head, watching Kit closely. When Kit concentrated on her stew, hardly in a hurry to reply, Cicely huffed. "I don't like helping a girl that won't give us answers."

"She's being hunted! Like a deer, oh, like that poor deer we found that had been shot by an arrow the other day. Poachers, it was." Wyn clasped her hands to her chest, bemoaning its loss. "You want to let that happen here?"

"No! I just want to know something. I don't like a mystery. We could be inviting danger to our door." Cicely leaned forward, fixing a harsh gaze on Kit. She was so close to her that in the orange firelight, Kit could see the moles that were scattered across the older woman's chin. "You want to know where the north road is? Then tell me something."

"I could just wait until the sun rises, then see which way is north," Kit pointed out.

Wyn giggled. Cicely seemed to fight her own smile before nodding.

"You have a head on your shoulders, a smart one, I'll give you that," Cicely nodded. "We've given you food, and if my sister has her way, a bed for the night."

"I am getting my way," Wyn insisted.

"So, I will have something my way." Cicely placed her hands on her knees and leaned even further out of her chair. "Where are you going?"

"To the Highlands," Kit explained slowly. "A friend of mine went missing. I intend to find him." Her words prompted the sisters to look at one another.

"She's an odd one, isn't she?" Cicely said to her sister.

"A rescue?" Wyn said with awe.

Kit grimaced at the idea, praying it didn't come to that. "I don't know where he is." She was aware of Cicely fidgeting in her seat, her manner becoming more comfortable and her spine less rigid.

"Don't like the idea of a girl going all that way on her own," she murmured.

"I can take care of myself." Kit's words merely earned raised eyebrows from Cicely and Wyn. When Kit returned to her stew, Cicely sighed.

"You'll need what help you can get, then. The north road is that way." Cicely gestured through the window. Kit sat straight, startled by the sudden reveal. "When dawn comes, turn left beyond this window, then just keep going. You'll get to York, and then go on. Keep heading that way and you'll eventually reach the border. You got a long way to go yet."

"I know." Kit ate the last of the stew, doing everything she could to scrape up the remaining dregs. When she realised that she would have to go back to York after all, she paused with the spoon in her mouth and her eyes on the fire.

"What is it?" Wyn asked, sensing her discomfort.

"The men I was running from." Kit lowered the bowl. "They might be waiting for me in York."

Cicely and Wyn exchanged nervous looks. Kit didn't know what more to say or do. These two strangers had been kind enough to take her in. Fidgeting and pulling at the edges of the smock, she wished to make her gratitude known.

"Thank you. Truly," Kit whispered. "I would not have blamed you for leaving me on that riverbank."

"You are most welcome," Wyn beamed.

"My sister brings home every injured thing she finds," Cicely huffed. "Last week, she found an injured badger. He was content for a day or so, wrapped up in our rug, before he became quite aggressive, and we had to kick him out of the door."

"He just didn't know how to say thank you," Wyn insisted. "Kit, dear, when these men look for you, will they be looking for you as you are? In these clothes?" Wyn gestured to the clothes drying over the mantelpiece.

"Yes." Kit nodded, wondering where Wyn was taking the conversation.

"No, Wyn. No, before you go any further —" Yet Cicely was cut off.

"Maybe there is a way to get you through York, dear, without any of these men seeing you are there."

Cicely looked ready to argue again, but Wyn waved a hand at her sister, urging her to be quiet.

Kit sat forward on her knees. "How?" she asked.

"Keep your head down, Kit. If they know your face, then don't give them a chance to see it." At Cicely's hasty whisper, Kit followed the order and bent her head down. "And stop fidgeting. You'll draw attention to yourself."

"I've never known a dress to be so itchy." Kit shifted on the cart, where she was sitting between Cicely and Wyn. "Is there lice in this?"

"No!" Wyn declared rather quickly, though Cicely laughed as she whipped the reins of the two horses drawing them forward.

"It may have been home to our hedgehog for a while, though." Cicely's words made Kit wrinkle her nose and lift her head away, suddenly understanding where the odd smell that surrounded her was coming from.

Fixing her eyes on the road ahead, Kit could see they were not the only cart and horse heading into York this morning. There was a whole line of carts they were following. Amongst them were lonely riders and the occasional walker. Some peeled off in different directions, and some were heading for the northern side of town, toward a tall gate set in the stone city walls.

Kit tried to stay still in the dress that had been given to her. Underneath the rather tight bodice, made of pale blue wool, she wore the same smock she had been in the night before. If she stood off the cart, it would have been noticeable that the dress was a little short for her, so Cicely had insisted she stayed sitting, with a wide-brimmed grey hat low on her brow. Behind her was her saddlebag, bearing her usual clothes and her weapons belt, in which she'd hidden Queen Elizabeth's letter. More than once Kit found herself glancing toward the saddlebag, checking it was still there, until Cicely glared at her, warning her to be still.

"Now, Kit, listen here," Wyn said, leaning toward her as they rode closer to the north end of town. "At the gate, they sometimes search passers-by."

"Why?"

"They say they're looking for criminals. Hmm. Who knows, really?" Cicely warned on Kit's other side. "I say they just like to nose into other people's business."

"Shh. We're nearly there," Wyn whispered. "Best stay quiet, dear. We'll handle this conversation."

Kit was only too happy to agree. She slumped down at the front of the wagon as Cicely and Wyn struck up a conversation, talking about chickens and eggs, something so domestic and boring they evidently hoped to disarm the guards that stood at the northern gate.

Once the cart in front of them had passed under a stone arch, flanked by two riders, Kit set her eyes on the men that walked toward their cart. There were guards for the city, who reported to the Sheriff of York, dressed in dark blue uniforms and the occasional shining piece of armour that sat heavily on their shoulders. Amongst them, another man moved, someone dressed far too ostentatiously to be just another guard.

When Kit's eyes fell on the rather pointed shoes and the elaborate moustache, she slumped further down at the front of the cart, beginning to think that hiding in plain sight was a bad idea. As their cart pulled to a stop by the gate, the guards moved toward them, along with the moustached man, Graham Fraser.

"Ho, there," one guard said and approached the cart on Cicely's side. "Where are you off to today?"

"Since when is it your business where we go?" Cicely asked, sniffing in annoyance.

"Prickly, my sister is, sir," Wyn cut in with a warm laugh. "She don't want anyone to know our business."

"Well, all that pass must declare a reason and pay the toll. Where are you going?"

Kit jerked her head up at the word toll, then set her eyes on Graham Fraser. He wasn't looking at them but at the carts behind them. He appeared to curse under his breath then turn to talk to a guard nearby, passing him a few coins. It didn't take any great leap of Kit's imagination to realise that Fraser was bribing the guards to let him search the passing carts.

"To see our sister," Wyn answered the guard before Cicely could rebuke him again. "Our niece here needs to see her mother. She's sick. It's north of here."

"Let us hope we do not bring the sickness back with us," Cicely said with a soft laugh. "Who knows, maybe we carry it with us already?"

Kit bowed her head and hid her smile at Cicely's words, seeing what she was doing. It worked well, for the guard backed up instantly.

"We don't want sickness here. Pay your toll and throw your money on the ground." He told them the price and gestured to the earth at his feet.

Kit hurried to put her hand in her pocket and offered the coins to Cicely to toss away. Flicking her eyes to Fraser, she could see him walking past their cart, still talking to the guard he'd paid beside him. As they passed, she caught a fragment of their conversation.

"She'll be here, I know it."

"And who are we looking for? A sheep dressed in wolf's clothing?"

"Ye could say that…"

Soon, Fraser was gone, off to search the other carts. As they were beckoned forward through the city gate, Kit blinked a few times, not quite believing that the plan had worked. It seemed that Fraser was so intent on looking for a woman in man's clothes, travelling alone, he couldn't even look close enough to see she had been sitting before him.

For a minute or so, their cart travelled on in silence, until they reached the river at the other end of town. Turning into the side of the road, Cicely pulled on the reins, drawing them to a stop.

"Well, that was more amusing than I thought it would be," she laughed to herself and shook her head.

"He was there," Kit murmured. "I cannot believe he didn't see me."

"Sometimes, people can't see what's in front of them." Cicely jumped down from the cart, allowing Kit to do the same, before she unlatched the second of the horses that pulled the cart forward. "Now, dear, you take this horse and keep on riding."

"I'll bring it back to you someday, I promise," Kit said, taking her saddlebag from the back of the cart and preparing to leave. Wyn passed her the reins but didn't release them yet. When Kit moved her gaze to her, she saw there was a wetness in her eyes, one she was trying to fight.

"You stay safe, now," Wyn pleaded, keeping her voice level. "I don't want to hear of a girl being killed on the road."

"You have seen her weapons," Cicely called from the cart. "No man's going to kill her easily."

Kit smiled then latched the saddlebag over her shoulder and pulled herself onto the horse. For now, she would ride in the gown, and change as soon as she was far enough away from York. Pausing before she left, she turned to face Cicely and Wyn. They were both staring at her with a mixture of uncertainty and worry in their gazes.

"Thank you. Both of you."

"No need to thank us," Cicely said, shaking her head. She then flicked her finger at the open road. "We'll go back to hedgehogs and badgers after this. Now go, before you really do draw danger to our door." She smiled, showing she was in jest.

"Until we meet again," Kit said and bowed her head to the two of them before turning the horse and flicking the reins. The horse galloped away, kicking up dust behind it.

CHAPTER 12

"God's blood, it's cold," Kit muttered as she pulled the horse to a stop at the summit of a hill. She'd been riding through Scotland for a few days and was at last near her destination. Delving a hand into her open doublet, she reached for a pocket inside the wool lining and pulled out her map. Even though she was wearing her red leather gloves, her fingers struggled to move in the bitter wind that was picking up the loose locks of her hair and whistling past her cheeks.

Kit was beginning to understand what Iomhar had meant about winter being worse in the Highlands than in England. Never had she known this sort of cold; it had left her toes numb for so long that her legs were beginning to twitch in the stirrups of her saddle.

"Where are you?" Kit murmured as she stared down at the map. She'd folded the parchment over at an angle. At the far edge, by a crease, there was a dot circled in ink. This was Iomhar's house, and it was supposed to be merely a short ride away.

As Kit jerked her head up, the wind nearly took her hat. She had to press down on it as she searched the horizon. On one side, looking down from the hill she was on, she could see a small town with smoke rising from chimneys. On the other side, there were open fields and a dense forest. It was this forest that caught Kit's interest. Leaning forward in the saddle and squinting, she caught sight of something gleaming in the morning sunlight. It could have been a window, she wasn't sure, but soon enough, smoke began to rise from this same spot, showing there was another chimney.

"That's it." With the words, Kit folded up the map and stuffed it away, pressing it into her doublet, before she clicked her tongue and urged the horse down the hill in the direction of the glinting light.

Passing through the forest, Kit had to use her compass more than once to be sure she was heading consistently in one direction, watching as the needle danced about the brass instrument. She rode slowly over gnarled roots and earth that was frozen solid. When the house did appear, it was sudden.

Stepping between two trees, Kit pulled on the reins of the horse, agog.

"That is not a house, Iomhar," she whispered, as if he would be able to hear her. "It's practically a castle."

The front of the building consisted of grey stone with tall, narrow windows, three storeys high. On one side, there were brown timbers, with white wattle and daub and a pitched roof. On the other, there were two small towers. It wasn't much bigger than Walsingham's house, but the style suggested a family of greater grandeur.

"To be an earl's son, eh?" Kit whispered as she pulled on the reins.

The horse trotted forward gently, moving out from the trees and across open grass toward a gravel drive. Kit paused by the door, flicking her eyes between the many windows, though she couldn't see a single face or any sign of life. As she climbed down from the horse, the mare snorted, tired. Kit patted her neck and let her walk away slowly as she moved toward the door.

Climbing up the first steps, she knocked lightly on the wood. At first, there was no answer; then Kit spied a doorknocker, broad, black, and shaped like a falcon's beak. Taking hold of the iron handle, she knocked louder. It wasn't long before there were sounds on the other side.

Kit felt nerves flutter in her stomach. Aside from Niall, she'd only seen Iomhar's family in the portrait that hung in his house in London.

"I'm going, I'm going," a voice said from the other side of the closed door. "Aye, our poor steward is run off his feet these days."

Kit cocked her head to the side, listening to the voice that crept nearer. Soon enough, the door opened to reveal a woman. Her hair was as black as Iomhar's, though the eyes were different, more of a pale blue. A smattering of freckles covered her nose, which she wrinkled at the sight of Kit.

"If ye're looking for a stable job, we have enough workers. Head to town and ye might find work there, boy." The young woman went to close the door again, but Kit placed a hand against the heavy wood.

"I am not here to look for a position." Her voice caught the woman's attention, for she pulled back the door sharply.

"Ye are a woman?" She pointed at Kit, stepping forward to reveal a dark blue gown with a plaid skirt.

"I am." Kit nodded.

The woman came closer, forcing her down the steps and back across the drive. "A woman in men's clothes? Wait a minute." She snatched the hat off Kit's head. "Ye are! Ye are a woman."

"I have just told you that," Kit said wryly, though the woman didn't appear to hear her.

"Ma! Ye have to see this," the young woman called inside.

"What is it?" another voice called back.

"Quite the enigma, aye, I'll give ye that." The young woman crossed her arms. When Kit cocked her head to the side, narrowing her eyes, the woman fell about laughing. "Nay need to take offence. Ye have to admit, ye are an entertaining mystery to find at the door."

"I wasn't aware I had come dressed as a jester," Kit replied dryly.

"Ma! Come!" the young woman ordered again.

Kit was growing frustrated. She'd ridden all the way here to see Niall, and to give him news of what she had discovered, only to be greeted by a woman who found her presence so amusing, she could barely stand still. Kit took in her dark hair and bone structure, realising that she had to be one of Iomhar's sisters.

"What's all this clamour?" someone called. The voice was familiar to Kit. She stood straight, listening as his footsteps neared the door. "Abigail, ye'll shout the house down with that voice of yours."

"I am not that shrill!" the young woman, Abigail, protested. She placed her hands on her hips as the other figure appeared at the door.

Niall stepped forward and covered his ears with his hands. "Aye, ye declared so shrilly my eardrums may have burst." He laughed as Abigail swatted his arm in reprimand. "What has tickled ye so?"

"I believe it was my presence," said Kit.

Niall jerked his head so sharply that he appeared to crick his neck and lifted a hand to soothe it. "Kit?" he murmured.

"Kit?" Abigail repeated. "Wait… This is Kit?"

"Kit!" Niall jumped out of the door and down the steps, reaching Kit's side. "In the name of the wee man, ye've ridden all this way since I saw ye?"

"Yes," Kit replied, backing up when she saw how excited he was to see her.

"This is Kit?" Abigail said again, hurrying down the steps to keep up with her brother.

"She knows me?" Kit asked, looking at Niall.

He smirked. "Well, Iomhar might have talked about ye. A wee bit."

"A wee bit?" Abigail scoffed. "More like —"

"That's enough, Abigail," Niall said quickly, waving a hand at his sister. "Aye, to your last question. This is Kit."

Kit watched as Abigail examined her. Her blue eyes darted down Kit's clothes then back to her face.

"She's not what I was expecting," Abigail said, wrinkling her nose.

Kit felt the corner of her lips curve into a smile. "Iomhar said you were rather good at making your feelings known to others," she replied, watching as Abigail's lips parted. Niall laughed, tipping his head back as Iomhar sometimes did.

"I am not sure I like her very much," Abigail murmured, pointing at Kit. "Why is she here?"

"Maybe ask that of her instead of me." Niall gestured to Kit. "Forgive my sister, Kit. She can be rather…" He glanced at Abigail, who raised her eyebrows.

"Will ye dare finish the sentence?"

"Perhaps not." Niall turned back to Kit. "What are ye doing here? It's a long way to come from London. I should know — I did it not long ago."

"I have news," Kit whispered.

Niall nodded slowly, showing he understood.

"News? News of what?" Abigail asked, looking irked. "In the wee man's name, what is going on?"

"Does everyone say that around here?" Kit asked Niall. "Pleading with the *wee man*?"

"More of us than ye would think." Niall took her arm. "Come. Ye need to meet everyone."

"Everyone?" Kit repeated as she was drawn toward the steps that led up into the house. "I have only come to tell you something."

"And ye expect to stand out in all this wind to tell me?"

Kit let herself be dragged further forward, conscious that Abigail was following.

"She is still not what I was expecting," Abigail said slowly.

"Quiet, Abigail." Niall's order was ignored, for Abigail continued to mumble as Kit was taken into the house.

In the hall, Kit managed to retrieve her arm from Niall, stumbling to a stop and looking around the house. It was grander than she had pictured it from Iomhar's descriptions. A staircase stretched out on one side of the hallway, disappearing into the timbered rafters of the building, built from dark mahogany wood. The stone wall beside it was peppered with portraits and the occasional weapon pinned to the stones. On the other side of the hall were three large doors, all leading to different parts of the house. Niall called through one of these doors.

"Rhona! Duncan! Come see who has paid us a visit."

"I am not an entertainment, Niall," Kit retorted.

He turned and smiled at her. "Aye, ye must forgive me. They've wanted to meet ye, after all."

"Meet me? Why?" Kit didn't get an answer, for Abigail was still standing beside her, looking her up and down as two more people appeared in the doorway.

"Why is there all this shouting this morning?" a man asked, stepping through the doorway with another young woman at his shoulder. This man was tall, almost as tall as Iomhar was, though he was lankier, and his face was longer too.

"Meet Kit." Niall stepped back and gestured. "Kit, these are our other siblings. Duncan, my brother, otherwise known as the Earl of Ross, and my sister, Rhona."

"I didn't have so formal an introduction," Abigail objected.

"Ye introduced yourself," Niall pointed out. "In an ill manner, I'd say."

Abigail looked ready to argue once more when the two other siblings stepped forward. Unlike the others, Rhona had brown hair, but her eyes were like Iomhar's.

"Ye are Kit? Ah! How nice it is to meet ye at last." Rhona hurried to curtsy then grasped Kit's hand, as if they were old friends. Kit took her hand, but rather limply, looking at Niall in confusion. He said nothing, though he chuckled under his breath.

"She is not what I expected," the Earl of Ross muttered from behind Rhona. His voice was deep and gravelly.

"That's what I said." Abigail moved to her brother's side with the words. "She looks rather like a stray."

"Abigail!" snapped Rhona, turning to her younger sister. Abigail just offered an innocent look.

"That's what riding on the open road will do," Niall assured as he elbowed Abigail. "Ye said the other day when I returned that I looked like I had been dragged through a hedge backwards."

"Ye did," the earl and Abigail said together.

"Ye must be tired?" Rhona turned to face Kit, who was trying to extricate her hand from her grasp. "Would ye like a drink? Some rest?"

"Niall?" Kit said, looking at him. "I just wanted to deliver my message."

"Were ye expecting to run back out of that door again?" he chuckled. "Ye do not stand much chance of that."

"Oh, what is all this noise?" A new voice joined them. Kit was startled by the sound and turned her gaze to the staircase.

A woman was walking calmly down it, lifting her plaid skirt as she moved. When she was halfway down, she froze, with one hand on the banister. Her hair was light brown and beginning to grey, and the lines in her cheeks were visible, as if carved into white stone. Her green eyes were like Iomhar's and Rhona's, recognisable even at this distance. Kit became aware that the woman was staring at her.

"Katherine?" she murmured.

"Katherine? Is that her name, Ma?" Abigail asked, leaning against her brother. "I thought Iomhar said it was Kit?"

Kit said nothing. She stared back at the woman, unsure what to say. She could only presume that at some point Iomhar had told his mother her real name.

The woman continued to stare at Kit, not saying anything and not even blinking. Still, she clung to the banister and her skirt.

"Ma? Are ye well?" Niall was the next one to break the silence.

"Aye, of course." Their mother seemed to shake herself out of a daze. She forced a smile and then hurried down the stairs. "Kit? I am so happy to meet ye at last." She curtsied and took Kit's hand as Rhona released the other one.

"And you," Kit said hurriedly and curtsied too, aware that behind her there was a snort of laughter.

"It looks odd to see someone in men's clothing curtsy," Abigail blurted out.

"Abigail!" Niall and the earl's joint warning seemed to silence her.

"Kit, this is our mother, the Dowager Countess of Ross, or Lady Ross," Niall finished the introduction.

"You called me Katherine," Kit started slowly, staring at the woman.

"Aye, I did." Lady Ross appeared a little wrongfooted. She suddenly smiled then released Kit's hand. "Forgive me, ye prefer Kit, is that right?"

"I do not mind, my lady." Kit remembered her manners, addressing the countess properly, who smiled a little more in response.

"Goodness," the countess said. "I have asked Iomhar many times when we would meet ye, and now, here ye are."

"You have asked?" Kit looked at Niall, but he only smiled.

Rhona giggled. "I wonder why that is?" she said, prompting her brother to shush her.

"Ma, Kit is here to tell us something." Niall stepped forward, taking command of the situation.

"I am," Kit confirmed. "It concerns Iomhar."

The atmosphere in the room appeared to change. The occasional laugh and glimpse of humour vanished. In its place, there was tension. Kit didn't need to look round to know all the siblings were exchanging glances. The countess was the only one staring straight at her, with those deep green eyes never once leaving her face.

"Do ye know where he is?" the countess asked, her voice breathy with hope. She stepped forward.

"I do not," said Kit. The countess fell still again. "Yet I have managed to find something. Something that might give us a clue to his whereabouts." She was about to speak of everything that she had found, but the countess nodded, and spoke again before Kit could.

"Ye will need a drink first after your long journey. I will not have Iomhar's friends treated discourteously here. Duncan, call for some refreshments. Kit, come, follow me. Once ye are rested, ye can tell us what ye have found."

The countess took her arm and urged her through the nearest door. Behind her, Kit could hear the siblings muttering together. She was aware of the strange way in which they all looked at her — with hope and fear. It was plain that they were impatient and longed to know what she had to tell them of Iomhar.

Kit was quickly pressed down into a settle bench in a stone room, lofted with timber beams overhead. More than once Kit protested that her clothes were dirty from the ride and she didn't wish to see the bench dirty, but the countess still insisted that she sat. In the end, only Kit's cloak and grey hat were taken from her. Once the hat was gone, she became aware of the countess staring at her even more, as if she was puzzled by something.

The earl took the grandest chair in the room, and Abigail sat on a stool nearby. Niall opted to stand, his stance wide, waiting to hear the news, and Rhona bustled around, pouring drinks for them all. Kit leaned back on the settle bench when the countess took a Savonarola chair and brought it close, sitting in front of her.

"Drink this," Rhona said, pressing a glass of mead into Kit's hand. "Ye may need it."

Kit found Rhona was right. The first sip was not enough, and Kit managed half the glass before she turned her attention on the countess.

"What have you found?" the countess asked. Kit then noticed the lines on the countess's face even more. There were heavy bags under her eyes, as if she'd had sleepless nights and had spent some of them crying. Kit flicked her eyes to Niall, thinking of what he had said about his family struggling with the disappearance. Kit longed to bring the countess some comfort, but she had a feeling that what she had to say would not alleviate her distress.

"I discovered a letter."

"Where?" the earl asked.

"That is not the important thing. The important thing is what it said." Kit turned her eyes on Niall. He must have known she had taken it from Walsingham, for he nodded, urging her on. "It was written in code and seems to follow a first letter in which the sender asked for a meeting in Scotland with an intelligencer. The sender wished to deliver information in exchange for a pardon for his crimes."

"What crimes?" Abigail asked.

"What information is more important," Niall noted.

"I know something of his crimes," Kit said, looking down into her mead cup and playing with it, remembering when she had last seen Oswyn. "He was an intelligencer, but he betrayed that honour for money. In return for his pardon, he promised information on Mary Stuart's aims, and her most loyal subject's plans, Lord Ruskin."

Kit watched as everyone in the room shifted. They all knew the name, for they had been told by Iomhar of Lord Ruskin's revelation — that he'd been the one to kill their father. Rhona looked tearful and jerked her head away. The earl held himself still and Abigail began muttering curses under her breath. Niall rested his hands on his weapons belt, as if ready for action at the mere mention of the man's name. Lastly, Kit turned her focus on the countess. Her lips trembled before she pressed them firmly together.

"Katherine, ye believe that Iomhar was the intelligencer sent to meet this man with his pardon?" The way Lady Ross kept calling her by her full name interested her, but Kit chose not to comment on it.

"I do." Kit nodded. "He knew the person who sent the letter, so he would have been ideally placed to go and meet him."

"Who wrote the letter? Who was the betrayer?" Niall asked, jerking his head up and stepping forward.

"We spoke of him to you," Kit said. "I believe it to be Oswyn Ingleby, the man we met in Northumberland."

"That turncoat? He betrayed ye all once for money — is there really any reason to think he would hold true to his word on this occasion?"

"Who knows?" Kit shrugged. "What we do know is this letter was sent, then Iomhar left to meet him. He went to The White Hart in Inverness."

"It's a tavern," the earl said, his voice deep. Kit looked at him, trying to deduce something of his character. He was quieter than his siblings, and sterner too. He did not smile as easily as the others. "I have been there once." He glanced at his brother. "Crime is as common as the stars there. Nay, it would not be a safe place to be for very long."

"Iomhar can handle himself in a pub brawl if that's what worries ye, brother," Niall pointed out.

"That is not what worries me," Kit said. She leaned forward, resting her mead cup between her palms. "What worries me is why Oswyn asked for this meeting. Like you, Niall, I do not believe he would truly want a pardon. He made his choice. It's possible that all of this was —"

"A trap?" the countess finished before Kit could, pain etched on her features.

"It is only possible at this time, my lady." Kit stood slowly. "Now, I have delivered you my message, so I will move on."

"Move on? Where?" The countess stood too, blocking her path.

"I intend to go to Inverness, my lady."

"What? Nay." The countess shook her head then appealed to the earl behind her for help. "Duncan, tell her she cannot do that. The risk is too great." Before the earl could say anything, the countess turned back to Kit. "If what ye said is true and Iomhar was caught in some trouble meeting this man, then ye cannot go to that same trap, Katherine. Ye cannot. Ye must stay here whilst we think of another way to tackle this."

Niall approached on her other side. "Ma, may I remind ye that Kit is an intelligencer. Better than Iomhar, if his words are to be believed."

"He said that?" Kit asked, straightening her spine.

"He said, in some ways. Not in others," Niall added quickly. "He believes ye do not think things through."

"That sounds like Iomhar."

"Even if Katherine is an intelligencer, we cannot take that risk," the countess said firmly. "One person is missing as it is. We cannot face losing another." Her words became louder, echoing across the stone room.

"Ma." Rhona approached, resting a hand on her mother's shoulder. "Nay one else will go missing."

"Ye do not know that." The countess shook her head, looking tearful and breathing heavily. "Nay. Nay, we will think of another way."

"Ma —" Niall tried to interject, but Lady Ross was not going to have her mind changed.

"That is the end of the matter." She waved a hand sharply in the air, making her plaid skirt billow with the sudden movement. "We will discuss it at dinner. Katherine, ye will stay for dinner, aye?"

Kit parted her lips to refuse but felt a sharp dig in her side. She turned to see it was Niall. "Ow, what was that for?"

"She doesn't have brothers or sisters, Niall," Rhona explained. "My brother is trying to tell ye to stay for dinner."

"And the night too," the countess said hurriedly. "Aye, ye must. It will give us time to think." She was still trying to fight her tears. "If ye would excuse me, I must speak to Cook about another place for dinner." The countess hurried out of the room, her skirt flapping behind her. When a door closed in the distant regions of the house, the heavy sound made Abigail and the earl jump.

"Well, that was interesting," Abigail said with a huff.

"Do not be flippant, Abigail." The earl's reprimand didn't seem to bother her as she looked to Kit.

"So, what are ye going to do?"

Kit didn't answer, though she knew exactly what she was going to do. She was still going to Inverness, but it seemed Lady Ross's objection would make that task a little more difficult.

"I'd place money on her answer," Rhona said, topping up their mead cups.

"You would?" Kit murmured, watching as Rhona winked at her.

"Well, ye have not ridden all the way here just to deliver a message that could have been sent in a letter, have ye? Ye are still going to Inverness, are ye not?"

"I am." Kit nodded.

"But Ma said ye could not go," Abigail protested. It was then that Kit noticed how young Abigail was, practically still a child, and petulant at times.

"She is not my mother," Kit reminded Abigail. "I go where I like, not where others choose to send me." Taking a sip from her mead, she noticed Niall and Rhona exchanging looks.

"Ye are really going to go after him?" Niall asked.

"Wouldn't you?"

"Och, definitely. I have already decided I am coming with you."

"Niall!" Abigail protested, stepping forward. "Ye heard Ma."

"She may be my mother, Abigail, but I do not have to do what I am told. When do we go, Kit?"

"Well, if I'm now staying here for the night, I'd say tomorrow, early. Before your mother realises that we are gone."

CHAPTER 13

Kit stood waiting in the hallway of the house, so restless that one of her heels kept bobbing up and down, dully thudding against the stone. She had struggled to sleep at all, despite the comfort of the bed, and the warmth of the fire that the countess had insisted be lit in her chamber.

All night Kit's mind had been stuck between two things. Firstly, she kept wondering if Abigail would tell the countess of what was afoot. It wouldn't stop Kit from going, but it was a complication she wished to avoid. Secondly, Kit thought of Inverness, and who Iomhar was going to meet.

"Oswyn, what were you up to?" Kit whispered.

Trying her best to push the thought away, she glanced out of the nearest window. The moon was high tonight, and the sky clear, revealing the dappled stars. The cold wind that whistled outside kept creeping into the hall through gaps in the windows, prompting Kit to shiver.

When the stairs creaked, Kit looked up, certain it would be Niall. Tipping her grey hat high and pulling her cloak tight around her neck, she prepared to leave before she realised who it was.

"Rhona?" Kit said in surprise.

Rhona smiled and hurried to the bottom step, her face illuminated by the moonlight through the windows. "Aye, that's me. Before ye ask, I am coming too, and ye cannot stop me."

Kit's lips parted as she gawked at the woman before her. "This is not a good idea."

"Ye are starting to sound like my Ma."

"With good reason," Kit whispered harshly. "You cannot come, Rhona. It is too dangerous."

"Och, why not?" Rhona said wildly, huffing as she wrapped a cloak around her shoulders. "Ye are going. Ye are a woman."

"Aye, but she's a trained intelligencer." Niall's voice joined them as he appeared on the stairs, evidently having overheard their conversation. "Not to mention she is pretty good with a weapon." He took the stairs two at a time to cross to their position, his voice a sharp whisper. "Rhona, go back to your chamber."

"Nay." Rhona reached for the door. Niall barred the way with his arm, refusing to let her pass.

Kit sighed and pinched the bridge of her nose. She needed to be on her way to Inverness now, and she did not have time for a sibling argument. "By God's blood, this will not do." She pushed past them both and reached for the door.

"What are you doing?" Rhona asked.

"I am going." Kit opened the door and stepped out. Niall and Rhona stopped arguing and hurried after her. They rounded the house quickly, with Kit leading the way to the stables.

"Rhona, this is not wise," Niall muttered.

"Ye are not stopping me."

"I could! I could pick ye up and carry ye back into the house and lock ye in your room."

"Ye're my brother, not my gaoler, Niall."

Kit ignored them and stepped into the stable. Gradually, her eyes adjusted to the darkness, and she found her mare fast asleep.

"Do you have a horse I can use?" Kit asked Niall. "Mine is too tired."

"Aye. This one. It is Iomhar's." He gestured to a horse at the back of the stable.

Kit flinched when she turned to face it. Tall and black, he towered over the other animals. "He will do," she said and stretched forward, greeting the horse with a pat on his nose.

"Rhona, go back in the house."

"Nay!" Rhona insisted. "Niall, listen to me. Iomhar is my brother too. Ye are not the only one who has watched this family struggle whilst he has been gone. If there is even the slightest chance of finding him, do ye really expect me to wait here and do nothing?"

Niall buried his face in his hands, growling in frustration. As Kit moved to saddle the horse, she glanced back at Rhona and Niall in the doorway. As with the countess, she could see signs of grieving in Rhona's face.

"Let her come," Kit said softly.

Niall jerked his head up. "What?" he spluttered. "This is not an adventure. This is a hunt!"

"That it is," Kit agreed as she threaded some reins over the steed's nose. "In my experience, a hunt is conducted much faster with more pairs of eyes on the task." Rhona looked thoroughly pleased, much to Niall's annoyance.

"She cannot fight, Kit," Niall said fearfully, stepping toward her. "I am telling ye this, she is not ye. She was not raised as ye were. The closest she has come to a knife is the one she uses to cut meat at the table."

"Aye, it's true," Rhona accepted with a nod.

"Then we'll keep her safe," Kit said as if it were no great matter. "In my experience, one does not have to know how to handle a knife to be useful." She thought of Wyn and Cicely, and how she would not have come this far had it not been for their help. "Rhona, find yourself a horse, and pray your mother doesn't hate us both for taking you with us."

"She's used to Rhona. She knows she likes her mischief," Niall said, though he didn't look comforted.

Together, they prepared their horses and left before the sun had risen. Kit followed the path Niall carved, back through the forest and toward the hill from which Kit had first approached the house. When they reached the peak, the sky began to lighten, and the stars faded from view.

"This is how Iomhar left us." Rhona's words made Kit pause on her horse, holding the reins back a little. Slowly, Rhona drew level.

"How do you mean?" Kit asked.

"He said goodbye and that he would leave soon, but he did not tell us he would leave so early in the morning. Nay. He crept out before any of us could wave him off." Rhona shook her head, dismayed. "I've been wondering why he did that."

Kit wondered too as she urged Rhona to ride faster, so that they could both catch up with Niall. "Perhaps he didn't want the pain of a real farewell." Kit thought back to how Iomhar had said goodbye to her. Had he known he would be gone a long while? Or had he known he was walking into a trap, and might not come back at all?

"I see what Duncan meant about this place," Rhona fretted as she followed Kit down the cobbled street. It was narrow and lined with drunkards. Some swayed, struggling to stay on their feet, and some looked ready to throw up against the wall on the far side. "It is hardly a cloud in heaven, is it?"

"Not quite," Kit agreed as she beckoned Rhona to follow her closely. Up ahead, Niall was leading the way, heading to The White Hart.

Inverness hadn't been too difficult a ride, but they had decided to wait for night to fall, to ensure that the tavern would be filled with people. Kit's eyes darted, searching for Oswyn.

"Kit? What does this man look like?" Rhona asked.

"Rather scrawny. His face is not dissimilar to a rat's." Kit watched as a drunken man stumbled toward them. She reached out and grabbed Rhona's arm, pulling her sharply away before a collision could happen. The drunkard fell against the nearest wall, much to the amusement of his friends.

"Charming," Rhona murmured dryly.

"Wrap your cloak tighter," Kit urged with a wave. "That is an expensive-looking dress, and you do not want a drunkard to take too keen an interest in you." Rhona did as she was asked. Kit's words caught Niall's attention and he looked back at them, his eyebrows raised.

"Ye think this place poses that kind of danger?" he asked, his tone wary.

"They are drunk, Niall. There is no way to bet on what a drunk man will do."

When Niall stopped and fixed his eyes on his sister, clearly concerned, Kit pushed past him. It didn't take long to find the tavern.

At the end of the alley between two narrow buildings was a rather squat thatched cottage, with its doors open wide and as many tables outside as there were in. Lanterns were placed in the windows and there were candles on the tables, with so many dancing flames that it had to be a fire risk, not that the visitors cared. Most customers were men, laughing and drinking, but there were women too. Some had come for a drink with friends, and others were pushing a certain sort of business.

Kit didn't need to look hard to see there were criminals amongst the crowd. More than one thief picked a pocket before her eyes, and one man's hand kept twitching toward a blade at his hip, apparently nervous of who he was waiting to meet.

"Well, this bodes well," Niall said wryly as he stopped behind Kit. "Ye try to take a man out of there forcibly, and we run the risk of many of them turning on us. Ye may be stronger than ye look, Kit, but we cannot fight them all."

"I know, I know," Kit said. Her eyes lingered on the women who were trying to peddle themselves to earn a few coins, then she looked at Rhona.

"What is it?" Rhona asked.

Kit began to smile. "Maybe there is a way to persuade Oswyn out of that tavern, rather than us having to go in to get him."

"We do not even know if Oswyn is going to turn up. He may have come here last year, but that doesn't mean he's a frequent visitor." Niall paused, flinching as he seemed to realise exactly where Kit was looking. "Why are you staring at Rhona like that?"

Kit didn't elaborate but returned her focus to the tavern. "It may not be important. As you say, Oswyn may not come." She moved into some shadows in the street to keep watch. Rhona and Niall followed her, with Niall rather pointedly pulling the cloak tighter around Rhona when it slipped a little.

Kit had barely leaned against one of the nearby buildings when there was a commotion and two men stumbled out of the tavern, one chasing the other. The older man swatted the younger one away, accusing him of being a thief. The movement made his clothes become skewed and the high collar of his doublet opened, revealing a flash of ink on his neck.

"I do not believe it," Kit whispered.

"What?" Niall asked.

"The tattoo. Look." Kit gestured to the older man.

Niall saw it just before the man retreated inside, turning his collar back up. "The unicorn," he murmured. "It's the symbol."

"I know. If he's here, then any number of men from this group could be here, including…" She didn't finish the sentence. Before the man could step in through the doorway, someone called his name.

"Myers? You been in another brawl?"

Kit knew that voice. She looked down the road to see the scrawny figure of Oswyn Ingleby approaching. "That's him," she whispered.

Niall stepped forward, his face instantly tense, but Kit grabbed his arm. "Kit, ye have told me that is the man my brother went to meet before he vanished. Ye surely do not expect me to stand here and do nothing, do ye?"

"Yes, I do." Kit tugged on his arm, pulling him backwards. When he didn't move much, Rhona took hold of his other arm and tugged so hard that he fell against the wall in the shadows beside her.

"Kit is right," Rhona said. "We do not want to cause a commotion of our own, Niall. Do ye want all of these men turning angry eyes on ye?"

"Not particularly." Niall winced. "It seems the group have accepted a Northumbrian man as their own."

"So it would seem," Kit agreed and watched Oswyn as he followed Myers into the tavern.

He hadn't changed much since she had last seen him. It was possible he was not quite so thin, showing the money he had changed sides for was at least buying him more food. His clothes were a little scruffier than before, and there was a staff loose in his hand as he stepped through the door.

"Any ideas?" Rhona asked.

"One." Kit looked at her again. It was a risk, she knew that, but Rhona could blend in, in a way that Kit knew she could not. "*You* could bring him out."

"Me?" Rhona flattened her hands to her chest.

"Do not say it, Kit," Niall pleaded, but she went on regardless.

"I cannot go in there, for Oswyn knows me. He would not come out to talk to me, but likely run for the hills. Niall, you are obviously a soldier — he is just as likely to walk away from you. There are criminals here, but Rhona…" Kit paused and smiled at her. "You can walk amongst them."

"How?" Rhona asked, then her eyes landed on the women in the crowd. "Oh, I see. It could work."

"Nay, it could not!" Niall blocked the path. "Ye are not going to pretend to be a harlot just to draw that man out of there."

"Do ye have a better idea? Niall, I can do this. Charming a drunken man is rather easy."

"And how do ye know that?" Niall was growing more and more panicked.

"Oh, calm yourself. Ye look ready to burst your bowels." At Rhona's words, Kit attempted to hold back a laugh and failed. Niall was ready to argue again, but when Rhona elbowed Kit in the rib, she took the hint.

"Niall?" Kit stepped forward.

"Aye?"

"Your weapons belt is undone." Kit bent down, as if to grab the falling weapons that were actually fixed in place. Niall flinched and looked down too. At the distraction, Rhona took off. When Niall realised what had happened, he slowly stood straight, glaring at Kit.

"Ye did that just a little too easily," he murmured, then turned and leaned on the wall beside her, resting his eyes on the tavern.

"For Iomhar, remember?" Kit reminded him.

"Ye have just sent my sister to…"

"To what? To greet a man kindly? To charm him with a smile? It is hardly asking her to take a knife to a man, is it?" Kit asked, watching as Niall fidgeted.

"Iomhar was right. Ye do take unnecessary risks."

Kit winced, feeling the insult. She wished Iomhar was there so she could argue with him herself. "I judge it to be a necessary risk."

She fell silent, watching the door of the tavern. She didn't have to wait long for a result. Soon enough, Rhona stepped back outside. Her cloak was open now, revealing her fine gown. Her arm was outstretched behind her, and she held Oswyn's hand. He followed, tottering as she pulled him toward their hiding place. He had left his wooden staff behind.

"Be ready," Kit warned as Niall stood straight. They both rested their hands on their weapons belts.

"Where are we going, fine lady?" Oswyn asked, his Northumbrian accent thick.

Rhona didn't answer but pulled him into the shadows. Oswyn's smile slipped as her hand fell away. Kit stepped forward, tilting her head back so that his eyes found hers.

She saw the fear in his face. The skin around his eyes tautened, his jaw clicked, and he backed up.

"Good evening, Oswyn," Kit said coolly.

He turned, plainly intent on running, but he didn't manage a step before Kit lashed out. She grabbed hold of the collar of his jerkin and hauled him backward, keeping him firmly in the shadows.

"No! Help —" Before he could say more, Kit placed her hand firmly over his mouth. Using her arms to keep his body in place, she dragged him down the alley, far away from the street that was lit by the tavern's lanterns.

"To your left," Niall ordered, once they had moved a little way and were hidden from the tavern. Kit followed the direction, finding a small alcove between two buildings. She then released Oswyn, tossing him against the wall.

A tiny lantern attached to the building swung in the wind, casting Oswyn in streaks of orange light that danced back and forth across his face. He shuddered as he plastered himself to the wall, trying to get as far back from Kit as possible.

"I think he remembers ye," Niall said with humour. Behind them, Rhona wrapped her cloak tightly around her torso.

"I'm interested in what else he remembers." Kit stood firmly in front of Oswyn. When he made a sign of moving, she laid a hand on the dagger in her weapon's belt, and he fell back. Then his lips flickered, as if attempting to smile.

"Kit," he said quietly. "It's good to…"

"I do not wish to hear it." Kit shook her head firmly. The suddenness of the movement made him jerk, bumping the back of his head on the brick wall. "Are you still Lord Ruskin's pet?"

"Pet?" Oswyn took offence, standing taller. "I am one of his soldiers."

"Ye do not look like a soldier," Niall scoffed.

"Who's this?" Oswyn nodded at Niall, then his eyes flicked to Rhona. "And who is that?" Niall shifted to stand in front of his sister.

"No, Oswyn. Tonight, I am going to ask the questions." Kit stood her ground. "The last time I saw you, you were scrambling away from Holy Island, trying to row as if your life depended on it."

"I think it did," Oswyn mumbled.

Kit could remember that night clearly. She could also remember something Oswyn had done for her. He had pleaded with Lord Ruskin not to hurt her, and even diverted a pistol when he had tried to take a shot. Oswyn had as good as saved her life, though she had never known why.

"Ask him, then we can be gone," Rhona called to Kit. "Och, I do not think it a wise idea for us to be here much longer."

"Aye, I agree," Niall murmured, stepping forward. He took a sword from his belt, thicker and broader than a rapier, and pointed the tip in Oswyn's direction. Oswyn squealed like a rat that had been trodden on, and cowered back.

"That will not be necessary." Kit glanced down at the sword. Niall lowered it, but he did not return it to his belt. "Oswyn, you are going to tell me what I want to know, and I will leave you alone. That is a fair exchange, is it not?"

He harrumphed at the idea, attempting to stand straight now the sword was lowered. "I cannot be certain you'd stick to your word."

"You can be certain. Because when we worked together in Northumberland, I kept my word. You were the one to break your own."

Oswyn shifted and looked down, almost embarrassed. "It was necessary."

"No. You were persuaded by money."

"You have no knowledge of —"

"Enough." The way Kit curled her hand around the hilt of the dagger in her belt was enough to silence Oswyn. He kept his eyes on the blade, and his teeth chattered. "You sent a letter to Taurus, did you not?" She used the codeword she knew he was familiar with, from when he had been loyal to Walsingham.

His eyes widened in surprise, before he nodded.

"And Iomhar came to meet you," Kit finished, watching as Oswyn smiled a little.

"You been missing him, pet?" The return to the old name he'd used for her in Northumberland angered her.

"Can I use it now?" Niall asked, lifting his sword.

"He's persuading me you can," Kit said, without taking her eyes off Oswyn. When he whimpered and slinked back, Kit stepped forward. "Tell me what happened, Oswyn, and I will keep my word. You can return to your drinks, and I will not drag you across the border and into Taurus's hands."

"You wouldn't get that far." Oswyn tried to laugh. "You'd be stopped."

"Not when she has a soldier and his regiment to escort her," Niall cut in.

Oswyn's eyes darted over him, taking in the weapons at his belt. The only sounds were the distant catcalls from the tavern.

"Tell me what happened, Oswyn. Iomhar came to meet you, didn't he?" Kit hissed. She could hear her heart thrumming in her ears.

Oswyn looked between her and Niall before making a decision, nodding ever so slightly. "He did," he said, his voice deep.

"Here?" Kit asked, gesturing in the direction of the tavern.

"That was the plan. He turned up in disguise. That wasn't supposed to happen," Oswyn muttered angrily. "I was bait, that was all."

"Bait for a trap?" Rhona asked, her voice a little shaky.

"Aye, that was it. The roads were being watched by Ruskin's men. He'd had enough. It was carefully orchestrated. He'd be done with Iomhar Blackwood for good, see him dead in his grave, but those watching for Iomhar missed him. He turned up, walked into the tavern like a regular, then got me by the throat." Oswyn motioned to his neck madly. "Demanded information from me on Ruskin's whereabouts. When I refused…" He grimaced. "Aye, the tavern keeper was not best pleased."

"You fought?" Kit urged him on.

"Aye. Ended up in the street, brawling like drunkards. I think my ribs are still cracked in places from it." Oswyn rubbed a sore spot on his chest. "Next thing I knew, we were descended on. Clan Mackintosh do not take kindly to outlanders causing trouble."

Kit became aware of Niall cursing beside her. He thrust his sword back into his belt.

"Mackintosh?" she repeated, looking at him.

"The clan we are in now," Niall explained in a hurry. "The neighbour to our own clan, the Rosses. The Mackintoshes have a habit of locking up those they see as troublemakers. Is that what they did to Iomhar?" he asked Oswyn.

"Night watchmen descended on us both." Oswyn shifted awkwardly. "Turned my own staff on me, they did — left their marks too." He rubbed his back. "Took us to a castle out of town. Took Ruskin a few days to get me out, but he did."

"And Iomhar?" Kit asked. "What of him?"

As the wind whistled up the road, it rattled the lantern above them. Oswyn jerked his head toward it, looking into the light. It made his cheeks appear gaunt, as if he were a dead man.

Kit grew impatient and stepped toward him. "Speak," she demanded.

Oswyn snapped his eyes to hers, his body trembling. "Ruskin told them they'd caught a spy, and to keep him locked up," he whispered. "So, that's what they did. Ruskin judged it to be enough. Iomhar was not dead, but he was gone, and would be no trouble anymore."

"A castle? Ye mentioned a castle?" Rhona asked excitedly, moving to Kit's shoulder. "Which castle?"

"Urquhart Castle." Oswyn breathed out, as if giving up. "Last I heard, he was still there."

"He's alive, then?" Rhona whispered.

Kit's hand tightened over the hilt of her dagger. "Of course he's alive," she muttered. "He has to be." She didn't need to look at the siblings to know they were exchanging a glance at her words.

"Aye, you have a weakness for the man, do you not?" Oswyn asked with a deep laugh.

Kit had had enough. She pulled the dagger out and pushed it toward him. He made a choking sound and slapped his head on the wall in his effort to get away from the blade, wincing at the pain.

"You did this to him, and yet you do not care, do you?" Kit murmured. Slowly, she lowered the blade. The frantic fluttering of Oswyn's eyelids ceased, and he sighed with relief. "You do not care about much, I think." Kit stepped back. She had the information she needed.

She'd taken two steps away with Rhona at her side when she heard the woosh of a sword.

"No!" Kit snapped, spinning on her heel to see Oswyn cowering against the wall. Niall was standing in front of him, the sword dangerously close to his arm. "Niall, do not hurt him."

"He deserves to be hurt. This man is the reason Iomhar is where he is. This man is the reason he has been gone for so long. For all we know, Iomhar could be… He could be…"

"Och, do not say it, Niall," Rhona pleaded.

Niall cursed instead. His blade was so close to Oswyn's chest that he began to cry, and his breath came in great, heaving gasps.

Kit stepped forward, seeing what punishment Oswyn was enduring. "Fear is enough for him." She placed a hand over the flat side of the sword and lowered it, pushing it away.

Niall stepped back. "He deserves more than fear. After what he's done… There should be pain, Kit," he seethed.

"Not from me." Kit took hold of Oswyn's jerkin and hauled him off the wall, making him stand. He hurried to dry his tears on his sleeves. "Sadly, I owe him my life." Her words caught Oswyn's attention.

"You remember that?"

"I do." Kit nodded. "You could have let Lord Ruskin kill me that night on Holy Island, yet you didn't let it happen. Why, exactly?"

Oswyn looked down. "Not all of Ruskin's men are demons."

"Perhaps not," Kit acknowledged. "You may not be his devoted servant, but you are loyal to his money, aren't you?" Oswyn had no defence for this and merely looked down at his feet. "I owe you, so today, that debt is repaid." She took his shoulder and steered him past Niall, shoving him down the road. "Keep quiet, Oswyn. Do not tell Lord Ruskin that you have seen us, or next time, I will not stand between you and a blade."

Oswyn stumbled before finding his balance and standing straight. "I give you my word, Kit." He bowed to her. She could not remember him having done so before, but she supposed it was a mark of respect. Wiping one last tear from his cheek, he turned and fled down the road.

"Kit," Niall said quietly, moving to her side. "Is it wise to let him go?"

"To hurt him would raise suspicions, and we don't want that," she pointed out.

Once Oswyn had retreated, his figure nothing more than a shadow dancing in the orange lantern lights, Kit turned to Niall. Behind him, Rhona was pacing and twisting her cloak.

"What is wrong?" Kit asked her.

"Urquhart Castle. Of all places, that castle!" Rhona's manner was quite wild.

"Calm yourself, Rhona," Niall pleaded.

"Och, ye be calm! Ye were the one who just raised a sword to an unarmed man."

"I was angry."

"Well, I am angry now. If Iomhar is there... Nay, he cannot be. The thought is too awful." Rhona tipped her head back and looked to the sky, muttering something, perhaps saying a prayer.

"I have missed something, have I not?" Kit took hold of Rhona's shoulder. "What is so special about this castle?"

"That could take a while to explain," Rhona faltered.

"To put it succinctly," Niall sighed, "it's where the Mackintosh clan chief sends men he wishes to forget."

CHAPTER 14

"Ye did what?" Lady Ross's voice rang so much between the stone walls that Kit nearly turned and fled the other way.

"Don't ye dare," Niall commanded over his shoulder.

Kit was forced to stay still, watching as Lady Ross stood in the hallway of the house, glaring at the three of them in the early morning light. Behind her were the earl and Abigail, and all three were in various states of dress, having heard the horses return.

"Urquhart? Are ye sure?" the earl said, stepping forward. There was clear hope in his voice. Abigail listened too, as she twisted her hair into a plait.

"That is what this man said," Kit replied. "There is only one way to be certain, though. We go to the castle."

"Oh, in the name of the wee man and all his angels!" Lady Ross tossed her hands to the sky and marched away across the hall, before pacing back toward them. "Ye have all just returned from one dangerous trip, and now ye wish to go off on another?"

"Nay," Niall and Rhona said together, making Kit's shoulders slump.

"I may be a fool, but I am not hoping for my own death," Niall explained succinctly. "I would not go there, Ma."

"Neither would I." Rhona shook her head and reached for the nearest door. "I need something to drink."

"Aye, so do I after hearing of this chaos!" Lady Ross snapped and followed her daughter into the sitting room. "Rhona, how could ye do this? The danger ye were in … unthinkable!"

"All clouds bring not rain, Ma. It was just a tavern. It was nothing we have not seen before."

The voices began to drift away as the two ladies left, followed closely by Niall and the earl.

Soon, only Kit and Abigail were left in the hall. Kit stood very still, and Abigail stared at her, still fidgeting with her hair.

"He's there? Truly?" she asked, her manner so anxious that Kit couldn't help offering a smile.

"At least now we have hope, Abigail."

Abigail smiled back with evident relief.

"Abigail!" At Lady Ross's bark, Abigail hurried into the room. "Katherine, I hope ye are coming too."

Kit couldn't hold back her laugh, though she lifted a hand to cover her lips as she followed them into the room. Lady Ross's outbursts felt a little soft compared to Walsingham's.

"Ma, Kit is her own person. She does not have to follow your orders," Niall reminded his mother.

Lady Ross didn't argue, but she crossed toward Kit and took her arms. Kit was so startled that she stood very still, her eyes going wide. All Lady Ross did was spin Kit around, apparently examining her.

"Nay injuries? Nay damage?"

"No, my lady," Kit said, turning back to face her.

"By blood and this light, thank God for that." Lady Ross exhaled loudly then stepped forward and embraced Kit.

Stunned, Kit didn't move. She stood there like a wooden plank, unsure what else to do. She couldn't remember the last time she had hugged someone. Somewhere in the back of her mind, she rather suspected Doris had given her a few hugs when she was little, but that was many years ago.

Kit didn't raise her hands to embrace Lady Ross back, but merely stood there, unsure what to feel.

A second later, Lady Ross released her. The panic was still evident in her face, her green eyes somewhat narrowed with the anger she was restraining, but her relief overpowered this. "Ye operate by your own rules, Katherine, that I can see. It rather reminds me of someone." She turned and hurried into the middle of the room.

Kit wobbled, trying to stand straight after the awkwardness of the embrace.

"I should clip ye two around the ears." Lady Ross crossed to Niall and Rhona, who were both sitting at the far end of the room in settle benches, drinking cups of small beer.

"Ma, we are not children anymore," Rhona reminded her.

"And I am a soldier." Niall held up a hand.

"A soldier should know not to take his sister to a place frequented by criminals."

"Perhaps we should change the subject slightly," the earl said, sitting beside his brother on the bench. His sudden entrance into the conversation left them all a little stunned. "Urquhart Castle. If that's where Iomhar is, then…"

"Then it explains his silence," Abigail offered, taking a seat beside her sister. Kit approached with interest, looking between the four siblings that now sat opposite each other on the two settle benches.

"Something doesn't make sense." The earl shook his head.

"What's that?" Kit asked, aware that Lady Ross was presenting her with a chair. When she tried to offer the seat to the countess instead, Lady Ross took her shoulder and pushed her into it.

"If Iomhar were arrested, a clan chief would send a letter to me. He would explain the arrest or make a plea for his release, try to get some money, or write to tell me they were going to execute —"

"Do not say it!" Lady Ross demanded. Everyone fell still and silent. Kit's eyes darted between the faces, noting how the siblings kept their eyes on the tankards in front of them. Lady Ross sat forward. "Kit, ye are not drinking. Here, take this."

"Oh, I do not need it." Kit tried to turn down the cup of small beer but found it pressed into her hand regardless.

"Nonsense. Ye have been riding all night — ye need it. Drink." Lady Ross's words were firm, but she gave a quick smile. Kit did as she was told, rather unused to the way this woman was fussing around her.

"Niall, didn't you say that Iomhar left things here when he departed?" Kit asked.

"Aye, that's right." Niall nodded.

"Then he has nothing identifiable on him, does he?" Kit pointed out, watching as the earl's eyes widened in realisation.

"Ye think they do not know who he is."

"Even if he told them who he was, would they believe an earl's son to be brawling in a tavern? If Lord Ruskin had already accused him of being a spy, then he wouldn't want to admit his identity, in case the clan turned their attention here." Kit's rather plain way of explaining things made Abigail drop her cup. Fortunately, Rhona caught it before it could go far.

"She's right," Niall said slowly. "If Iomhar is accused of being a spy against Clan Mackintosh, then he's not going to want to link himself to us."

"Then, how do we release him from Urquhart Castle?" Rhona asked.

"Simple. We write to them," the earl said firmly.

"What?" Kit leaned forward in her chair. She nearly tipped it over, but Lady Ross's hand on the back stopped it from going anywhere. "If you write to the castle now, and tell them the spy they have in their dungeon is your brother, do you think that will do any good? They would not release him. It simply casts this whole family into suspicion."

No one answered her for a minute. She supposed they must have thought her right, for the silence was uncomfortable. They looked at one another, apparently hoping someone would come up with another idea.

"I'm not sitting here and doing nothing." The earl stood and downed what was left in his cup.

"Do not go to see them," Niall warned. "Kit's right. We will be under suspicion then. If ye turn up at the door and say he's your brother, they may arrest ye too."

"Then I'll write a letter." The earl marched out of the room, his boots heavy on the floor. He slammed the door behind him, shaking the timber beams overhead.

"Well, that went well," Rhona said drily.

"It's not over yet." Lady Ross turned her eyes on Kit, making her sit up. "Kit, I need to speak to ye later."

Having bathed, dressed and walked the halls, Kit finally found Lady Ross on one of the upper floors. She was sitting on a coffer at the edge of her bed, staring into space. Kit hovered by the open door, uncertain what to say. When Lady Ross didn't notice her, she tapped lightly on the door.

"Come in, Katherine," the countess said, offering a smile that did not last long.

Kit took one step into the room, but she went no further. Her eyes danced about. The chamber was grandly decorated, with furs on the bed to keep Lady Ross warm on cold nights. They would be needed, for snow was beginning to fall, like drifting feathers from the sky. There were two more coffers in the corners of the room and a table surrounded by high-backed chairs.

"How are ye?" Lady Ross's question surprised Kit so much that she nearly backed out again. "I've never seen anyone so startled by a kind question. Ye are like a young buck at the end of a crossbow." She smiled a little more, genuinely this time. "I am merely checking ye are well, Katherine."

"I am fine, thank you, my lady."

"Oh, nay more of this 'my lady' nonsense." Lady Ross waved a hand in the air and stood, then turned and lifted the lid of the mahogany coffer. "Ye must call me Moira."

"Moira?" Kit stepped further into the room, encouraged by the informality.

"Iomhar spoke so much of ye, I feel as if I know ye. It is odd to me to hear ye call me 'my lady'." She spoke with confidence, then reached into her coffer and pulled out a fresh gown, which she laid on the bed.

Kit couldn't help admiring the material. Made of dark green plaid and wool, it would no doubt ward off the bitterness of the snow.

"Ye like it?" Moira asked, gesturing to the dress.

"I do," Kit confirmed. There was something about the gown's style that reminded her of the dress she had hidden back at home — the one in the box that she had taken from Walsingham's wardrobe. The one she was so certain she had been wearing the day she had nearly drowned.

"Well, I know ye like your doublets and hose, but if ye ever want a gown, ye can borrow one of mine," Moira said with ease and reached into the coffer, pulling out another gown. She held it up to Kit's shoulders. "There, it would suit ye well. Very well indeed."

Kit smiled and looked down at the gown. "I mostly like to avoid gowns. They are uncomfortable."

"Ha! I cannot argue with ye there. Oh, the gowns may be beautiful, but they sometimes hurt." Moira dropped one of the gowns into the box. Kit returned to stand beside the bed, where the green gown lay. Reaching out, she trailed a finger across the square neckline that was hemmed with pearls, just like the gown she had hidden.

"The style... I saw another dress like it once."

"Ye did?" Moira said, moving to her side. "I would not be surprised. It is very Scottish in fashion."

"It is?" Kit asked, jerking her hand back from the gown.

"Aye." Moira lifted the dress, holding it up so the light that bounced off the snow outside shone across the pearls.

Kit was reminded of how Doris had once said that when she had come to Seething Lane, she'd had an accent, possibly Scottish. She was now faced with the possibility that the gown was Scottish too.

"Forgive me, Moira. You wished to speak to me." Kit cleared her throat and returned to the matter at hand. Now was not the time to think of that dress. She had to focus on Iomhar and Urquhart Castle.

"I did." Moira sighed and laid the gown down. "I can warn my children not to take risks, for they are my own, but I know well enough I cannot give ye the same warning." She turned and sat on the edge of the bed. When Kit didn't move, she pointed to the very edge of the bed, urging her to do the same. Kit sat gingerly, feeling quite out of place. "So, ye will have to forgive me for intruding on your life, but I would like to say something if I may."

Kit nodded, urging her on.

"Take care, Katherine."

Unsure how to respond, Kit just sat there, looking down at the dress between them.

"The risk ye took last night might not seem great to ye —"

"It was not, my lady, I assure you. We were all quite safe."

"Moira," she reminded Kit with a small smile. "My name is Moira."

"Moira," Kit said hurriedly. "It was no great danger. I wish you to know that."

"Then I choose to believe ye." Moira sat back a little, sighing. "Yet Urquhart Castle is another matter entirely. It's fiercely protected by the Mackintoshes, and they do not look at the Ross Clan as friends. The clan rifts go back too long and run too deeply to be solvable overnight. If we are to find Iomhar inside that castle's walls, then it must be done with care. As nay one has followed ye here to watch over ye, and keep ye safe, I will happily be the one to do it."

Kit shifted a little on the bed, unsure what Moira meant.

"I will not see ye hurt, Katherine." Moira's words reminded her of another.

"Iomhar said that to me once," Kit whispered.

"He did? Then I am glad I raised a man with a good heart." Moira smiled, clearly full of pride. "Now, I must get dressed. Duncan wishes to discuss his letter, and if I do not visit the steward soon, we will not have meals at all today."

They both stood. Kit was about to leave but hesitated in the doorway.

"Moira?" she said, turning back.

"Aye?"

"If you do not mind me asking, when you saw me yesterday, you knew who I was right away. You knew my name." Kit hadn't managed to shake that moment from her memory. "How were you so certain who I was?"

"The clothes were a good sign." Moira smiled. "Iomhar told me before of your liking for doublets. In truth, though, I have a confession to make to ye."

"What is that?"

"When I said your name, Katherine, it was not because I knew it." Moira shook her head. "It was because ye reminded me of someone." Moira paused with one hand over the dress on the bed, looking up at Kit. "Even now as ye stand there, ye are very like someone I once knew."

Kit felt a coldness wash over her as Moira stared at her face.

"Ye reminded me of this person. Absurd, I know. Ye are from London, after all, not to mention ye are very different in age. It must just be one of those things, a casual likeness," Moira said easily. "Her name was Katherine too, though."

"Oh…" Kit didn't move.

"It is natural for me to call ye Katherine, I suppose. Do ye mind?"

"No. You can call me Katherine."

Kit longed to know more about this woman she looked so like. Where had Moira seen her before? Was the likeness really so great? Yet it was not the time to ask such questions.

"Would you close the door, Katherine? I will be downstairs soon."

"Yes, of course." Kit closed the door behind her and hurried along the landing, not looking where she was going as she thought of what Moira had said.

Ye are from London, after all…

What if Kit wasn't from London, though? What if the accent she'd had and the dress meant she was truly from Scotland? Was it possible that Moira knew something about where Kit had come from?

Kit hovered at the top of the stairs, looking back down the corridor in the direction of Moira's chamber. She didn't have time to think of any more questions, for Niall appeared on the stairs.

"Ah, Kit, there ye are. Ye should hear this."

"Hear what?"

"Duncan's letter. He's insisting on writing to Urquhart Castle, and I fear nay good can come from a letter like this."

CHAPTER 15

"What could be wrong with such a letter?" the earl asked, quite wild as he waved a sheet of parchment in front of his brother for what felt to Kit to be the fourth or fifth time.

Kit's eyes flicked between them. They were all sitting at a long mahogany table, and there were trenchers of food in front of them. The smell of smoked fish kept curling under her nose, making her feel rather sick, though she would occasionally look down at it with a small smile, remembering that it was Iomhar's favourite.

As the brothers argued, the sisters ate, and Moira struggled to keep control of the room.

"Would ye two settle down and eat at least?" she pleaded, banging a pewter jug on the table to get their attention. The heavy thud made both Niall and the earl sit up in their high-backed chairs, with the wood creaking beneath them. "Nay result will come from arguing. We must keep our heads. Aye, we must."

Kit was certain Moira was trying to convince herself to stay calm, as well as her sons. More than once Kit had seen Moira's hands quiver as she picked up her cutlery or her cup. The pewter rim seemed to tremble before it reached her lips. Kit could see her sadness, though she tried to hide it.

"To think he could have been there this last year," Rhona muttered, poking at her food.

"Are ye eating, Rhona? Or making sure it's dead?" Moira asked.

"I'm struggling to eat, Ma. I cannot help thinking…" Rhona didn't need to finish the sentence.

Kit swallowed some of her mead and looked down at her uneaten smoked fish. Like Rhona, she had not stopped thinking about Iomhar. If it were true that he was at Urquhart Castle, and had been there for this last year, then the horrors he might have endured spooked her to her core. "Urquhart Castle," she began slowly, lifting her eyes from her plate. "Would you tell me more about it?" The family exchanged nervous glances before Moira nodded at Niall, encouraging him to speak.

"It keeps shifting between different clans," Niall said, his voice deep. "It was once part of Urquhart Clan itself. It's changed hands since then, thanks to raids on the land. Most recently, it was occupied by the Grants, allies of the Mackintoshes. They both use the castle to this day as a sort of joint military base. Nay soul wishes to go there. Myth has it they keep their worst reputed men there."

"Do they ever..." Kit paused and placed her cup down on the table. She had to ask, though her nerves crawled. "Do they execute their prisoners?"

Moira dropped her cutlery, making it chink loudly before she hurried to pick it up again.

"Aye," Niall said slowly.

"Yet they still have a court of law," the earl reminded his brother. "They could not hurt Iomhar on the say of one man, even a man like Lord Ruskin. Nay, if they believe him to be a spy, then they will have kept him within their walls. Nothing more."

"You are sure?" Kit asked, leaning forward, desperate for reassurance.

"I am." The earl nodded. Kit noticed, though, that Niall wasn't in a hurry to agree with his brother. If anything, he seemed to be avoiding meeting her gaze. "If we are to get him out, it must be through diplomacy." The earl went to rest a hand on the discarded letter beside him, but Niall slapped it before he got there. The sudden thud made Abigail jump.

"*This* letter? Ye think this will help?" Niall asked, waving it in front of his brother's eyes. "Nay. It is a foolish idea, Duncan. Ye are blind to reality."

"I am not."

"Ye are!" Niall snapped. "Ye write this and admit one of their prisoners is our brother, then they will simply have cause to suspect us, just as Kit said. Ye cannot write such a letter." He held it out of reach and passed it down the table. "Kit? What do ye think?"

Rhona took the letter, then passed it to Kit. She grasped it hurriedly and flattened it out, her eyes dancing over the words that had been written in haste. It was neat script, but Kit could tell that the tone was desperate.

"You cannot send this," Kit whispered after a minute of reading.

"Why not?" The earl was losing his temper again, though Moira waved a hand at him, pleading with him to be quiet.

"Because it puts the power in their hands." Kit lowered the letter to the table. "You have made it plain you will do anything to have Iomhar back. It gives them control over you." These words seemed to calm the earl a little. He sat back in his seat and breathed heavily, his nostrils flaring.

"Then what else do we do?" he asked, looking around the room.

"Is there anyone else we could appeal to?" Abigail offered. "Anyone who knows of the castle?" Her question hovered for a minute, unanswered, until the earl and Niall looked at one another.

"There is," Niall said eventually. "We know a soldier. He frequently visits Urquhart Castle to discuss clan relations for the king. Aye, he could know something more of what goes on in that castle, better than we do."

"How quickly can you talk to this soldier?" Moira asked. She seemed to have abandoned her food, her pewter plate pushed away.

"It may take a few days to find where he is."

"A few days?" Kit repeated, already shaking her head. "If we are right about this, then Iomhar has already been there for over a year."

"Then we must have patience and wait a few days more." The earl's voice was sharp. He evidently thought it would quieten Kit, but it did no such thing.

"It is still not a safe plan," she pointed out, her voice as firm as his. "If you tell anyone of Iomhar's true identity, then you put this house in danger, and Iomhar himself."

"She's right," Niall agreed. "The relationship between the Mackintosh clan and our own is hardly a good one, is it? The Rosses and Mackintoshes have been tense for years. Old rifts and betrayals have not been forgotten. If they know where Iomhar is truly from, then they are more likely to hurt him. Maybe even…" He didn't finish his sentence, but he waved his hand in the air, the meaning explicit.

Kit felt a sudden lump in her throat and looked down at her plate. For so long she had persuaded herself that someday soon Iomhar would walk back through the door. For so long, she had convinced herself that he was not hurt. That he was alive and well somewhere, just away from her. Now, she was forced to accept that she was wrong. Iomhar was in danger.

"Katherine?" Moira whispered. "Ye all right?"

"I am well," Kit replied hurriedly. Her eyes stung, and she realised she was close to tears.

"We cannot just sit here and do nothing," Rhona muttered, stabbing the fish on her plate. "For all we know, Iomhar is hurting this very moment, and what are we doing? We're *discussing* what to do and attempting to eat." She thrust her plate away.

Kit did the same and stood.

"Katherine?" Moira turned to her.

"Excuse me," Kit murmured, leaving the room as quickly as she could. She didn't want to let Iomhar's family see what the fear was doing to her. Hurrying through the door and closing it behind her, she put as much distance between herself and the dining room as she could as the tears began to run down her cheeks.

When the door to Kit's chamber creaked open, she jumped from the coffer in front of the window, where she had been staring out at the snow.

"I apologise for interrupting." Moira's head appeared in the gap between the door and the frame.

Kit hastily tried to dry the tears on her cheeks. She didn't know how long she had been up here, staring at the snow. "I should apologise. I should not have walked out."

"Oh, ye think I worry for that?" Moira asked and stepped into the room, closing the door behind her. "After this last year, I have walked out of many such scenes myself. Like ye, I hoped to hide my tears from my children. I did not succeed." She moved swiftly toward Kit. There was something in her hands. "Ye have been up here for a long time, Katherine."

"Have I?" Kit sniffed, stopping more tears from falling. She shifted back on the coffer and looked out of the window.

"Ye do not need to hide your tears from me." Moira appeared beside Kit, perching on the other end of the coffer. "Ye should not be ashamed of them."

Kit nodded slowly, uncertain what to say.

"Aye, ye must care for my son."

"I'm sorry?" Kit jerked her head toward Moira, nearly hitting her nose on the cold glass beside her.

Moira offered a rather sad smile. "Ye rode all the way from London to the Highlands, in the hope of finding him."

"Niall came to see me. He explained you were all struggling. I couldn't bear that thought." Kit shook her head.

"Was that the only reason ye came?" Moira asked, knowingly.

Kit didn't answer but crossed her arms over her body and looked out at the snow. She couldn't put it into words. All she knew was that she had to find Iomhar.

Glancing down, she caught sight of the belt around her waist, reminding herself of the other reason she had left London. The letter to Mary Stuart was still hidden, but that task would have to wait for now.

"Here, take this." Moira presented Kit with a handkerchief. "I have many of them, after this last year. I cry when I think the children cannot see me, though I am not sure it always works."

Kit thanked her for the handkerchief and took it, drying her tears.

"There is something I wished to show ye." Moira opened her palm, revealing what she was carrying.

Kit sat forward, startled to see the glint of gold. "What is it?"

"Do ye recognise it?"

Kit thought hard, then remembered exactly where she had seen it before. When she and Iomhar had gone to Northumberland, they had come back to their rooms once to find them searched. In Iomhar's room, a golden chain had rested on a small table, shining in the candlelight.

"It was Iomhar's," Kit whispered.

"Aye, he liked to keep it hidden. He told me he either wore it beneath his shirt, or kept it at home, where nay one would see it." Moira held it up. In the light that danced in the window off the snow, Kit saw that it was a golden circle, with wire knotted in the middle. "Here, take a look." Moira passed it over.

Kit turned the pendant over, pressing the wire between the pads of her fingers. She knew Iomhar must have kept it well hidden, since she could only remember seeing it once.

"What is it? This symbol?" Kit asked, trailing her fingers over the knotted wire.

"We call it the Celtic shield knot," Moira explained. "It is supposed to protect the wearer."

Kit cursed under her breath as she looked up from the pendant. "Yet he left it behind?"

"So it would seem." Moira sat back with a sigh, leaning on the glass. "As ye say, he went in disguise and left anything identifiable here. *This* belonged to his father. Aye, there is a chance someone may have recognised it, had he worn it."

"He kept it very well hidden," Kit murmured.

"Ye should wear it."

"Me?" Kit spluttered, attempting to pass it back to Moira. "No, I could not. It belongs to your family."

"Aye, and I am giving it to ye to wear for now." Moira pushed the pendant back into Kit's hands. "Someone should wear it, and if Iomhar is not here, it seems to me ye are the person who takes the most risks."

"Thank you," Kit murmured. Laying her hand flat over the pendant, she clung to it, as if part of Iomhar were in the room.

"It's a long way to come, Kit, a long way indeed from London," Moira whispered. "Ye are intent on finding him, are ye not?"

"Yes," Kit said.

"Would ye tell me why?" Moira asked, her eyes boring into Kit's. "Not all friends would risk coming so far."

"I…" Kit struggled to put it into words. She shrugged instead and looked at the pendant. "I miss him." She was aware of Moira shifting.

"Aye, now that is a good answer." Moira took the necklace from Kit's hands. "Here, let me help." She threaded the chain around Kit's neck, then fastened the lock as Kit held her hair out of the way. She felt rather like a child. Doris had once done this, many years ago. "May it keep ye safe, Kit. Come down soon. We have persuaded Duncan not to send his letter, but we must think of something else to do."

"I'll be there soon," Kit promised.

The two shared a sad smile, then Moira stood and left. The moment the door was shut, Kit sighed and looked out at the snow, raising a hand to fiddle with the pendant at her throat.

Her mind worked quickly, thinking over every option that had been suggested by the family. If they contacted this soldier, it could take days to hear anything from him, and she didn't have that long, not if she was going to deliver her letter to Mary Stuart. What was more, it was possible that the soldier's enquiries could put Iomhar in more danger.

They didn't need someone to raise the matter diplomatically, for it would draw attention to Iomhar's identity. No, Kit realised the safest way to get him out of that castle was to do something unexpected. A plan was forming in her mind, but it was a risk, and would have to be undertaken alone. If she acted by herself, then there would be no danger to Iomhar's family.

"I have broken into a prison before," she whispered to herself. "I can do so again."

CHAPTER 16

This time, Kit was careful to make sure no one came with her. She woke in the early hours of the morning, when the darkness was still thick. With no moon out tonight, and dense clouds, it was hard to see what she was doing as she climbed out of bed and dressed. Knowing she couldn't take too great a risk, she took off her belt and slipped out the small silver case in which she'd hidden the letter from Queen Elizabeth. Stuffing it into the bottom of a coffer, she left it there and hurried out of the room, wrapping the belt around her waist again.

Wearing a thick woollen doublet, gloves and her grey hat, she crept through the house, being careful to listen for sounds, but no one moved. She checked the weapons at her belt — she carried her daggers and a crossbow, with a few loose bolts strapped up in a thin leather bag that hung from her hip. Heading to the sitting room, she found where Niall had discarded a map. Lifting a candle, Kit checked it was the right map — it showed not only their current position, but also that of Loch Ness and Urquhart Castle, right on the edge of a protrusion of land that stretched out into the loch. Snatching the map up from its place on the table, Kit blew out the candle and made her way to the door.

Outside, it did not feel so dark thanks to the snow. She trudged through the ice to the stable. Inside, she found Iomhar's black steed, snorting to her in greeting. Kit clicked her tongue, urging the steed forward, and hurried to saddle him. Once the reins were in place, she left, leading the horse down a path where the snow was at its thinnest. The horse still occasionally complained, stomping his hooves a little too harshly, but he obeyed her orders, nevertheless.

At the edge of the forest, Kit looked back at the house. No candles were lit, and every window was dark with the curtains drawn. The family had retired to bed late, having made no other decision than to stick to Niall's resolution to hunt for the soldier they had mentioned.

Kit reached beneath her doublet and held onto the Celtic shield knot at her throat, then turned the steed and rode away through the forest, heading for the hills in the distance.

As the sun came up, Kit found Loch Ness. She had been riding for what felt like hours. It was bitterly cold, with the wind nipping at her cheeks and nose until they were red, and her hat frequently attempted to escape her head. The horse's nose was beginning to droop with tiredness after walking through the snow for so long, but she wouldn't let the steed slow his pace. They had to stay consistent, if they were going to reach Urquhart Castle soon.

The vast loch stretched out before her, the blue surface almost like glass, appearing to freeze at the edges thanks to the cold in the air. Not many people were on the road Kit stood upon, merely one or two horses, which were heading to a village at the edge of the loch.

Pulling the horse to a stop, Kit glanced at the map in her grasp, then twisted it round, seeing that Urquhart Castle was not far away. Halfway down the loch and atop a land protrusion, it should have been easy to spot. Kit put the map away and lifted her eyes, seeing the castle was indeed in view.

In the distance, she could see the morning sun glinting off the grey stone. It was expansive, with two towers spread across undulating mounds of earth in the loch, and a drawbridge that connected it to the mainland. Around it, Loch Ness was frozen.

Kit urged the horse on, heading to the castle. Once she reached the main road leading toward it, she found it was a busy place. People were moving in and out over the drawbridge, some carrying barrels, others shifting crates, as if replacing the castle's supplies. One man stood on the drawbridge, overseeing it all, with a crossbow firmly at his hip.

Pulling the horse into the cover of nearby trees, Kit soon saw he was not the only one who was armed. Along the top wall that overlooked the gate and risen portcullis, there were five other guards, each one carrying a crossbow or pistol at his hip. The guards seemed rather lost in conversation, not watching the land around them too closely.

Slowly, Kit climbed down from the horse. The snow was so thick here that it rose halfway up her shins. Shivering, she wrapped the reins around the nearest branch, then felt herself being nudged in the shoulder by the steed. Laying a hand on his nose, she tried to comfort the animal, yet it continued to push against her and snort.

"You think this is a bad idea?" Kit whispered, feeling a smile tug at her lips when the horse snorted again. "Or maybe you are just angry with me for riding you through the snow?" The horse seemed to agree with her. "All will be well," she said, more to herself than the horse as she left him behind.

Pulling her hat low over her face, she crept between the trees and moved toward the edge of the copse. In front of her, the land dipped down, revealing a harsh cliff face. This cavern was covered by a short drawbridge that led to the gate of the castle. Beyond it, the curtain wall was high, far too high and smooth for Kit to consider climbing.

Kit's eyes flicked to the frozen water, and another idea arose, one so mad that she cursed.

"No. Iomhar would think I had lost my mind." She looked away, trying to think of another idea, but nothing presented itself. "God's blood, what other choice do I have?" She began to scale down the side of the hill, crossing the short distance toward the water. Beside the hill, there was a small sandy section of earth, dappled with rocks that were covered in snow. Beyond the rocks was the water, frozen solid.

Holding her breath, Kit placed the toe of her boot on the ice. It didn't crack, nor shift beneath her. She darted her gaze up to the main road and the drawbridge. She couldn't see the road from where she stood, which meant she was partially hidden. Only able to see the underside of the drawbridge, she stood a chance of reaching the castle walls this way, without being seen.

Kit's hands shook as she stepped further out onto the ice. She kept as close to the cliff edge as she could. The loch was so vast that even at this distance she could see the middle of it was not frozen over, so she kept to the very edge, fearful of crashing through. She hated being in water enough as it was and didn't think plunging through ice would help that fear.

Walking around the headland, she found trees and rocks forming the castle embankment. Once she was far out of view of the road and the drawbridge, she turned to the trees. One quick step, and there was a crack under her boots.

Kit froze, looking down at the ice. Two long lines began to stretch out from beneath her right boot. They moved like lightning forks, growing bigger.

Kit grasped at the nearest rock and pulled herself off the ice, just as she felt the solid sheet give way beneath her. With her weight fully on the rock, she glanced back, seeing a small hole where her foot had been. Sighing deeply, Kit rested her forehead against the rock for a minute. She may have made it to the castle this way, but she was not sure she could get back out using the same route.

Trying not to make a sound, she climbed up the rocks and trees. When she reached the castle wall, she flattened her body against it. She was standing on a small stretch of earth, with the wall on one side and the drop back down to the ice on the other. As she peered at the distance she had covered, the wind buffeted her face and doublet, making the woollen material ripple.

She knew she couldn't stay here for long. With the wind as strong as it was, it could push her into the water any minute.

Stepping over the sods of snow, Kit moved along the castle wall. As she had feared, the castle wall was too smooth to climb easily, but there was another possible route in. The wall curved in front of her, revealing the makings of a slim tower, and in that wall was a narrow window.

Moving to stand under the window, Kit raised herself on her toes and peered through the glass. Beyond the window, there appeared to be some sort of formal apartment, perhaps one of the resident's chambers, yet it was empty. The furs on the bed were flat, and the fireplace was dark.

Digging one boot into the only nook in the stone she could find, Kit lifted herself up, peering through the glass. There was no way to open it, for it was fixed firmly to the frame. Kit took her dagger from her belt and turned it over, then braced the hilt of the weapon against the glass and struck once.

One pane of the lead-lined glass shattered. The shards fell away, revealing enough of a space for Kit to slip through. With her head poked through, she listened for any sounds, but no one appeared to have heard the glass smashing. Bending her body as much as she could, she inched through the space and stepped into the room, crunching some of the shards beneath her boots.

The chamber was not as big as she had first thought it to be, but it was certainly grand and there were signs that it was occupied, with a plaid doublet loose over a coffer and a pewter tankard left on a table nearby.

Hurrying to the door, Kit moved on her toes, knowing she had to escape this room as soon as possible to avoid discovery. When she heard no sounds beyond the door, she opened it an inch and peered out to find an empty corridor. Stepping out, she closed the door soundlessly behind her and moved on.

She knew she couldn't walk far dressed as she was. The moment she met someone, she would be caught and revealed as an intruder. With this in mind, she paused by a window in the corridor, looking into the inner courtyard of the castle.

There were many people moving back and forth, delivering supplies. It could be easy to disappear in such a crowd, if she was dressed the right way. There were guards that moved amongst the men, wearing scarves over their faces to ward off the snow that was beginning to fall lightly once more. Kit smiled a little, a plan forming in her mind, before she hurried on down the corridor.

Reaching a spiral staircase, she descended quickly, then found the perfect target at the bottom of the stairs. Standing in the open door was a guard facing the courtyard, humming a tune to himself and bobbing on his toes. He was in full view, but that could change.

Kit crept around the bottom of the spiral staircase, hiding in the shadows, then whistled once. The guard flinched and looked round, trying to see into the shadows.

"That ye, Mason? That dog gone wandering again?" His question amused her. When she whistled another time, he hurried forward. "That damn dog, I'll get him —" He broke off when he stepped into the shadows and his eyes found Kit's.

With her hand curling around the dagger in her belt, she quickly raised the blade toward him.

"Take off the cloak and hat," she warned. The man didn't hesitate to obey. He slipped off the garments, tossing them to the ground. "Now, what's through there?" She gestured to a small door behind him, so short that it only reached his shoulder.

"It's a store. A cupboard."

"Open it and step inside."

The guard hurried to the task. The store was full of boxes that he knocked over as he stepped inside. Kit reached for the rapier in his belt and slid it out.

"Do not make a sound until I come back," she ordered, uncertain if he would listen or not. As far as she was concerned, she just needed enough time to find where they kept their prisoners. She closed the cupboard door on him, being careful to drive the rapier through the looped handle of the door and into the stone wall beside it.

Stuffing her grey hat in her doublet, she put on the guard's hat and cloak, then wrapped a loose stretch of plaid material around her face, hiding her features. Now disguised, she could walk freely.

Stepping out into the courtyard from the tower, no eyes turned to look at her. She moved slowly, as if she had no real purpose, walking past other guards and those delivering supplies. More than one argument seemed to break out between the men, with some saying the wrong barrels had been brought, but Kit ignored it all. The commotion helped her to walk unseen.

She passed through the cobbled courtyard and headed toward the gatehouse, where she soon saw the doorway of the dungeon. Another guard stood in front, plainly announcing the location of their prison, yet he was distracted. There was a dog at his feet, tied to the end of a thin end of a rope that he held in his hand. The dog kept straining, desperate to be free.

"Dumb animal," the guard muttered, trying to keep the dog in place. Kit remembered what the first guard had said about a dog running off and took a chance. Deepening her voice to sound like a man's, she approached and patted the animal.

"Good boy," she said softly. "Well behaved dog ye have here." She adopted a Scottish accent, watching as the guard laughed.

"Nay, he's not. He'll run and chase anything as soon as he has the chance to." As the guard spoke, Kit lowered her hand to the rope at the dog's throat, pulling to loosen the knot, unseen.

"Ye need to tighten your rope, then."

"Tighten it?" The guard barely finished his sentence before the rope was loosened completely. The dog sensed it and bolted. "Dumb dog!" the guard cried and ran after it. Darting between the men in the courtyard, the dog was keen on chasing those bringing in the supplies. The guard followed but couldn't get close enough to grab him.

With her smile hidden by the plaid strip, Kit opened the door to the dungeon and stepped inside.

The stench was instant, and one of the worst she had smelt. Pushing her nose more firmly into the plaid, she hurried down a spiral staircase that moved deep underground. The air around her grew colder still, until her hands were balling into fists, making her leather gloves squeak.

At the bottom of the staircase, the dungeon opened out into a narrow corridor. There were more cells than she had imagined, so many that it was impossible to know which way to go. They were covered in iron gates and some had windows, for light streamed through and cast shadows onto the walls.

There was the occasional cough of a prisoner, and she thought she heard one man retch. In the cell beside her, there was an old man, shivering in the cold. His woollen blanket was not thick enough, and he clutched it with fingers that were as white as bone.

Kit looked back and forth, knowing she did not have long before the guard returned to the dungeon door and realised that she was inside. With desperation, she tried something she had not done for a long time.

She whistled a slow and gentle tune. The short ditty was one she and Iomhar had heard on the road once, and something she had used as a signal to him in more than one crowd. The buoyant tune of 'Leave Lightie Love' filled the air, sounding eerie in this damp and dark place. The last time she had whistled it, they had been at Nottingham Castle, and had discovered there was a plot to kill the queen.

Kit fell silent, waiting for a response, but none came. Turning on the spot, she grew panicked. It wouldn't be long now before she was discovered. In desperation, she whistled it again, louder and slower this time. The old man beside her looked up from his blanket, glaring at her, but she didn't stop until she'd hit the end of the chorus.

Then another whistle answered her. It was sudden and soft, and had come from behind her.

Kit took off toward it, running so fast that her boots slipped on the damp stones. At the end of the corridor, she came face to face with a cell barred by iron struts. The whistle stopped as she struck the metal, making it ring.

"Iomhar?"

CHAPTER 17

Kit breathed heavily as her eyes landed on the figure beyond the iron struts. As he lifted his head, she saw that his hair had grown longer. It was untamed around his ears, dirty too, and his beard was matted in tendrils, like a dropped bird's nest.

But his eyes were the same. His bright green gaze turned toward Kit, illuminated by the light from the window.

"Iomhar?" Kit murmured again, watching as he shifted forward abruptly. He tried to move to the bars but was wrenched back, a groan escaping him. Kit looked down, seeing what fixed him in place. There was an iron chain fastened to his ankle.

"Kit? That ye? Or am I imagining ye?"

"I'm here," Kit said quickly. She lowered the plaid from her face and pushed the guard's hat back. At the sight of her, Iomhar jerked forward again, cursing at the irons clamped to his ankle. He managed to clasp one of the iron bars that separated them this time, staring at her in disbelief. "You're alive." Kit felt relief washing over her body. She was aware of how wide her smile was, but she didn't care.

"Barely." Iomhar's answer made her smile falter. "Kit, what are ye doing here?" His voice was panic-stricken, and his eyes shot behind her. The scar on his cheek was almost hidden by his wild hair, but she could see it as he strained against his chains, trying to get closer to her.

"Why do you think?" she asked, scoffing. "Do you think I just wished to say good day?"

He narrowed his eyes. "This place is dangerous, Kit. Ye cannot be here."

"All the more reason for you not to be here either." Her words made him smile a little, his beard twitching with the movement. "Time to get you out, don't you think?"

He strained against the irons. "Kit!"

"What?"

His hand moved on the bars and found hers. His fingers were dirty, but she didn't pull away. "If ye are found…" He grimaced, not wanting to finish the sentence.

"Then we best not be found." She reached into her doublet, finding the secret pocket in the wool lining. Taking hold of the compass she had so often used, she flipped the lid, looking inside. She had used gunpowder once to get someone out of prison; there was every chance it could work again. This far underground, it would be difficult for the sound to be heard if she didn't use too much.

"I do not understand," Iomhar said, quivering. "How did ye find me?"

"You did not make it easy," Kit snapped.

"Did ye think I could send a message?"

"It would have helped if you had left with a touch more information about where you were," she argued, lifting out the glass vial she kept behind the needle of the compass.

"Aye, it's good to see ye too," Iomhar said, with a gentle laugh.

Kit smiled briefly, before she urged him away from the bars with a wave of her hand. "You will need space for this."

"Kit, we do not have time." Iomhar looked up, listening, but Kit wasn't paying attention. She had to get him out. Tipping the glass vial into the lock of the gate, she was careful to add just a small amount of gunpowder, enough to be lit by a spark. "Kit! A guard is coming."

Kit froze and straightened up. There were footsteps on the spiral stone staircase, moving closer.

"Hide," Iomhar ordered, backing up from the bars. "Please, Kit. Hide."

She nodded then retreated into the shadows. At their end of the corridor, there was a small alcove, hidden in darkness. She pressed herself flat into the shadows and held her breath.

"What's going on down here?" a guard barked as he stepped into the corridor. "Anyone come in to see ye lot? Anyone wish to talk? Or do ye wish to be flogged again for me to get the information out of ye?"

"He went to see the spy at the end." The old man's croaky voice made Kit curse inwardly. He raised his bony hand through the iron bars of his cell and pointed in Iomhar's direction.

Kit's eyes shot to Iomhar. He sat very still on a ledge in the stonework of the dungeon, staring at the guard who was quickly approaching, his boots thudding against the stones.

"Ye, spy, who came to see ye? Who was it?" the guard demanded.

"A guard," Iomhar answered. "Shouldn't ye know who your guards are?"

"This was nay guard!" the man snapped in answer. "One of our men has been found locked in a store cupboard, his uniform taken."

Kit could see Iomhar's lips quirking into a smile, apparently amused by what she had done. She, however, was irked to find her ruse had been discovered so quickly.

"Tell me who it was!" the guard yelled, but Iomhar gave no answer. "As ye like it then, spy. Ye will be made to talk." The guard reached down to his belt for a key.

Kit realised what could happen if the key was pressed into the lock. It could create a spark, if it was done with just enough pressure.

"Are ye going to flog me?" Iomhar scoffed. "It hasn't made me speak before."

"Then we'll have to find something worse," the guard snapped.

Kit's eyes darted to the loose shirt on Iomhar's back. It looked torn, and could have been destroyed in such torture. She feared for him, but she couldn't think of that now.

The guard thrust the key into the lock. The spark was made quickly, followed by the bang of the gunpowder that caught light.

"Argh!" the guard roared and jumped back. The powder caused a small explosion, burning his skin. As he raised his hand high in the air, Kit could see the red and white marks, with smoke curling off the flesh.

"Now!" Iomhar barked.

Kit was already moving forward. She turned over her dagger and used the hilt to strike the back of the guard's head. He was dazed for a second, then his body tipped forward. He fell like a plank, landing flat on the stones with his burnt hand outstretched and loose straw that had been used for prisoners' beds scattering around him. After the heavy thud, there were murmurs from prisoners, who were unable to see what was taking place at this end of the corridor.

Kit took the keys that had fallen out of the guard's hand then grasped the cell door, opening it. Iomhar stood, his eyes wide as he looked at the open gate.

"I'm free," he murmured.

"Not quite yet." Kit lifted the keys, revealing how many there were on the iron loop. "Any idea which one opens your irons?"

"Small iron one, carved with a cross."

Kit found it quickly and bent down, thrusting it into the lock around his ankle and prising it open. When Iomhar stepped out of the irons, he limped, growling at the pain.

"That has been around my ankle every day for… How long has it been?"

Kit didn't answer him. Instead, she stepped out of the cell.

"We need to be quick, before he wakes up." Kit stepped over the guard and Iomhar followed her, but he didn't let her get far. Kit felt a hand on her arm, and she was swung back. "Iomhar?"

He wrapped her in an embrace. Kit was so shocked that she just stood there for a second, before her arms came up and she clung to him too.

"You're alive, Iomhar, and you're getting out of here," she promised him, her voice just a whisper. He held her tighter still. This close, Kit could smell the stench that hung on his clothes, but she didn't pull back. The tension in her body left her and she breathed deeply.

"Ye came all this way," he murmured as they eventually stepped back from each other. Here, the shadows were greater, and Kit could not see his expression, but the softness of his voice showed his relief.

"Did you think I wouldn't?" she asked. "We need to be quick. If they know about their locked-up guard, then it's only a matter of time before they find us."

When some of the other prisoners saw one of their own was free, they began to wail, calling for help, but Kit ignored them all, as did Iomhar as they walked on. She reached for the spiral staircase, realising as she hastened up the steps that Iomhar was not close behind her. She looked back, watching as he limped and breathed heavily.

"Iomhar…"

"Do not tell me to hurry, Kit," he pleaded. "I have nay energy in me. The last thing I ate may have just been dirt."

"Dirt?" Kit took a closer look at Iomhar as he stopped behind her on the steps. His shirt hung off his body. He was thin, too thin, and had clearly been starved.

"I will not be able to run," he whispered as she walked forward, leading the way to the dungeon door.

"Then we'll have to find another way out." When Kit reached the door, she held on to Iomhar's shoulder, keeping him in place as he leaned against the wall, needing it for support. He heaved, out of breath from the climb. "You look as if you need carrying out of here."

"I think I do," Iomhar sighed, finally catching his breath and tipping his head forward. He was a shell of the man he had been, and that thought crushed Kit.

She clamped down on the feeling and pulled open the door a crack, peering out. She had to be practical now, and couldn't afford to be scared of the state Iomhar was in.

"I thought I imagined that whistle."

"You didn't," Kit assured him.

"Thank the wee man for that." He seemed to shake himself, trying to return to the matter at hand. "What do we do now?"

Once more, Kit looked through the gap, out to the courtyard. The supplies were still being delivered, but there was one cart unattended. "We ride out of here," she whispered.

By the time she had finished explaining her plan, Iomhar was staring at her in bemusement.

"I was about to ask if ye were mad," he hissed, "then I remembered that ye have just broken into Urquhart Castle of all places, dressed as a bloody guard. I think I can answer that question myself."

"Do you have any other ideas?" Kit asked. When Iomhar shook his head, she didn't waste time. "Then we go ahead with it."

"Kit, wait!" Iomhar snapped, but she didn't give him time.

She walked out of the door, pulling the plaid up around her face to hide her features, and closed the door behind her. Across the courtyard, she could see some of the guards talking, their heads bent together. They looked fearful and were pointing in different directions across the castle, apparently planning where to search for their intruder.

Meanwhile, Kit walked amongst them, easily hidden, then reached for the empty wagon in the courtyard. She laid a hand on the side of the cart just as a man appeared, carrying an empty crate in his arms.

"What are ye doing?" the man asked.

Still dressed in the uniform of a guard, Kit stood taller. "Ye shouldn't have left this here," she said sternly, adopting a deep Scottish accent. "Who said ye could?"

"Well, I..." The man looked wrongfooted. "I left it there last time."

"Aye? The matter has changed. Ye should ask for approval before ye leave your cart here." Kit shook her head in dismissal. "Go collect your other crates. I will move it for ye."

"Aye, sir. Very well." The man dropped the empty crate onto the back of the cart and walked off, allowing Kit to climb into the driver's seat and whip the reins of the one horse pulling the cart. The horse ambled forward slowly, until they drew level with the door to the dungeon. Pulling on the reins, she urged the horse to stop, then whistled the beginning of 'Leave Lightie Love'.

A few seconds passed, and Kit had to whistle again before the door opened. Iomhar was there, only this time, he was wearing the cloak and hat he had taken from the unconscious guard lying far below in the belly of the dungeon. His dirty tartan trews gave him away, but Kit was clearly the only one who looked that closely.

Iomhar walked slowly out of the door, keeping his face hidden beneath the brim of the guard's hat. He limped toward the cart, though he did his best to cover it up. When he reached the side, he pulled himself up into the driver's seat beside Kit.

"Are you well?" she whispered.

He offered one dark look, apparently unable to answer the question. "Get us out of here, Kit," he pleaded.

She did as he asked and pulled on the reins. It was only when they reached the drawbridge that others began to realise something was wrong.

"Get ready," Kit warned. Iomhar nodded and gripped the wooden cart.

"Och! Ye cannot bring that thing back over here yet." One of the guards stepped out onto the drawbridge. "Wait, who are ye two?" he called.

"Do not stop, Kit," Iomhar begged.

"I have no intention to." She whipped the reins of the horse. The steed neighed in surprise before galloping across the drawbridge.

There was a commotion, with people jumping out of the path of the cart, and one man even falling over the edge of the drawbridge, clinging desperately to the wooden railings.

"It's our intruder! Stop him!" a voice cried from the courtyard behind them.

"Stop!" the guard on the bridge ordered, and lifted his crossbow, aiming it straight at them. Kit whipped the reins harder, and the guard could not fire in time. Forced to scramble to the side of the drawbridge for safety, he lowered the crossbow, and they escaped past him, riding out onto the open road.

It was difficult, and the wagon began to slow down, struggling through the snow.

"We cannot escape like this," Iomhar called, looking back over his shoulder. "We are moving too slowly!"

"Then we'll find another way. Iomhar, you are going to have to ride."

Iomhar grimaced but nodded, showing he was prepared to do anything at this point.

Kit directed the cart up the hill, toward the place where she had left the steed, then hastily pulled it to a stop.

"You take your horse." She practically pushed Iomhar out of the wooden seat. He limped toward his steed as Kit reached for the horse pulling the cart. There was no saddle, but she could adjust the harness and bridle to act as elongated reins, and it would have to do for now. Unlatching the horse from the cart, she climbed onto his back and prompted him forward.

Seconds later, Iomhar appeared at her side, patting the neck of the black steed that was snorting in approval, pleased to have his master back.

"They're coming," Iomhar said, his voice deep as he looked behind them.

Kit saw horses advancing through the snow with other guards beside them on foot, lifting crossbows. "Time to go," she ordered and whipped the reins, leading the way. Iomhar followed, then moved to her side.

They took the same path Kit had arrived on, where the snow was at its thinnest. Here, the horses could move faster, but it was not enough. If they were going to escape, Kit knew they would have to do something more than just outrun the guards of the castle. Casting a glance at Iomhar, she could see he was weak, bending over the neck of his steed. He would not be able to ride for long.

"We'll hide."

"What?" he called to her.

"We cannot outrun them, so we'll hide. This way." Jerking on the bridle, Kit urged her horse in a different direction, curving around Loch Ness. Iomhar followed, the steed keeping up with ease despite the rider's tiredness.

Their sudden change in direction helped a little, for their chasers dropped back. Kit steered onto a path down toward the village she had seen before. Here, the snow on the roads had been partially cleared, making it easy for them to ride into the town.

"This is your plan? To hide here?" Iomhar asked in panic.

"Well, who would be mad enough to hide so close, eh?" Kit's words made him shake his head in disbelief.

They rode down a nearby road between thatched houses. Partway down, Kit stopped and jerked on the reins, and Iomhar came to a halt a short distance in front.

"Down," she said. He didn't question it, but did as she asked, allowing her to tug the horses into a gap between the houses, looping their reins around an iron hook. Turning to Iomhar, she could see him leaning against a wall. "Now, we rid ourselves of these." She pulled off the guard's cloak and hat, urging him to do the same, then returned her grey hat to her head. Iomhar was still noticeable in his torn clothes, so she reached toward the steed and pulled off a blanket she had thrown there that morning, to keep her warm on the ride. Wrapping it around Iomhar's shoulders, she made sure his clothes were hidden. "There, just look cold and hungry as we walk, like a beggar man."

"I do not need to pretend for that," he grumbled as she walked him forward, taking his arm.

Moving out of the narrow lane, they entered a main street, beyond which she could see the guards heading into the village on horseback. Kit urged Iomhar through a tavern door, pushing him in so hurriedly that he tripped on the doorjamb. It was busy enough in the tavern that no one looked their way, all far too interested in their own business and the drinks in front of them.

"Sit." Kit pressed Iomhar into a settle bench in the corner of the room. He sat back, yawning and leaning against the wall, as she went to the tavern owner and ordered as much as she could: beer, umble pie, bread, cheese, and smoked fish. She kept a passive face and tried not to show any excitement when the guards and their horses hurried past the windows.

"They must be looking for someone," another drinker in the tavern said. No one seemed very interested, though, and they all soon turned their gazes away from the passing horses and back down to the cups in front of them.

Taking the tankards of beer that were offered to her, Kit returned to the table and placed two in front of Iomhar, and one in front of herself. He said nothing before he took the first cup and began to drink. When it was empty, he lowered it to the table, the pewter gently tapping the wood.

"Thank ye," he said. "I needed that."

"Wait until you see what else we have coming." Kit's words seemed to go unheard, for Iomhar flinched as more horses raced past the window. She kicked him under the table, catching his attention.

"Ow, what was that for?"

"If we are to hide in plain sight, then that means not reacting, Iomhar," she whispered. "We cannot raise anyone's suspicions."

He nodded, then turned his attention to the second tankard. As he gulped, the tavern keeper delivered their food. The trenchers were laid out in front of them, and Iomhar stared as if he were before the gates of heaven.

"Iomhar?" Kit said softly. "Are you all right?"

"I just…" He struggled for words and reached for the trencher bearing an Arbroath smokie, the fish he loved so much. "I didn't think I would be able to eat like this again."

"Then eat up," Kit said with a smile.

Yet he didn't. His hand hovered over the fish as he lifted his gaze. "Kit, we could be found any minute."

"Then do you not want to eat before that happens?" Kit asked.

"The wee man and all his angels, I do not want to go back, Kit," he hissed, bending over the table.

"I'm not intending to let them take you back." Her voice was solemn as she held his gaze.

"Ye expect to defeat that many guards in a fight, Kit? I am not sure I will be much use at the moment." Iomhar gestured to himself.

"They are looking for two people hiding, Iomhar," she continued, her voice deep and careful. "They are not looking for a pair sitting in a tavern, eating, as if they have no worries in the world."

"Ye think it will work?"

"When people hunt, they look for prey. They look for those who seem scared and those who run. You hide here for long enough, and they will not notice you. How many of them know your face?"

"Only a few," Iomhar said quietly. "Nay, not many were allowed to see me."

Kit took off her hat and dropped it on Iomhar's head. "Then that will do for now." She motioned to the table. "Eat. Before I take it."

Iomhar delved in. He started with the fish, attacking it like a wild animal who had not eaten in days. Kit swiftly returned to the tavern keeper to order more beer.

On occasion, she would let her eyes slip to the windows. The guards were searching hard, but they were quickly losing hope. Some guards ended up in an argument, no doubt blaming one another for the escape. At one point, a guard knocked on the door of the tavern and asked the owner if two people were hiding. The tavern owner said no, but it didn't stop the guard from turning over the back rooms. He left again quickly enough, not thinking to check those that were sitting at ease in the tavern.

The moment the door shut behind him, Kit smiled and lifted her beer to her lips, watching as Iomhar rested his gaze upon her.

"I never thought that would work," he murmured.

"People do not see what's in front of them sometimes."

Iomhar smiled. It was the first full smile she had seen from him. They returned their gazes to the window, watching as the guards retreated. One was ordering the others to search the countryside.

When the food was gone, Iomhar sat forward, staring at the empty plates.

"Did that help?" Kit asked. His eyes snapped toward her, with so much intensity that she sat back. "Too much yellow bile? Iomhar, why are you so angry?"

"Do ye need ask me that?" Iomhar's voice was gentle, despite the suggestion of ire in his eyes. "Ye were supposed to stay in London, Kit. Far away from this place."

"That worked well, did it not?" Kit asked, lifting her cup to her lips. "I didn't know where you were, your family were going mad grieving for you, panicking that you might have been…" Her breath hitched, unable to say the word. "We had no way of looking for you." She swallowed past the sudden lump in her throat. "Next time you go missing, at least make it a little easier to find you."

"I didn't know I would end up here."

"You suspected it was a trap, though, didn't you?"

He leaned forward, resting his elbows on the table. "How much do ye know, Kit?"

"I know that Walsingham received a letter from Oswyn, offering information on Lord Ruskin in exchange for a pardon, and he sent you. You went to meet Oswyn in disguise; then you were caught fighting by nightwatchmen and were taken to the castle. There Lord Ruskin accused you of being a spy, and they have held you there ever since. Is there anything I am missing?" Kit asked.

Iomhar nodded in approval. "Ye did well."

"Thank you." Kit took another sip of her beer, watching as Iomhar did the same.

"There is only one thing ye have not said."

"What is that?"

"Why did ye come to find me?"

Kit nearly dropped her tankard. "I had to get you out," she murmured, avoiding his gaze. Lifting a cloth that was under one of the pewter plates, she mopped up the beer she'd spilled.

"Why?" Iomhar asked again.

Kit paused, still not looking at him. She had answered this question when Moira had asked the day before, but she didn't feel like she could tell Iomhar that she had missed him yet. The mere thought of saying it made her fidget. "I wasn't going to leave you there, you fool," she whispered, her tone very gentle. "I had to get you out."

A deep sigh came from the other side of the table, prompting Kit to look up.

"Thank God for ye, Kit," Iomhar said, tipping his head back and closing his eyes. Kit sat taller in her seat, smiling at his words. "Thank God indeed."

"You're alive," she whispered. "I'll thank God for that instead."

He chuckled and opened his eyes, meeting her gaze. "They couldn't kill me. They had nothing but an accusation against me." Suddenly, the smile vanished from his face and he looked behind Kit.

"What is it?" She knew that expression of old — it was fear mingled with worry. When she heard the tavern door close, she didn't need to look round to know someone had walked in whom Iomhar did not want to see.

"He'll recognise me, Kit," he hissed.

"Who? Who is he?"

"The captain of the guards from the castle. He may have come here for a drink, but he knew my face, aye, better than anyone there. He stood there and watched my face as they flogged me for information."

Kit looked over her shoulder to see a guard standing by the tavern keeper. His uniform was different from that of the other guards; his hat was broader and his cloak more tightly fitted. He ordered a drink then looked around the room, searching for a table.

There was no time to hide Iomhar. When the guard's eyes landed on Iomhar, his body stiffened.

"There ye are, spy."

CHAPTER 18

"Run," Iomhar said quietly. He and Kit jumped to their feet as the guard advanced.

"Do not move!" the guard roared and lifted the wheellock pistol from his belt. It had to be loaded, so Kit reached for the table between her and Iomhar. He had the same idea and they pushed it over, diving behind the wooden surface as the shot rang out.

The bullet sounded so close that Kit's eyes darted to Iomhar. Between them, there was a bullet hole in the wood, mere inches from their ears.

"He'll have to reload," Kit said. Iomhar nodded, knowing it was their chance to escape. They both scrambled out from behind the table and launched themselves around it.

The guard was hastening to reload his gun, but it took too long, allowing Kit and Iomhar to run for the door of the tavern. Other customers crouched beneath tables, demanding to know why shots were being fired. Kit darted through the door first, with Iomhar behind, barely reaching it in time as a second shot rang out. It splintered the doorframe, narrowly missing their heads.

They sprinted down the street, heading in the direction of their horses in the narrow lane. Iomhar struggled, his limp slowing him down. Kit looked around, but no other guard seemed to be here. They had to be back at the castle or in the countryside, searching for them.

They dived down the lane as Kit glanced back, seeing the guard hurrying out of the tavern and reloading the pistol. His eyes found her before she disappeared into the lane.

"He's seen us," Kit called to Iomhar ahead of her.

"Then we take the horses and ride as fast as we can. Hiding will not help us now." He reached the horses first and pulled on the reins, releasing them from where they had been tied to the iron hook.

Kit heard rapid footsteps and looked back. The guard was advancing, lifting his pistol and preparing to take his next shot.

"Down!" Kit grabbed Iomhar's shoulder and pushed him into the alcove where the horses had been hiding. The shot struck the stone wall, making the black steed buck, spooked by the sound.

Kit reached for the weapons in her belt and snapped up the crossbow, loading it quickly with a bolt.

"Don't miss, Kit," Iomhar pleaded, leaning against the wall beside her. She nodded, then angled her head around the corner of the wall, watching as the guard hurried to reload his shot. She aimed carefully, then released the bolt.

It whipped through the air and landed in the captain's hand. He roared at the pain and dropped his gun. The bolt was still in his hand as he reached for another weapon in his belt with his other hand. This weapon was a broadsword. He lifted it high as he advanced their way, his face red and sweaty.

"On the horse, Iomhar." Kit's order was quickly adhered to. He pulled himself onto the steed, just as the other horse grew so spooked that it tried to bolt. Iomhar moved after it, attempting to draw it back. With so much distance between her and the horse, Kit couldn't get there in time, not before the captain was with her.

Lowering the crossbow, she rounded the corner, preparing herself for the fight. The captain was closer than she had expected, and he thrust out at her with the sword. Kit lifted the crossbow, using it as a shield to bat the strike away. It shattered to pieces in her grasp.

"Kit!" Iomhar's voice called out in panic, but she couldn't turn to look at him. She was too busy batting away the pieces of the broken crossbow and reaching for another weapon as the captain lifted his sword.

Snatching up her daggers, she thrust them in front of her, making a cross. The sword landed where the blades met, prevented from going any further. He tried to drive the tip forward and Kit backed up, lowering the daggers and creating space between them.

She was reminded of Graham Fraser, who'd followed her on the road with orders to kill her. This guard didn't know who she was, but he plainly had no qualms about hurting her, for he struck out again, aiming for her chest. She barely batted it away in time, before striking out herself. With her shorter blade, she managed to cut him across the cheek, forcing him to veer back.

"Out of my way, Sassenach," he growled. The insult meant he must have heard her accent, to know she was English. "Betrayers are killed round here."

He struck out, and this time, Kit couldn't back up in time. His blade collided with one of her daggers, with so much force that she was knocked from her feet. The knife fell away.

"Kit!" Iomhar called.

Looking up, she became aware of the captain standing over her. He lifted his sword, about to drive it down into her chest.

Her death was coming. She could sense this man would not hold back; he had no misgivings about killing someone who stood between him and one of his prisoners.

Looking down at the one dagger she had in her hands, Kit made a bid for survival and lifted it sharply against the man's leg. He roared, louder this time, and fell to one knee. The blade of his sword came so close to her face that Kit cowered, curling into a ball and driving her dagger upward.

The blade found its mark. She felt it plunge into something then heard the groan, and opened her eyes just enough to see what was happening.

His sword had landed by her face, buried in the dirt. Her dagger, on the other hand, had found its way into his chest.

The man's face had paled, and his breath was stuttered.

Realising what she had done, Kit pushed the man's shoulder and rolled him off her, scrambling back. When she found the dagger still in her hand, she dropped it, watching as the blood shone on her palm.

"Kit?" Iomhar was behind her. His arm wrapped around her waist and tried to tug her to her feet.

Kit could see that the captain was dying, staring up at the sky. "No…" she whispered. "I killed him. I didn't mean…" She trailed off, horrified at what she had done.

"Kit, get up!" Iomhar managed to raise her to her feet and snatched the dagger up from the ground, putting it in her weapons belt. She was certain she would be sick at any second. "We need to get out of here. Now."

She nodded numbly and hurried for the horse, pulling herself up and tugging on the bridle straps. Iomhar led the way this time, out of the lane. Kit couldn't help looking back. The man had stopped moving, with his sword limp at his side.

"Oh God," Kit murmured, looking down at her hands on the reins. She was spreading blood on the leather.

"Kit." Iomhar reached over and jerked the reins. "Not now, aye? We'll deal with this later. It will not be long before news spreads of what has happened here, and we cannot afford to be found."

She nodded, then gestured to a lane out of town. "Take that road. We can reach the hills that way."

He led the way. With some insistence, Kit managed to make her horse run faster through the snow, so frightened of what she had done that her hands shook.

They climbed up the nearest hill, far out of the village. When they were near the summit, the horses slowed down, struggling with the incline and the snow. Kit stared between the loch, Urquhart Castle, and the village.

"What have I done?"

As they escaped across the hills, they soon found themselves caught in a snowstorm.

"We need to find cover!" Iomhar called to Kit.

The snow was falling heavier and faster, and Kit kept having to wipe flakes from her eyelashes. She couldn't see very far. They had made it to the hills some time ago, but the clouds were so thick and the snow fell so quickly that she couldn't see beyond Iomhar's horse in front of her.

"It's growing worse," Kit agreed. "We have to stop."

"There. Look!" Iomhar thrust a hand into the air. As Kit forced her steed on, she soon saw what Iomhar was pointing to.

It was some sort of croft with a stone building, half covered in snow. There was no candlelight shining out of the windows, suggesting that whatever shepherd usually rested there had been wise enough not to stay out in the hills.

They made their way toward it. When they reached the door and Kit stepped down, her horse as good as kicked her off, glad for the break. Kit pulled the steed around the back of the croft, urging the animal to take cover under a small wooden roof set on posts, before hastening to the stone building.

Iomhar still had the plaid blanket wrapped around his shoulders, the one thing he wore to ward off the cold wind. It seemed to be doing little good, for when he braced his shoulder against the door of the croft, breaking it open, Kit could see he was shivering and the snow had landed in his unruly beard and hair.

The door broke open under his weight and Iomhar stepped inside, with Kit following closely then shutting the door behind her.

It was a small building, but large enough for a shepherd to make his bed on one side of the room and cook over the fire on the other. A small fireplace was set beneath a chimney and beside it there were logs. Iomhar wasted no time in dropping in front of the grate, piling the wood high.

Kit followed, intent on helping him, but she capitulated a few steps away from the fireplace. Leaning against a wall, she sank down to the ground and stared at her hands. They trembled, still bloodstained.

"Ye did what ye had to, Kit." Iomhar's words were sudden in the silence and made her hands shake all the more.

"What I had to?" Kit murmured. "I killed a man, Iomhar. Nothing is right about that. Nothing."

"What would ye rather? Be dead yourself?" Iomhar asked and began to light the fire with a tinder box. A flame danced to life and licked the nearby logs of wood, stretching slowly across the fireplace. Iomhar turned to look at Kit, his eyes sincere. "I told ye before. When it is between ye and them, what choice do ye have? It is not murder, Kit. It's survival."

Kit winced all the same. Closing her eyes, she thought back to the moment the man had died as she had climbed onto her horse and ridden away.

"I'd rather ye were alive, than him. If that is the choice, then I'm more than happy with the outcome." Iomhar's voice was closer than she had expected it to be. Kit opened her eyes to find him reaching down to her, offering his hand. "Ye need me to carry ye to the fire?"

"I'm fine where I am."

"Nay, ye are not."

"Iomhar!" Her protest did little. Taking her hand, he pulled her to her feet and tugged her toward the fire before he let her drop down again.

"Ye can nurse your regrets here. At least ye'll be warm then."

Kit had no words as she leaned on one side of the stone hearth, feeling a lump in her throat. She kept trying to push away the memory of the man, but it was no good. His face returned, as did the feeling of the dagger in her hand.

Iomhar was on his feet soon enough. Moving to the side of the room, he found bowls of water under wooden lids. His movements became frantic, as if he hadn't seen clean water in a long time. He splashed himself, washing his face and hands before placing the second bowl in front of Kit.

"Wash off the blood. It will help. Trust me."

Kit chose not to ask why he knew it would help and did as he said, slowly washing the blood off her hands. When the water turned pink and her skin was clear, he took the bowl away and sat in front of the fire.

The flames were so strong now that yellow light danced across the room. Kit turned to Iomhar, trying to think of the good of the moment. Two days ago, she would have exchanged nearly anything to know he was alive.

"You're here," she whispered, startled that the words had escaped her lips.

Iomhar looked up, a softness appearing in his eyes. "Glad to see me, Kit?"

"Well, you look a little scruffy," she attempted to jest, even as her hands continued to shake.

Iomhar laughed. "Aye, a dungeon will do that to ye."

"Your clothes," Kit murmured, staring at the torn shirt. "You said they flogged you."

"Aye," Iomhar answered swiftly. "When Lord Ruskin accused me of being a spy, but did not say much more, they thought I was a spy for another of the clans. They wanted information out of me, information I could not give, and would not give. Rest assured, Kit. Any secrets of Walsingham's that I know have stayed hidden."

"That was not what worried me." She kept her voice quiet, her eyes dancing along the marks upon his skin. She could see now as he warmed his hands near the fire that his arms were grazed too.

"Aye, worried for me?"

"Well…"

"Ye must have been to come all this way to find me." Iomhar smiled. "Ye missed me, Kit?"

She paused, breathing deeply before she answered him. "Perhaps a little," she confessed, watching as Iomhar's smile grew.

"Aye, I missed ye too."

"You did?" Kit tried to clamp down on her excitement at his words.

"Aye. I really did think I had imagined ye whistling today. I thought my mind was playing tricks on me." He placed another log on the fire. "I did not think ye would come all this way to look for me, nor be so foolish as to break into Urquhart Castle."

"Oi! I think I did rather well. I got you out, didn't I?"

"Aye, ye did." Iomhar smiled and lifted his gaze from the fire. "How did ye know where to find me, Kit?"

"There is much to tell you." Kit rested back on the stone hearth. Iomhar's eyelids were closing, and he yawned. "You are tired."

"I am. I never had a good night's sleep in there. It was so cold my bones felt like icicles, and flies buzzed in my ears all night." Iomhar huffed and gestured to the croft around them. "This is luxury in comparison."

"Then sleep." Kit rose to her feet and pointed to the straw bed across the room.

"What?"

"Sleep, Iomhar. You need it. I'll keep watch." She knew he needed to rest, but she had another motive too. She couldn't stop thinking of the man she had killed, and she needed to be alone with those thoughts for a little longer yet. "Come." She offered her hand. Iomhar took it and let her pull him to his feet, then walked to the bed across the room. When he lay down, he didn't release her hand straight away.

Kit smiled at him. "No guards are coming through this door, you have my word on that." She took back her hand and moved to the door.

"After today, I believe ye, Kit," Iomhar whispered as he closed his eyes.

Kit walked to the fire, glancing between the door and the bloodstained dagger in her belt. She began to fear what she was capable of if another guard did find them.

CHAPTER 19

"Iomhar, you have to wake up." Kit nudged Iomhar's shoulder. It was still dark, but it was no longer snowing. Iomhar began to stir on the bed, then sat bolt upright, so suddenly that Kit jerked backward. "By this light! What is wrong?"

Iomhar turned to look at her, then blinked hard. "I thought I was…" He sighed deeply, catching his breath. "I thought I was still there." He pinched the bridge of his nose. "I thought it was all a dream."

"Do you want me to pinch you?" Kit asked, nudging his shoulder.

"Knowing ye, a pinch would hurt." They both smiled and Kit stepped back, giving him room to swing his legs off the bed and look out across the croft. "How long was I…?"

"Asleep? A couple of hours I think, maybe three. The snow has stopped. It's not melting, but it might be clear enough to get you home."

"Nay, Kit. I meant, how long was I at Urquhart Castle?"

Kit's brow creased. "You have no idea?"

"A few months, would be my guess. Nay … your face tells me it's longer than that." He looked fearful and pushed a hand through his hair. "How long, Kit?"

"Just over a year." With these words she reached for the door and opened it wide, stepping out into the snow. Before she could move very far, Iomhar gently took her arm.

"A year?" he murmured in disbelief. "But … my mother. Did she think I was dead?"

"She may not have been the only one who feared it." Kit eyed him carefully, watching as he too stepped out into the snow.

"Ye feared it too?"

"No. I knew you couldn't be dead."

"How?" Iomhar smiled, clearly thinking her conviction absurd.

"I don't think you die easily." Kit walked around the croft, heading toward their horses. "And I didn't want to believe it was possible," she mumbled, rather hoping he wouldn't hear.

"To get this horse," Iomhar said, patting the black steed's neck, "ye must have been to my family home."

"That I have," Kit nodded. "Speaking of which, you need to answer something for me on the journey to your house."

"What's that?" Iomhar asked.

"Why do your family know so much about me? Niall said you talked about me. How much did you talk?"

"Only a little."

A few hours later, they stepped out from the trees to stand in front of Iomhar's family home. Kit's eyes danced across his face. Despite the mass of beard and unruly hair, she could see that he swallowed, as if holding back tears.

"How does it feel, to see it again?" she asked.

"If it wasn't so bloody cold, I'd think it was heaven." Iomhar stepped down from his horse and examined the building before him. "Aye, there was a time when I thought I would not see it again. Ever." He glanced at Kit as she too stepped down from her horse. "I thought I would die in there, Kit."

"What else did they do to you, Iomhar?" she whispered.

He grimaced and looked away. "Nay, I do not want to talk about that now." He took a step toward the house but didn't get far.

Kit watched as the door was flung open, so vigorously that the heavy oak clattered against the wall. Abigail was there, stumbling forward, tears in her eyes. She hurried down the front porch steps as quickly as she could, moving toward her brother in a flurry of plaid skirts.

"Iomhar?" she whispered.

"Evening, Abigail." At the sound of Iomhar's soft voice, she ran forward and embraced him. Iomhar lifted his younger sister easily off the ground.

Kit smiled as she patted her horse's nose. There was a commotion inside the house.

"It's him. Ma, he's here!" Rhona's voice was shouting.

"Ah, Rhona. Do ye need to shout in my ear?"

"Be quiet, Niall, and look outside. Ye will not believe it. I do not believe it!"

More cries followed, then the siblings appeared. Rhona was first, and practically tore Abigail out of Iomhar's arms to be the next one there.

"Ergh, Iomhar, ye stink," she complained tearfully as he put her back down on her feet.

"Aye, that's what happens after spending so long in a dungeon."

"Och, a dungeon." The earl was the next one to appear and hurry toward his brother. "Ye!" He thrust a finger in Iomhar's direction. "Ye have driven us all mad for this last year."

"I know, I had a feeling — ah!" Iomhar couldn't finish what he was saying. He was first struck in the arm by his brother, then pulled into an embrace. "Good to see ye too, Duncan."

The earl was in no hurry to let go of his brother, even as he complained of the stench. "Ye need a wash."

"I know," Iomhar chuckled.

Niall was the next to appear. Kit peered around the horse's nose, watching as the last brother came to a stumbling halt on the steps outside of the front door. For a second, he said nothing. He merely stared, his lips parted in amazement, then he leapt down the stairs. "Ye! Ye have been gone too long."

"I've already hit him for that, brother," the earl said with a smile as he stepped back from Iomhar, allowing Niall to take his place.

Iomhar and Niall clasped hands first, nodding at each other before they embraced.

"I knew ye were alive," Niall sighed. "Nay way ye would die yet. Not so easily."

"Easily? Pah! I'll tell ye what it was like some time."

"Please, do!" Abigail pleaded, at which point the earl shook his head, apparently unsure whether he wanted to hear the details.

Kit felt a stinging in her eyes as she watched the family together. She was rather reminded of the theatre, standing at a show she had no part in, unable to tear her eyes away.

"We were going to write to get ye out when we heard where ye were," the earl hurried to explain. "I do not understand. How are ye here?"

Then Iomhar nodded in Kit's direction. As their gazes turned on her, she flinched and busied herself with the horses.

"Ye have Kit to thank for that," Iomhar said. Kit looked up to meet his gaze and smiled gently. She could see there was something he wished to say, though he seemed to be hesitating. Before he could continue, though, the last person they were waiting for appeared in the doorway.

Moira hurried down the steps and into the snow, with a hand covering her mouth. She didn't bother holding back her tears, and her breaths were great, heaving gasps. "I-Iomhar?" she stuttered. Iomhar stepped away from his siblings and toward his mother. She lifted a hand and pushed back the long wisps of hair from his eyes. "Ye have come back to us. Thank the Lord for it."

Moira clung to Iomhar as if he were the very thing keeping her alive, her fingers turning as white as the snow around them. She continued to cry in his arms as he held onto her. Kit was mesmerised, and she could not look away until Abigail complained of the cold and pointed out it was high time that they all went inside to continue their reunion.

Kit plunged her hands into the basin of water, trying to remove any last specks of dried blood. She scrubbed vigorously, turning her skin bright pink. She didn't let up, not until she was certain every trace of blood was gone.

Looking down at the doublet she was wearing, she saw some stains upon it, splattered there from when she had delivered the fatal blow. She remembered the stuttered sounds passing the guard's lips, then the way his body had become still.

A wave of nausea returned, and she hurried to take off the doublet, tossing it across the room with such strength that it struck the wall and dropped to the floor. Kit hurried to change, her hands still damp and her body shivering in the cold that bled through the window. She put on clean linens and fresh hose, then slung a waistcoat-style doublet over her body, leaving it loose as she looked down, checking all signs of blood were gone.

She tried to remind herself of what Iomhar had said — that the death had been necessary in order for her to live — but it didn't help much. Her hands still shook with the knowledge that she had killed someone yesterday, and they could not be clean enough. She plunged them into the water basin repeatedly, trying to wash off the blood that was no longer there, when she heard a gentle tap at the door.

"Who is it?" Kit called.

The door opened a little and Moira pushed her head through the gap. "Katherine?" she whispered. "Oh, Katherine, look at ye."

The words made Kit freeze. She looked up into the mirror that was attached to the wall and mottled with age. Kit saw how wild she looked, her hands frantic and her hair ragged from the number of times she had pulled on the tendrils, unable to keep still.

Moira stepped into the room and closed the door behind her, before hurrying to Kit's side. Kit didn't take her hands out of the bowl, not until Moira forced her to do so.

"Where is Iomhar?" Kit asked distractedly.

"Bathing. Aye, he needs it," Moira explained with a small smile. She took a nearby towel, drying Kit's hands for her. Kit was reminded of being a child, when Doris had dried her hands in such a way. She could remember Walsingham doing it once too. "What a feast we are making downstairs. We are to celebrate. Aye, Katherine, we must celebrate. My son is home!" Moira gushed and blinked, stopping more tears of happiness from falling.

Kit felt a tear on her own cheeks, though she was uncertain what it was for. Was it the relief that Iomhar was alive? Or was it from the knowledge that a life had been taken?

Moira's smile faltered as she lifted the towel to Kit's cheek. "Something happened yesterday, did it not? When ye helped my son."

"We should not talk of it." Kit shook her head. "It does no good."

"Then let me say something else instead." Moira took Kit's hands in her own. "Ye saved him. I will never be able to thank ye enough for what ye have done for me and my family today."

"No. You do not need to thank me so." Kit tried to take her hands back, but Moira held onto them a little longer.

"Nay, Katherine. I do. Thank ye. With everything I have, thank ye." Moira smiled, holding Kit's gaze and refusing to release it. "Ye are shaking."

"I know." Kit sighed deeply, trying to stop.

"Whatever happened yesterday, I hope it will not scar ye. Sometimes, we do things we do not think we are capable of for those we care about." Moira's words made Kit's breath catch in her throat, before she nodded slowly. "Now, ye cannot hide in this room all night, washing your hands. Ye must come downstairs, so we can celebrate Iomhar's return."

Kit had spent too long this last year wondering when Iomhar would return and fill the empty space beside her. That thought prompted her to nod and Moira reached forward, tying up Kit's waistcoated doublet for her.

"Here, let me help ye," Moira said, her smile growing. "There, quite dapper indeed."

"Thank you." It had been a long time since anyone had made such a simple effort to care for her.

"Now, will ye come?" Moira asked and offered her hand to Kit. Kit found herself accepting it and nodding.

CHAPTER 20

"Here, Kit, this one's for ye." Niall pushed a particularly tall tankard toward Kit, so full of mead that she had to hold onto it with two hands.

"Me? What's this for?"

"What do ye think?" Niall asked with a laugh, stepping back. "I knew I was right to come to see ye in London. Ye brought Iomhar back." He winked. "Ye are the reason he is here. If that doesn't deserve the biggest drink we have, I do not know what does." He stepped away, hurrying to pour more.

Kit smiled, turning her gaze on the room. Conversation was fast tonight, with each person looking toward the door in anticipation of Iomhar's return. He'd been in his chamber for a while, so long that Kit suspected he may have fallen asleep again.

Moira sat beside Kit on a settle bench, with Abigail perched on a footstool nearby. Rhona could not sit, but continued to walk around the room, sometimes lighting more candles to fend off the darkness, and sometimes moving toward the door.

"Shouting to him will not make him any faster, ye know," the earl said with a laugh as he took a settle bench opposite where Kit sat.

"I'm still tempted," Rhona replied and turned her back on the doorway. "He has been gone for over a year! Can ye blame me for my impatience?"

"Is that how long it has been?" Iomhar's deep voice made them all jerk their heads toward the now open door.

Kit sat forward, surprised by the transformation. His long hair had gone, as had the overgrown beard. He looked more like his old self, aside from the shadows under his eyes, the scars on his forearms revealed by the rolled-up cuffs of his dark green doublet, and the fact that he walked with a limp.

Niall moved to Iomhar's side with another tall cup of mead. "Are ye in need of this all of a sudden?"

"I think I'll need two," Iomhar stammered, staring down into the cup. He took the first swallow, then marvelled at it.

"Did they not give ye something to drink there?" Abigail asked.

"Dirty water, nothing more." Iomhar promptly swallowed nearly half of what was in the cup, making his brothers smile sadly.

"I'll get ye another." Niall turned away to collect the second cup as Iomhar was steered further into the room by Rhona.

"It does not matter how long ye have been away, Iomhar," she said, her tone buoyant. "Ye are home now."

"Aye. Ye are right." He nodded, though he did not look convinced as he was urged down into the settle bench beside the earl, wincing at the pain in his leg.

"For the wee man's sake, Iomhar," the earl muttered. "What did they do to ye?"

Iomhar looked around those in the room before he answered. "It is not for everyone's ears to hear."

"Ye think us feeble-minded, Iomhar," Moira said with a laugh. "Ye'd be surprised to hear what we've feared has happened to ye. I daresay we can stand to hear anything. Even Rhona here crept off in the middle of the night with Niall and Katherine to see an old spy friend of yours!" Moira gestured to Rhona manically, prompting her to grimace.

"It was not that bad, Ma."

"Not that bad? Pah!" Moira huffed then looked to Niall. "That's not what your brother said."

"Niall, have ye been trying to get me in trouble?" Rhona asked, putting her hands on her hips.

"I was being honest. Besides, Kit was the one who suggested ye go into that tavern and charm dear Oswyn."

"What —" Iomhar veered forward so fast on his settle bench that he nearly fell off it. The only thing that kept him there was the earl's hand on one shoulder, and Niall moving to grasp his other side. "Kit?"

"She was safe," Kit said hurriedly, sipping her mead. When he raised his eyebrows at her, in that questioning way he used to have, Kit allowed herself her first full smile. It seemed to crack something in him too, for he chuckled and sat back on the bench again.

"Thank the wee man I am home," Iomhar said softly. "I have dreamt of nights like this. Where conversation is this easy."

"Ye are home! And it is nay dream." Moira moved to her feet and crossed to her son, tapping him on the cheek. "And what a feast I have asked to be prepared for ye."

"Is there more smoked fish?" Kit asked, watching as Moira nodded eagerly. Kit grimaced, prompting Iomhar to smile.

"Now we are all here, and ye nay longer smell, Iomhar," Rhona said as Iomhar glared her way, "shall we move to that feast?"

"Ye try living in a dungeon and not smelling, Rhona." Iomhar shook his head. "Ye are surrounded by flies that crawl on your skin like ye are already dead."

"Iomhar!" Moira gasped.

"What?" Iomhar shrugged. "I thought ye said I could talk of what had happened?"

Niall laughed and clapped him on the shoulder. "It's good to have ye home. Come, let us get that food." Niall and the earl both helped Iomhar to his feet, and Kit watched as he winced, putting pressure on his injured ankle.

She followed the rest of the family as they began walking to the dining room, feeling as if she was somewhat out of place, until Iomhar reached the door. He disentangled his arm from Niall's, letting his brother move ahead, before he turned and looked back to her.

"Ye trailing to avoid the fish?" he whispered, leaning down.

"Ah, you saw through me," she replied. They smiled together, as the others took their seats at the table.

"If I may open our dinner, I would like to make a toast." The earl raised his cup at the head of the table.

"A toast?" Moira said. "To Iomhar?"

"Aye." The earl's answer made Iomhar snap his gaze away from Kit, looking to his brother. "If he'll come and join us at the table." The earl gestured to the chair beside him. Iomhar shot Kit one look before he moved to take it, and Moira beckoned Kit to sit beside her. "To your return, brother." The earl's voice deepened with the words — it was sudden, and the air in the room seemed to change with it. They all held their cups out in front of them. "And to the person that made it happen." The earl's gaze shifted to Kit. "Ye may have crept out of this house for the second time whilst staying here —"

"Shall I remind ye she is an intelligencer and can go where she likes?" Niall asked from the earl's other side.

"She always does," Iomhar added.

"Aye, thank God for it," Moira murmured. "To Katherine, for bringing Iomhar home."

The cups were raised, and they all drank in unison, except Kit, who was looking over the tankards toward Iomhar. She sighed with relief before she took a sip from her cup, thankful that she had taken the chance she'd had.

"Oh, enough sadness," Rhona said as she took her seat. "We have been sad this last year, and tonight, that ends."

"I quite agree," Moira declared, encouraging the rest of them to sit too.

"We should talk of good things instead, such as what Iomhar will do now he is home," Abigail said.

"Aye, he will rest that ankle first." Niall gestured to Iomhar as he passed over a plate of smoked fish.

"There are a few things I want to know before we discuss such things." Iomhar filled up his plate with the fish, then leaned forward, looking around Rhona so that he could catch Kit's eye. "How exactly did ye break into the castle, Kit?"

"I do not think you want to know that." She busied herself with drinking, aware of Iomhar's stare.

"Kit…" he warned.

She thought it best to explain fast. "Well, the loch was frozen over. It made for an easy entrance from the water."

Surprised sounds and laughs emanated from around the table. Niall laughed the deepest, guffawing, as Iomhar nearly dropped the plate of smoked fish.

"Ye walked across a frozen loch?"

"It worked, didn't it? Are you not glad I did?"

"Aye, very glad indeed."

"Iomhar, I think you need to go to bed." Kit nudged him. She was sitting on the footstool as he lay back on the bench, his eyes closing every now and then. "You need to sleep."

"Not yet." His eyes opened and peered at her in the candlelight. "If I sleep, I might wake up and find myself back in that dungeon."

"You won't." Kit stepped on his good foot.

"Ow!" He laughed and sat forward. "Aye, aye, I take your message. It is nay dream."

"No dream," she confirmed. Aware of whispers at the other end of the room, Kit looked away from him.

They had all eaten and drank steadily, to the point where Kit had felt uncertain on her feet and somewhat lightheaded. Everyone had insisted on feeding up Iomhar, until he had started pushing plates away, unable to eat anymore. Abigail, Rhona and the earl had retired for the night, but Niall and Moira were still whispering together.

"I don't want to sleep yet." Iomhar's words drew Kit's attention back to him. "I've dreamt too much of being out of that dungeon, Kit."

"You are free of that place now." She leaned forward, resting her elbows on her knees.

"Aye, thanks to ye."

"Thanks to Niall, really," Kit said, watching as Iomhar's brow creased. "He came to see me in London. Well, he broke into your house."

"He broke in?"

"He didn't know I was there." Kit shook her head. "When he explained the strange way in which you had left this house, and had not been in touch with them either, I knew I couldn't continue to sit staring at that front door."

"Ye stared at the door?" Iomhar asked, tilting his head.

"I may have been wondering when you were going to walk back through it." His growing smile made her fidget.

"Aye, as I said, I missed ye too." They chuckled together, before Kit looked toward Niall and Moira. They were both looking her way, and when she caught them, they turned back to talk to one another. "There is a question I have."

"What's that?" Kit asked, shifting her focus to Iomhar.

"Why did Walsingham let ye follow me?" At Iomhar's question, Kit sat back, staring down at her feet. When the silence stretched between them, Iomhar leaned forward, resting his elbows on his knees. "Kit ... should I understand from your silence that he does not know ye are here?"

She met his gaze, then slowly shook her head.

"I'll be damned," Iomhar muttered. "Ye disobeyed his orders, Kit? Ye do not often do that. In fact, when I first knew ye, the thought of going against him angered ye."

"I had no choice." Kit shrugged, as if it was no great matter. "He would not tell me where he had sent you. I had to do something. I found a letter from Oswyn in his papers, decoded it, then found myself here, at your family's home."

"Where does Walsingham think ye are?"

"That I will explain another time." Kit thought back to the letter that was still hidden in the coffer in her chamber. Soon she would have to deliver it, especially now she had found Iomhar, but she wasn't in a hurry to go anywhere.

"So, ye disobeyed Walsingham's orders and came all the way to the Highlands to look for me?" Iomhar asked.

"Perhaps. I'm afraid of making you conceited by admitting that is the case," Kit said wryly, looking away from him.

"Ye have risked a lot for my sake, aye. Do ye know what I was thinking, down in that dungeon?"

"That you were afraid you would die?"

"Aye, very much." Iomhar nodded. "I also made a promise to myself."

"What promise?" Kit's interest was caught. Half of his face was cast in shadows, while the other half was lit by the flickering candle flames.

"The life I live isn't the one I want forever." His words made her sit very still, her stomach tensed into a knot. "I wish to make a change, Kit."

"A change? What change?" She was aware that her voice had risen in pitch. Iomhar reached toward her, urging her to be calm. She shifted in her seat, breathing deeply. "What change?" she asked, her voice quieter this time.

"Ye know why I work for Walsingham, aye?"

"Aye." She mimicked his accent, making his eyes lighten briefly. "You wish to stop Mary Stuart from taking the throne, and to find Lord Ruskin. For your father." The mention of Lord Ruskin's name reminded Kit of her tangle with Graham Fraser in the streets of York. She knew she would have to tell Iomhar about it at some point, but now did not feel like the right moment.

"Aye." Iomhar agreed with a slow nod. "Justice will be done for my father's death. I will make certain of that. When Lord Ruskin sees a court for his crimes, I will change my life."

"How?" Kit asked, her voice barely audible.

"I will come back to Scotland," Iomhar said quietly. "Many times I thought I would die this last year and not see my family again…" He trailed off and shook his head, breathing in through gritted teeth as though the mere thought brought him physical pain. "That is not the life I want. I wish to see my family more. So, that is what I will do."

"You will leave London? Completely?" Kit stood, hardly able to understand the sudden panic that took her over.

"Aye, that is my hope."

"But it's home."

"Nay, it's your home, Kit. It's not mine."

"I…" Kit still struggled for words. She turned on the spot, frantic, then looked across the room, suddenly aware that

Moira and Niall were no longer there. They had left, leaving the door open behind them. "Your life is in London."

"Nay. It's not," Iomhar continued. "What I do is in London. My search for Lord Ruskin has been mostly in London, and when that is done, I can go where I like. Who knows how long it will take? Yet I do know I will not stay in London forever. It's not the life I want."

Kit turned, her hands on her hips. She marched away, increasing the distance between them. She was angry at him for this decision, though she couldn't blame him for it. His brush with death had made him see what was important, and that was his family. Kit was reminded of the moment she had stood on the drive when Iomhar had been greeted by his family. They loved one another dearly, as a family should, and Kit was separate from that.

"If that's the life you want, I understand." Kit found her voice, though she still couldn't look at him. She felt rather sick.

"It doesn't make ye happy, though, does it?"

She didn't answer him. She kept looking away, with her hands on her hips, aware that the settle bench creaked beneath him as he stood and crossed the room toward her.

"Aye, maybe this is the moment to tell ye my second thought."

"A second thought?" Kit repeated in confusion as he stepped in front of her.

"When I come back to Scotland, Kit, ye could come with me."

"What did you say?" Kit jerked her head up.

"Ye would think I'd suggested something awful."

"No, no," she said hurriedly, shaking her head. "Did you just say you want me to come back to Scotland? With you?"

"Aye. Do ye wish me to say it again?"

"But…" Kit was unsure what to think or feel. For so long she had wanted Iomhar back. Now he was here, but suggesting a future she had never considered.

"Do ye wish to always be in London, Kit?"

"It's my home. I've never thought of being anywhere else. And there's Walsingham." At her words, Iomhar grimaced. "What was that look for?"

"That look was because I am tired of that man ruling your life, Kit."

"He doesn't rule my life."

"Doesn't he? He gives an order and ye jump to it."

"That is my job!"

"Nay, it is more than that, and ye and I both know it."

"He raised me," Kit said pointedly. "Of course I do what he asks. Apart from…" Kit trailed off, realising how much she had disobeyed Walsingham's orders recently. "Apart from now."

Iomhar's lips flickered into a smile. "Aye, apart from now," he concurred and reached out toward her.

Kit froze as Iomhar took her hand off her hip and lifted it upward. She was reminded of the moment he had said goodbye to her, back in Seething Lane a year ago, and she held her breath as he raised her hand to his lips and kissed the back.

"You did this once before," Kit whispered. "I hope you are not saying goodbye this time."

"Nay, I'm not," he promised, lowering her hand, though he didn't let it go. "I'm making what I feel known." He breathed deeply, as if summoning the courage to say something, and looked down at their connected hands. "When I come to Scotland, Kit, I'd like ye to come with me. The offer is there, and it will always be, if ye want to accept it."

"Why?" Kit found the question falling from her lips. "Why do you want me to come too?"

Iomhar glanced at the open door, apparently wary of his family hovering nearby, then he lifted her hand to his lips again and turned it over. This time, he kissed the inside of her wrist. It was a more intimate touch and left her staring, open-mouthed.

"Maybe I liked it when ye and I lived in and out of each other's pockets," he said slowly. "Maybe I do not want that to end."

Kit smiled. She liked that idea too, she had to admit it, but as she looked down at their hands, other thoughts prevailed.

She had a job to do. She had a letter to deliver, to Mary Stuart, and a queen to return to with an answer. When she came back, Walsingham would have more for her to do, as he always did. Could she really imagine leaving that life? Stepping away from the existence that Walsingham had carved for her?

"Iomhar, I…"

"Ah, I hear it in your tone." Iomhar's grasp loosened. "Do not say it. I do not think I want to hear the words."

"I'm not saying no."

"Then what are ye saying?" Iomhar asked, holding her gaze.

"I don't know." She shook her head, none the wiser about what her answer would be. Abruptly uncomfortable under his stare, she lifted her free hand and pulled at her collar, then at some of the loose tendrils of her hair.

"Wait a minute — what is that?" Iomhar stepped forward. Kit's action had drawn his attention to the chain at her throat, mostly hidden beneath the doublet and the shirt.

Kit took her hand away from his and used it to lift the pendant from its hiding place, so he could see it. "It's yours," she explained. "Your mother gave it to me. She seemed to think it was good at keeping the wearer safe. For some reason, she thought I took a lot of risks and thought I needed it more than others."

"I see my ma knows ye already," Iomhar said and held the pendant in his hands. Kit lifted her arms to undo the chain, but he shook his head, stopping her. "Ye keep it."

"Maybe you should have it again, to stop you from disappearing into castle dungeons for years at a time." Her jest only made him smile briefly.

"As my ma said, ye take more risks than others. Ye keep it." He turned the pendant over in his hands as he spoke. "It was my father's. He wore it always, except for the day when he was guarding Mary Stuart, and Lord Ruskin came. The chain had broken, so he left it at home. Well, ye know what happened to him that day."

Kit nodded, remembering the story of how Iomhar's father had died.

"I intend to hold true to my promise, Kit, to my whole family. I want justice for my father, and I will do what I can to get it, even if that means hunting for Lord Ruskin forever more. Have ye heard anything of him? Since I've been…" He didn't finish the sentence but nodded slightly, uncomfortable with talking about the dungeon.

"There is something you should know." Kit glanced up at the ceiling, thinking of the letter that was hidden in her chamber. "It is part of the reason I was able to come to Scotland. It concerns the person who Lord Ruskin would do anything for. It's about Mary Stuart."

CHAPTER 21

The snow had stopped falling, though the path was still dappled white. It was a new morning. After telling Iomhar about the task the queen had given her, Kit had gone to bed and slept with difficulty, and was now gazing out of the sitting room window.

"Ye keep turning that letter over in your hands."

Kit looked over her shoulder to see that Iomhar had entered the room. He was walking a little more normally today, though still at an odd angle. He pointed to the letter she had clutched between her fingers. "Do ye have nay idea what's in it?"

"None," Kit confirmed, as Iomhar stopped beside her.

"Ye could open it?" Iomhar offered.

Kit shook her head firmly. "I would not do that. The queen asked me to complete a task, and I will do it, without invading her privacy."

"I would open it." Another voice joined them. It belonged to Niall, who appeared at the door and bounded into the room.

"Iomhar!" Kit gritted her teeth as she turned to face him. "You told him what this is?"

"Perhaps," Iomhar answered with a somewhat helpless smile. "I didn't see the harm in it."

"Let's see." Niall snatched the letter from Kit's hands. "We could open it, see what is really happening between the queens?"

"Niall! Give it back or I'll take it from you," Kit threatened.

"Believe me, she will, and she won't hold back," Iomhar warned his brother.

Kit rested a hand on her weapons belt. Niall thrust the letter toward her at once, apparently having thought better of his actions.

"Aye, aye, here ye go." He stepped back eagerly. "Do ye have to leave so soon, Kit? Ye should have seen Ma's face when I told her ye intended to leave today."

"Ye could stay longer," Iomhar added.

Kit rather liked the idea of staying and getting to know the family better. She didn't want to leave Iomhar so soon after finding him again, but she had no choice. "I have taken long enough about this as it is." Kit reached down to her weapons belt and unfastened it, opening the secret flap at the end. "I need to deliver the letter, and soon. Otherwise Walsingham really will suspect I have been defying his orders." She glanced pointedly at Iomhar, who just smiled.

"I'm glad ye did," he said softly.

"As are we all!" Niall added, much louder. "Had ye not, ah, it does not bear thinking about." He glanced through the window, looking out at the snow as Kit retrieved the small silver case and hid the letter inside it. There were still some signs of water damage to the letter, but nothing extensive. Mary Stuart would be able to read the contents.

"Who's that?" Iomhar asked, pointing through the window.

Kit looked up. Someone was riding madly toward the house, struggling through the last bits of the snow. Coming to a hasty halt, the horse neighed wildly, stomping his front hooves down into the earth beneath him. The rider jumped down off the saddle.

"I know him," Niall said, stepping back from the window. "He's one of the soldiers that reports to me." He took off in the direction of the door, followed by Kit and Iomhar. They reached the door at the same time as the soldier.

"Captain!" the young man called to Niall as the door was thrust open. The soldier shook some snow from the shoulders of his cloak and took off his low-lying cap as he bowed to Niall. The clan brooch was clearly visible in the hat, standing proudly.

"Good Lord, Bates, what has ye riding here so fast and so red in the face?" Niall asked with a laugh. "Ye'd think the flames of hell were at your heels."

"I have a message for ye, Captain." The soldier stepped forward. "It concerns the special task ye gave to me."

All humour drained from Niall's face. He looked at Iomhar, who clearly knew what this task was too.

"What task?" Kit asked.

Neither of them answered, though Niall motioned to the soldier. "Ye may speak freely, Bates. What have ye found?"

"It is not so much what I have found as what I have heard." Bates looked frantic, keen to deliver his message as quickly as possible. "Lord Ruskin was seen two days ago, leaving Edinburgh."

"Seen? By whom?" Iomhar asked, stepping forward. He looked strangely calm compared to Niall, who was moving back and forth.

"Another soldier. Lord Ruskin has taken to hiding in plain sight, trying to disguise his identity. Yet he was seen and what is more, we know where he is going."

"Where?" Niall asked impatiently.

"He is going to England, Captain," the soldier explained in a rush. "He is going to see his queen."

Kit rested a hand on the belt that was now back around her hips.

"Mary Stuart," Iomhar said, thinking aloud. "He is going to see her. Where? Where is she?"

"Chartley Castle," Kit answered when the soldier shrugged, unable to answer the question. "She is under house arrest in the castle."

"Then he goes to her, to do what? To see her? To free her?" Niall addressed all his questions to the soldier, but Bates backed up, still unable to answer.

"That is all I know, Captain."

"Very well. Thank ye." Niall hurried to be formal. He uttered some quick pleasantries to the soldier then beckoned him into the house. "Ye must be thirsty after your journey. Come through this door on your left, go down the stairs, and ye will find our kitchen. Take something to drink and eat."

As Kit turned, following Niall and the soldier with her eyes, she soon saw they were not the only ones to hear the soldier's message. On the staircase was Moira, and behind her were the sisters, with the earl standing at the rear. They were all staring forward, their faces expressionless.

Once the soldier had been hurried toward the kitchen, Iomhar stepped forward, looking at his family.

"It means we know where he is," he said slowly.

"Aye, and what are we going to do about it?" the earl asked.

"It's simple." Niall moved away from the door, walking with purpose. "Iomhar, ye and I should go to Chartley with Kit, to see if we can find Lord Ruskin."

"Aye, and he looks in a fit state to go, doesn't he?" Rhona pointed out, gesturing in Iomhar's direction.

"I'm not dead yet."

"Thanks to Kit." Rhona's words made Iomhar and Kit look toward one another.

"Iomhar," Kit began slowly, "you are still recovering. You're weak and you can barely walk straight. If it comes to fighting Lord Ruskin, do you really think you could survive such a battle?" She knew Iomhar was no fool, but he looked determined to go, no matter the consequences.

"I need to go."

"Are you not the one always telling me to think through a plan before I jump into it?"

"Well, maybe I've caught some of your habits," he answered wryly.

"Katherine is right." Moira's firm voice brooked no refusal. "Iomhar, we lost ye once, and I will not risk losing ye again to chase after a man who stole another from this family." Her words hung heavy in the air, making all the siblings shift.

"This is our chance," Iomhar hissed. "We cannot let that go by."

"I agree," Niall said with determination, moving to his brother's side.

"Then ye are not going alone. I am not ready to say goodbye to ye again yet." Moira stood taller. "This is not just your fight; it is our family's. Katherine, it seems ye have some new companions on your trip. We will all join ye on your journey to Chartley Castle."

"Is this a wise plan?" Kit asked, angling her mare close to Iomhar's side. They trailed behind the carriage, with the other brothers leading the way ahead on their own horses.

"My whole family on this trip, ye mean? Aye, marvellous idea," Iomhar said with sarcasm. "I know what my mother was trying to say. I am hardly at my strongest and in nay fit state to tackle a man alone. That does not mean this is a fight we should all be a part of."

"I think she didn't want to say goodbye to you yet." Kit's eyes lingered on the back of the carriage. They had been riding for two days, heading across the border into England and toward Staffordshire. No one had complained about the journey, despite its length. Most of the family seemed lost in thought, barely speaking to one another at times.

"What is the plan here?" Kit asked, looking ahead of the carriage. The hills were much smaller than in Scotland, but they still curved the landscape in knots and mounds. Clumps of forest seemed to absorb the sunlight, and a track ahead of them was well worn by cartwheels. "If Lord Ruskin is at Chartley Castle, we cannot all break in."

"Nay, that is not what will happen." Iomhar smiled. "I know my mother, and aye, ye are right. She is coming because she does not want to see me lost again. That is all. Aye, heed my words, Kit. We shall find some lodgings, and there my family will stay. Ye and I will go to the castle, that is all."

"I don't think Niall will let you go alone, not now," Kit murmured, her gaze resting on Niall as his horse walked alongside the carriage. He kept looking back their way, evidently checking on Iomhar with wary eyes.

"Ye may be right," Iomhar accepted with a sigh. "The rest… I will not let Lord Ruskin near them."

Kit smiled at his attempt to protect them, even when they were travelling so far to protect him. "You are fortunate." The words fell from her lips without much thought.

"Fortunate? Why?" Iomhar asked, steering his horse forward with the reins wrapped around one of his wrists.

"Your family." Kit nodded at the carriage ahead of her. "They love you very much." She kept thinking back to the moment Iomhar had been reunited with them. In particular, she thought of the embrace Moira had given her son. "There is devotion there."

"Of course, there is. We are family," Iomhar said, his tone nonchalant. When Kit shifted in her saddle, Iomhar seemed to understand her thoughts. "Aye, I see. Ye have not had such a family."

"No." Kit bristled as the wind picked up around them. She wrapped the cloak she was wearing tighter across her shoulders, fighting against the cold. "Walsingham is my guardian. Doris cared for me too, that cannot be denied, but *this*?" She waved ahead at the carriage. "It is not something I know."

She thought of how Moira had come to comfort her when she had been washing the blood from her hands. The care with which she had spoken to her was something Kit could not remember hearing before.

"Your mother is very kind."

"Ye could have a family of your own someday, Kit."

"What?" Kit jerked her head to Iomhar in surprise.

"Is that so mad to think of?" he asked with a shrug.

Kit sat very still as the horse trundled forward.

"Here!" the earl barked from up ahead.

Kit turned her head away from Iomhar, trying to focus on the matter at hand.

The carriage had come to a stop at the edge of a town, Uttoxeter, with either side of the road bordered by timber-beamed buildings. Above them, the sign of a coaching inn swung in the breeze.

"How far are we from the castle?" Niall called to his brother as he climbed down from his horse.

"Just over an hour's ride from here, if that," the earl called, looking down at the map in his hands. "It is a good place to find lodgings."

Kit longed to ask what Iomhar had meant by his words, but he was already climbing down from his horse. He limped once before concealing it, taking the reins and walking through the archway that led to the courtyard of the coaching inn.

Moira and the sisters descended from the carriage as the earl went inside to request rooms for them all. Kit didn't climb down from her horse just yet. With the knowledge that Mary Stuart was only an hour's ride from here, she longed to continue. She looked through the archway and out to the horizon.

With such a bright blue sky, the icy air was biting, and Kit's breath formed clouds in front of her. It would be a cold ride, but one she was happy to face.

"I will go on," Kit called to the family.

"Now?" Moira asked with obvious worry. "Is that a good idea?"

"We need to see the castle," Kit explained. "To know what it is we are dealing with."

"Then I will come with ye." Iomhar made a move to get back on his horse, but his shoulder was clasped by Niall, who refused to let him move.

"Ye are not going," Niall said, shaking his head. "Ye are still limping, and ye are tired after the ride. Ye have been stifling yawns for the last hour."

"I have not…" Yet Iomhar was trying to hide another even as he spoke.

"I'll go. Ye rest here." Niall climbed onto his horse.

Iomhar looked tempted to follow, before his eyes turned on Kit.

"Rest," she said. "You need it." Barely waiting for Niall, to whom the earl had tossed the map, Kit hurried out of the courtyard, racing ahead.

A sense of urgency was beginning to burn in her gut. She had to see Mary Stuart and deliver the letter.

"It's so isolated," Kit murmured in amazement as she looked up at Chartley Castle. It had taken less than an hour to reach the castle in the end, with the horse galloping beneath her. Niall had stopped beside her, their two steeds snorting as they hid between the trees, staring up at the castle close by.

Built on two hills, the castle stretched out wide with a curtain wall and three vast turrets, each one seemingly wider than the last. On the tallest tower a flag was rippling fervently in the wind.

"They would not want their guest to find a way out, would they?" Niall said. "Aye, keeping her isolated is the best way to keep her locked up."

Kit nodded, letting her eyes linger on the walls. They were tall, and would not be easy to climb to get into the castle. An inclined path led to two small turrets that bordered the gatehouse. At the gate, three guards stood, wearing different types of armour — some in kettle helmets, others in old-fashioned shoulder plates. All three carried pikes, one had a crossbow, and the second had a pistol latched at his hip.

"They will not make it easy to get in," Kit said slowly. "They do not seem to allow any visitors."

"They have let Lord Ruskin in, if our information is to be believed."

"It is an odd sort of house arrest then," Kit observed, turning to Niall.

"If Lord Ruskin posed as someone visiting the residents of this castle instead of Mary Stuart, he might just have found a way beyond those walls. Do ye think that could be your way in?"

"No." Kit turned back to the castle. It was a bitterly cold day, with the bare trees that surrounded the castle walls shaking in the breeze. Their branches moved like skeletal fingers, reaching out to be freed. Kit's eyes danced between the windows, looking for any sign of a prisoner. At this distance, though, she could see nothing. "If I am going to get in there, they cannot know about it."

"Then ye need a way to distract the guards."

"Even with a distraction, I could not walk through the entrance."

"Do ye see another way in?"

Kit's eyes danced across the front of the castle. To the side of the gatehouse, one of the turrets had two slit windows. One was so narrow it was barely wide enough for an arrow to fit through. The other was wide enough for a body.

"That way." Kit nodded at the window. "If someone could boost me to the window, then I could get in, unseen."

"Then we have a plan." Niall rode his horse a little distance along the trees, urging Kit to follow.

"How, exactly?" she asked. "We need a distraction that would be big enough to occupy all three guards. Do you have any idea?"

"Perhaps," Niall said with a mischievous smile as they came to a stop in the trees further down. "Leave the distraction to Iomhar, Duncan and myself. We can get ye in."

"You sound awfully confident." Kit was not so sure. Any distraction could raise suspicions from inside the castle's walls, especially as they were so isolated and unused to visitors.

"Trust me," Niall replied. "Aye, we know what we're doing, every now and then."

"Hmm." Kit watched the castle. The guards were now hidden around the corner from the main castle entrance. They stepped forward as the portcullis was raised. "Something is happening."

"Get back," Niall warned. "There's someone in the trees."

With soft taps on their horses' necks, urging them to be quiet, they steered themselves behind a thicker clump of trees and peered through branches.

On a path through the forest, there were four horse riders. Their faces were impossible to see at this distance, but they were riding keenly, with some speed. The horses' hooves thrust hard into the earth, thudding and echoing through the trees.

When the horses stepped out onto the inclined path that led up to the castle, they slowed at once, and the man leading the group of four lifted his head.

"Who is it? Can ye see?" Niall asked.

There were too many branches between Kit and the castle to possibly see a face. She could make out affluent clothes with a golden-coloured jerkin, and a cloak slung about the man's shoulders more for fashion than for warmth, with white fur lining the collar. Around his neck there was a ruff so vast that his head sat upon it as a cooked capon would sit in a bowl. A wide-brimmed burgundy hat brought low over his brow hid his face.

Cursing, Kit raised herself on the saddle, trying to get a clearer view. When she was afforded nothing better than before, she climbed onto the nearest branch.

"What are ye doing?" Niall reached for her horse, taking the reins to keep it in place.

"Finding a better view." Kit moved from one branch to another, spooking a nearby jackdaw that cawed and took flight. At the sudden movement, heads turned her way from the castle. She froze, keeping her body as close to the nearest tree trunk as possible.

The well-dressed stranger lifted his head and looked in her direction, just enough for her to see his face.

"I do not believe it," Kit whispered. She would know that face anywhere. His pale hair might have been hidden by the hat, but the eyes were unmistakable.

The guards soon looked away again, as did the man, turning to face the portcullis.

"Ye were lucky then," Niall hissed behind her. "How well this would have gone! For me to ride back to my family to declare, 'Wonderful news, Kit has been captured by the castle guards!'"

"They did not see me," Kit said, watching as the well-dressed figure walked toward the portcullis, followed by his attendants. They slipped inside before the portcullis was lowered and the guards moved to stand in front of the gate.

"Well? Did ye see who it was?"

"I did." Kit sighed and climbed back across the branches. When she reached the horses, she stopped in front of Niall, gripping a branch overhead and making more birds dance into the sky. "Something tells me you will like what I have to say."

"Why is that?" Niall asked.

"Because it seems your informant was right. That was Lord Ruskin going into the castle," Kit murmured, watching as Niall's eyes widened and his gaze shot back to the castle. His hands gripped the reins of both horses, turning his knuckles white. "Sometimes I worry what you and Iomhar will do when you meet him again."

"Do ye need ask?" Niall scoffed. "What do we do to murderers, Kit?"

The words grated on her. She jerked on the branch she was standing on, thinking of the man she had killed. She had made a vow to herself that she would never kill another soul, no matter what the consequences. The guilt was too much to bear, as if the man's spirit hung by her shoulder.

"We hang them, Kit," Niall continued when she said nothing. "He is a killer, is he not?"

"Yes, but the death was ordered by another," Kit reminded him and gestured to the walls of the castle. "She is in there too."

"When we find Lord Ruskin again ... what happens will be justice."

"Strange." Kit took the reins of her horse from Niall and climbed back into the saddle. "Something tells me your father would not have wanted you and Iomhar to become killers."

"This is our business, Kit."

"Not mine. I know." Kit looked at the castle that was just about visible through the branches. "I have come for a different reason entirely." Her thoughts turned to Mary Stuart as her eyes rested on the windows. "The question is, when do I break in?"

CHAPTER 22

"I am still not sure about this," Kit fretted as she hid between the trees, with Rhona at her side.

"What do ye not like about the plan?" Rhona huffed. "I think it a good one."

Kit turned to look at her. She was well-dressed and looked quite out of place on her knees, crouched between trees with her plaid skirt caught on brambles and nearby stones. Her arms were rather thin too. Rhona was supposed to be the one who would help hoist Kit up into the window, and Kit couldn't help thinking that this was not going to go well.

"I'm stronger than I look," Rhona said, apparently reading Kit's expression.

"I still think this a poor idea," Kit whispered, looking ahead through the trees toward the castle.

It was the early hours of the morning, so early that the sun had barely risen over the trees in the distance. A soft grey light had fallen on the castle, revealing the three guards by the gate. The first was standing to attention, playing with the pike in his hand and swinging it the way a youth would a staff. The second was leaning against the tower wall, his head lolling to the side, almost asleep. The third and final guard was trying to keep himself awake, tapping his own cheek repeatedly.

Between the trees and stepping out onto the incline were three figures Kit knew, though they were dressed like vagrants.

"Help! Help us! We need help!" Niall called ahead, adopting an English accent. Behind him, Iomhar was being helped to walk by Duncan.

"What is happening here?" one of the guards called out.

"We were attacked on the road by highwaymen. Please! Something is wrong with him. His head was struck." Niall waved a hand at Iomhar.

On cue, Iomhar buckled to the ground. Duncan tried to catch him, but Iomhar fell anyway, landing on the cobbles that led up to the portcullis.

"Aye, they're better actors than I gave them credit for," Rhona whispered at Kit's side.

As the three guards ran forward to help, the latter one dropping his pike in his haste to assist, Kit stood. When Rhona didn't follow straight away, she reached back and grabbed her arm, dragging her up.

"We are not here to watch a theatre show," Kit reminded her.

"It is rather interesting," Rhona confessed.

When they reached the edge of the trees, Kit checked to ensure all three guards were distracted.

"There, is that blood?" Duncan asked, forcing the three guards to lower their heads.

"Ah, our brother is dying!" Niall wailed.

"Fear not. I am sure he will recover." One of the guards tried to offer comfort, though it did little. Niall wailed some more, making Kit grimace.

"I have cause to question how good an actor you think Niall is," Kit whispered.

When all of the guards were looking down, she took hold of Rhona's arm and pulled her toward the side of the inclined path. Crouching beside the wall that lined the path, they used the cover to scramble up the hill, toward one of the towers in the gatehouse.

Standing beneath the window, Kit was not tall enough to reach it, and the wall was far too finely worked to find any sort of foothold.

"It's time, Rhona," Kit ordered, looking down the incline. Her eyes shot to Iomhar on the path, who wasn't moving. As her stomach knotted, she reminded herself it was all an act then turned and nodded at Rhona. "I hope you are feeling strong."

Rhona linked her hands together then held them out for Kit to step onto. Once Kit's boot was in her palms, Rhona thrust upward and groaned in pain.

"Shh!"

"Ye are heavier than I thought," Rhona huffed quietly.

Kit had to stand on Rhona's shoulder next, making the young woman curse, before she could reach the window. It was lined with lead in a square pattern, with the occasional stained-glass frame. Kit placed both palms to it. At first, it wouldn't move, and she glanced down at the path, nervous of the guards. When Rhona struggled under her weight and leaned against the wall, Kit was thrust toward the window. With the extra pressure, the glass swung open. It thudded off the other wall but didn't break.

"I'm in," Kit whispered and hauled herself up through the gap.

She landed on a stone floor, and curled herself into a crouched position, looking around the room. It appeared to be the chamber where they raised the portcullis, for ahead of her was a large winch, with a chain wrapped firmly around a thick metal rod.

Turning back to peer out of the window, Kit looked down to see that Rhona was already making her escape. Hiding behind the wall, she was crawling back toward the trees. The three guards were trying to raise Iomhar to his feet, but every time they helped him to stand, Iomhar purposefully pitched another way, forcing them to hurry to catch him.

"It worked," Kit murmured in disbelief and stepped away, focusing on the room as she closed the window behind her.

Creeping toward the nearest door that stood ajar, Kit peeked around the edge to see a corridor. With no sign of anyone, she stepped into it, reaching for the next door along. Opening this one wide, she revealed a stone staircase. Taking her chance, Kit hurried up the steps, being careful to run on the balls of her feet to make as little sound as possible.

She kept running, passing multiple doors until she reached the end of the staircase. A final door sat in the wall, short and squat. Taking hold of the iron handle, Kit opened the door and stepped out onto the roof of the castle wall, lifting the collar of her cloak up around her face to hide her features. Looking down either side of her, Kit could see out to the trees on one side and down into the courtyard on the other. The battlements stretched out ahead of her, and she walked across them with ease, hoping that if anyone glanced her way from the courtyard, they would presume she belonged there, for she walked with such confidence.

Judging it to be safe so high up, Kit began to circle the walls, looking down at the different turrets and the keep, trying to think of where Mary Stuart would be. At the far end of the castle, the walls hugged the keep, which was square and contrasted all the rounded towers.

Pausing at the side of the wall, Kit peered over the crenelations, looking down into the courtyard to see more guards outside the door to the keep. She felt a smile pulling at her lips, knowing that the guards' presence meant they had something or someone to hide.

Stepping back from the crenelations, Kit headed for where the wall met the keep. At first, there didn't seem to be an adjoining door, footpath, or any way to reach the keep. Then Kit's boot tripped on something in the stone wall beneath her feet. Looking down, she found there was a wooden trapdoor, set within the stone.

Reaching for the iron handle, Kit lifted the trapdoor, finding a wooden staircase inside. She hurried down it, landing in a timber-beamed room. It seemed to be some sort of storage space, with crates and barrels pressed on one side. Ignoring them all, Kit moved to the one door in the room and opened it a hair's breadth.

Pressing her eye to the gap, she found herself staring into a part of the castle that was infinitely grander than where she stood. The stone floor was covered in a deep red rug, and the walls were draped in golden tapestries. At the other end of the hall, a man walked, carrying a silver tray in one hand with a pewter jug on top. With his face turned away, Kit stepped into the corridor, keeping her boots on the rug to avoid making any sound.

Following him, Kit tried to catch up without raising suspicion. Either side of them, doors were closed, making Kit's chase unseen. When they reached the end of the corridor, the man paused. His head jerked, as if he had heard something.

Kit stepped off the rug and into an alcove set around one of the closed doors, pressing herself into the shadows. The man looked back, as if searching for someone, but he failed to check the shadows. Shaking his head, as if mocking his own foolishness, he walked forward again, and Kit stepped out, following him.

He walked through a door and into a second corridor, turning left then right, heading for another wing of the keep.

Kit stayed close, aware that in the distance she could hear voices. Evidently the man she was following was taking a drink to someone, but the question was, who?

The man turned and stopped abruptly before a door. He didn't raise his hand to knock right away, but sighed deeply and hung his head, as if going through the door was the last thing that he wished to do. Kit watched him closely, waiting as he raised his hand at last and knocked.

"Who is it?" a voice called from within the room. Her voice was quite deep and held the inflection of a strange accent.

"James, madam," the man answered. "I have brought your wine."

Her silence on the matter seemed to permit his entry, for he reached for the door.

Kit acted quickly. Reaching forward, she clamped a hand over his mouth and drew him backward.

He flailed for a minute, pushing the tray out wide, until Kit took one of the daggers from her belt and held it in front of him, so he could see the blade tip. He froze in her grasp.

"Place the tray down," Kit whispered in his ear. Slowly, he sank to the floor, with Kit moving with him, still holding her hand over his mouth. He discarded the tray on the ground. The moment it was out of his grasp, Kit lifted the dagger away and struck the back of his head with her elbow.

He swayed on his feet then began to tip, but Kit was able to catch him. She dragged him away, through the nearest door set a little way along the corridor. Peering inside, she found it was a privy. Propping him on the seat with his head resting back on the stone wall, she left him there, closing the door behind her.

"James? Where is that wine?" the deep voice called from inside the main chamber.

Kit adjusted her grey hat, pulling it lower to hide her face, then she put away her dagger and lifted the silver tray, walking into the room. Moving slowly, she kept her breathing quiet as she stepped in, her eyes dancing around the chamber.

It was long and had such high ceilings that the stonework arched far above her head. The vast windows on one side were a mixture of clear lead-lined glass and stained glass, coloured with red, green and yellow hues. The sun that shone through the glass painted the room in a myriad of colours. The chamber itself seemed to have more than one apartment.

The first was a space with a round table surrounded by high-back chairs. At one end there was an ample stone hearth, with the fire burning so strongly that it turned some of the room an odd shade of red.

Kit couldn't see the lady who had called out. Uncertain she had come to the right room after all, she moved toward the table and laid the tray down as quietly as she could, with her back to the window. Behind her, a floorboard creaked, as if someone was moving about and did not want to be heard or seen.

When there was a breath near Kit's ear, she lashed out. She reached to her far left, seeing a weapon out of the corner of her eye. A long silver blade glinted in the light.

Kit grasped the hand that was holding it, then spun the arm around, back behind someone's body. A woman yelped at the pain of it, releasing the weapon, before Kit elbowed her harshly in the stomach.

The woman fell back onto the table, making the jug and the tray dance, chinking loudly together.

Kit stepped back, the blade lifted, ready to defend herself again if she was called upon to do so, yet the tension left her body when her eyes landed on the woman before her. She knew that face, for she had seen it once before, in a portrait in Lady Ruskin's house. It was the same dark auburn hair, though unlike in the painting, it was beginning to grey, coiffed into two large humps at the back of the woman's head. The face was narrow, the eyes dark, and the nose hung low, hooking downward over her top lip.

"Mary Stuart," Kit whispered.

"Curious." Mary Stuart's voice was deep as her eyes flicked between Kit and the blade now in her hand. "Ye could have killed me. I could be pinned to this table now, bleeding my last, yet ye have not taken the strike. Ye are not here to kill me, then." With these words, Mary Stuart lifted herself up off the table, urging Kit to step back.

Kit could barely believe she was face to face with the woman she had heard so much about. She was tall, almost as tall as Kit, but she was also rather spindly in build and had such a narrow face that when she turned her head, she looked like a falcon, peering at Kit.

She did not seem like a killer, but Kit had heard the tales. She knew of how the woman before her had used a lover to murder her husband. She knew how the lady had attempted more than one coup, even against her own son, in order to be made Queen of Scotland. The former queen's name had been uttered many times in relation to plots in England, though they did not have certain proof that Mary Stuart was behind them.

"Why are ye here?" she asked, standing tall. She didn't fidget or straighten the creases in her high-collared green gown. She merely linked her hands together, staring at Kit as if they were discussing something menial, such as the weather. "Ye can lower the blade. We both know ye have not come to use it."

Kit did as she asked, watching as Mary Stuart's lips flickered.

"Curious indeed." She took a step toward Kit, peering beneath the hat. "Will ye speak, boy? Will ye tell me why ye have broken in? It's a feat few attempt. My jailors have sent many a man to prison for the crime."

Kit lifted her hat a little higher, revealing the fact she was no man.

"Hell may have angels yet," Mary Stuart muttered with awe as she cocked her head the other way. "Ye are a lass."

Uncertain what else to do, Kit curtsied quickly, without much deference, but acknowledging still that the woman before her used to be a queen.

"Even the servants here do not bother to do that anymore," Mary Stuart said with interest. "Are ye a friend?"

"No." Kit's English accent was noticeably different to the former queen's own voice. Though her Scottish inflection was strong, there was also the occasional French lilt, betraying the fact that she had spent much of her youth in France. "I have come to deliver a message."

"I have messages." Mary Stuart spoke with interest. "They are read by my captors, then passed to me on trays. People do not break in to deliver messages." She was fascinated by the idea, for she stepped forward with her hand outstretched. "Give it to me."

Kit reached for her belt and began to unbuckle it. Mary Stuart frowned at her as she did so, perplexed until Kit removed the silver case and lifted it for the former queen to see. Kit's hands shook as she opened the case and raised the letter.

Her eyes darted between the letter and the woman before her, thinking of all that she now knew about Mary Stuart. This woman had ordered the death of Iomhar's father — a man so treasured and loved by the family who had watched over Kit for the last few days.

When Kit hesitated, the letter was snatched from her fingers. Mary Stuart walked away with it, holding it close as she moved to the fire and peeled back the plain wax seal. Kit looked ahead through an archway into another apartment in the chambers. She could glimpse a bed that had been well made and a settle bench, along with letters that had been torn up and scattered on the floor. It was a glimpse of the anger that the former queen was capable of.

"I can scarcely believe it." The words tore Kit's attention back to Mary Stuart. She was poring over the letter in her grasp, before she smiled and scoffed, tipping her head back. A high-pitched laugh escaped her, one that was quickly dampened as she covered her mouth with her hand. "My cousin sent this?" she asked, turning her gaze on Kit. "My cousin who does not conduct a single order of business without her privy council has written to me?" She stepped toward Kit, the heels of her shoes clicking loudly on the stone floor. "And she sent ye to deliver it. Who are ye, may I ask?"

"No one of importance."

"Take off your hat, so I may see ye better."

Kit did not follow the order. She stayed very still, showing she had no intention of following such an instruction. Her defiance made the smile fall from Mary Stuart's face. Her cheek twitched.

"Remove your hat, or ye will not have the reply that your queen so desperately longs for."

The words left Kit with little choice. She took off the hat and revealed her face, standing with her back to the window, so that her face was somewhat in shadow.

"Perhaps she chose ye because ye are a woman. She hoped ye would not talk of things the men talk of." Mary Stuart laughed and stepped away, reading the letter. "She offers peace and hopes we can create a discussion that would benefit us both. To protect her kingdom, and … my son's." Her voice shook as she said the latter words.

Clearing her throat, she read part of the letter out loud. "*I implore you cousin, to heed my offer. You and I can be friends, and we can both live in this world without posing a threat to the other. Show willing in this friendship and concede your claims to both the Scottish and English thrones, then I can persuade my council to change your treatment. It would please me greatly to know you are better taken care of.*"

She paused, looking quite disgusted by what she'd read. She turned the letter over, apparently hoping there would be more, then wrinkled her nose.

"She neglects to mention that I have a right to the throne."

"Because your right has not been recognised, madam. Not by anyone." Kit found the words tumbling from her lips in anger. She supposed it was the effect of being face to face with a woman who carried death in her wake as if it were her shadow.

"Oh, the messenger speaks her mind. Aye, I can see why my cousin likes ye. Not quelled by royalty, are ye?"

"What royalty is there here?" Kit asked, reiterating her earlier point.

Mary Stuart stepped forward, her hand tightening around the letter. "How dare —"

"I am here to deliver the queen's offer of peace only, and to take back a reply. Do you have a reply you wish to send?" Kit kept her voice level.

The former queen hissed through her teeth. "Insolent. Aye, insolent, and nay doubt mad from the way ye dress." She marched toward her. Kit was forced to back up, to stop herself being struck. She stepped back further into the light from the window, and Mary Stuart froze.

She did not finish what she was saying but stared at Kit, her brown eyes wide beneath the heavy forehead.

"Are you ill, madam?" Kit asked, wrongfooted enough to fidget.

"I…" Mary Stuart swallowed. "I somehow think I have seen a ghost."

Kit stood very still, certain it had to be a trick of the light from the way the windows shone behind her. She looked back, half expecting there to be some spirit there, but there was nothing. She was standing alone before Mary Stuart.

"Tell me your name," the former queen ordered.

"Do you need it?"

"Nay. But I wish to have it."

"Kit." Kit saw no reason to give her full name. The name seemed to catch Mary Stuart's interest, for she angled her head the other way, watching Kit closely.

"Aye, the resemblance is strange, but that is all. It is a resemblance," she murmured to herself and stepped away. Kit at last understood what she meant and longed to ask who she had reminded Mary Stuart of, but she was prevented from doing so as the former queen wafted the letter in the air and continued her tirade. "This is an insult. Your queen tries to make peace and save her own life by pleading with me. It is the act of a child, desperate, begging for help in the darkness of the night. It is nay act of a true queen. Does she think I am some quiet woman who will sit silently in the castle? Imprisoned? I am a prisoner here."

"Some prison," Kit murmured, looking around the fine room.

"What was that?"

"I have seen my fair share of prisons, madam." Kit thought of Iomhar and the state he'd been in when she had taken him from Urquhart Castle. "If this is your prison, then you are fortunate indeed."

"Insulting. Insolent," Mary Stuart hissed and marched around the table. "Your queen is a fool. That is that." She folded up the letter neatly and placed it in the middle of the table, staring at it as if it were a weapon. "I once thought her a friend, aye, but plainly we are not, or she would not keep me here."

"You have tried to take her throne. Is that the act of a friend?"

Mary Stuart appeared ready to throw herself at Kit, with her hands curling into balls at her sides.

Kit spoke quickly to forestall the attack. "Will you write a reply?"

"Why should I?" Mary Stuart asked. "My silence will be enough of a reply to her. She will know without an answer what I make of her message." She reached toward her mantelpiece and retrieved a dagger, much like the one Kit had taken from her, which now hung loose in her grasp. Turning back, Mary Stuart thrust the dagger into the letter, pinning it to the table.

"Is that a threat, madam?" Kit asked, her hand shaking around the dagger. "A threat to the queen?"

"I made no such threat." Yet Mary Stuart's smile betrayed the truth. "Still, sacrifices must be made to enact God's will on this earth."

Kit was reminded of Iomhar's father and wondered if Mary Stuart saw his life as one of the sacrifices to be made for her greater cause.

"I have had enough of this conversation. Having satisfied myself with the reason ye are here, my curiosity is quite at an end." Mary Stuart stood straight off the table.

There was a knock at the door, one so light that it was barely audible. The former queen smiled at that sound.

"He knew ye would come," she whispered.

"I beg your pardon?" Kit asked, taking a step back.

"I have been waiting for a messenger to come, ever since he told me of ye. He heard that ye were leaving London. His men might have failed to catch ye on the road, but he knew ye would come here eventually. He was told of it."

Kit didn't need to ask who she meant. She could guess well enough.

"Enter!" Mary Stuart called, her voice echoing off the stone walls. The door opened, revealing Lord Ruskin.

CHAPTER 23

"Your Majesty." Lord Ruskin's voice was gushing as he stepped in and dropped to the floor, on his knees before his queen.

"Ah, Ruskin. My loyal servant." Mary Stuart stepped toward him as Kit moved back, colliding with the window behind her.

She looked through the glass, down to the ground below, but she knew there was no escape that way. The fall was too high, and she would be trapped within the castle walls even if she survived the drop.

"Ye were right," Mary Stuart said as she laid a hand on Lord Ruskin's shoulder. "The woman ye have been searching for. She's here. Ye said her name was Kit, did ye not?" Moving her hand to his chin, she lifted Lord Ruskin's gaze from her feet and angled his head across the room.

The moment those pale, milky blue eyes found Kit, she tensed. There was hatred there, reminding her of the moment she had seen Lord Ruskin again in Hampton Court just a year ago.

"Did ye not say she was to die on the road?"

"That was the plan, Your Majesty. Yet it seems I hired fools for the errand."

"I have had enough of my visitor," Mary Stuart said tiredly, stepping away from Lord Ruskin. "Ye can take her as ye like now."

Lord Ruskin hurried to his feet and moved across the room. Kit was careful to match his strides away, reaching for the other side of the table and keeping the distance between them.

Mary Stuart chuckled as she took a seat at the table, reaching for the letter that was still pinned beneath the dagger. She lifted out the blade and raised the letter to her eyes. "As much as I enjoy placing a wager on a bear or cockfight, Lord Ruskin, I cannot have blood spilled here. Ye know that, as I do." She looked toward Kit. "My captors will return soon. I do not think I could explain to them how a lass is dead in my chambers."

"Dead...?" Kit spluttered, scarcely believing it had come to this. "You cannot accept my death, madam." Her voice was firm. "Without my return to London, who will tell the queen what your response was to her letter?"

"Ye seem to have missed the part where I said I have nay intention of replying," Mary Stuart said with a frown. "My silence on the matter will make my rejection of her offer plain. Why would I need someone to deliver a message of silence?"

In the pause that followed, Mary Stuart nodded at Lord Ruskin. Kit ran in the other direction, heading for the door, but Lord Ruskin was too quick for her. When he reached her, she struck out with the knife she had taken from Mary Stuart, but he dodged the blow, thrusting his forearm up against hers. When a second blow was delivered straight to Kit's stomach, so hard that she buckled to the ground, the knife was prised easily from her hands.

Kit lay there, struggling to breathe as she curled up on the stone floor.

"How did ye know she was coming?" the former queen asked Lord Ruskin as Kit placed a palm to the floor, trying to move to her knees.

"We have men and women everywhere, Your Majesty. One of them told me of her commission," Lord Ruskin said calmly and kicked Kit hard in the back. She fell forward, barely stopping her nose from hitting the stone by thrusting her hands down first.

"Take her now. Before she is seen by anyone else."

Kit tried to raise herself up again and reach for the weapons in her belt, but her hand was grasped and her wrists were bound together with rope. Tugged to her feet as if she were a dog, she stumbled, holding out her bound hands before her. Lord Ruskin drew Kit toward the door.

"Wait." Mary Stuart's order made them both pause in the doorway.

"Aye?" Lord Ruskin said, yet Mary Stuart was not looking at him. Her eyes were on Kit as she leaned against the wall, breathing heavily and pulling against the ropes that bound her. "Who are ye, exactly?"

Kit didn't answer, but Lord Ruskin spoke for her. "Her name is Miss Kit Scarlett, Your Majesty. She is one of Walsingham's intelligencers."

"That is not what I mean." Mary Stuart sat back in her chair, eyeing Kit. "Aye, ye are a ghost," she murmured, speaking to herself. "Who are your parents?"

"I have no parents," Kit said, not seeing the point in hiding the truth.

"Who were they?"

"I do not know."

Mary Stuart stood and crossed the room. She grabbed Kit's cheek and tilted it upward, the better to see her face. "Aye, the similarity is there, I'll give ye that. Perhaps that is all it is."

"A similarity to who?" Kit asked, holding her breath.

Mary Stuart smiled faintly. "It does not matter now." She nodded at Lord Ruskin. "Take her. Do it somewhere far away from here. Somewhere she can be discovered, but do it so that it does not look like murder. I want the queen to know one day what happened to her messenger."

Kit was thrust out of the door before she had a chance to say anything more. She tried to run, but Lord Ruskin pulled on the ropes, jerking her back. As he closed the door, Kit was ready to launch an attack. Reaching for her weapons belt with her bound hands, she tried to grab one of the daggers, but before she could, Lord Ruskin struck out at her.

His hand collided with her cheek and temple with so much strength that she was knocked from her feet. With the skin around her eye stinging, Kit raised her bound hands to her face and felt blood beading. When Lord Ruskin had struck her, his rings had left cuts.

"Nay words, now. Or ye die sooner," he warned.

A second rope came up around Kit's face, but she was too dazed to fight against it. The blow had left her disorientated, limp on the floor as he gagged and bound her. Somewhere in her mind, Kit was aware of being lifted from her feet and thrust over his shoulder. She saw stars at the movement, then she seemed to swim in and out of consciousness. She imagined it like sleep coming for her, swallowing her whole, before releasing her again.

When her eyes opened fully, she could see a courtyard beneath her, and the heels of Lord Ruskin's boots walking across the cobbles. He was issuing orders in his deep, rumbling voice.

His orders must have been adhered to, for Kit found they stopped in front of a carriage. She just managed to lift her head enough to get a good look at it when he and another man held open the door.

"No…" Kit murmured.

"Aye, she's waking up."

Kit knew that voice. It was Graham Fraser, meaning he had to be one of the men who had accompanied Lord Ruskin to the castle.

"Then we do this fast," Lord Ruskin ordered and tossed Kit into the back of the carriage. She landed awkwardly, her arms bent under her, and the pain ricocheted through her head. Raising her bound hands, she covered her face and gritted her teeth.

When the doors of the carriage thudded shut, she looked up, trying to breathe deeply and understand what was happening. The carriage moved a second later, jolting from side to side, heading out of the courtyard.

Kit moved to her knees, trying to peer out, but the carriage had no windows. With blackened walls, it had not been built for fine people to ride in; it was more like a prisoner's cart. Scrambling for any opening, she ran her bound hands over the walls, but there was nothing there. When the carriage passed down an incline, possibly the long path that had led up to the gatehouse, Kit was thrust back, falling to her rear and gasping at the pain.

Raising her hands, Kit tried to take the gag away from her mouth. With her wrists tied so tightly together, it wasn't easy to get a grip on the rope. In the end, she scraped her face against the wooden floor, making the rope shift a little before she could grab it with the tips of her fingers. It grazed her cheeks as she managed to pull it down around her neck, freeing her mouth.

When the carriage levelled out, seemingly moving on flat ground, it picked up speed. Kit could hear horses' hooves on either side, which told her she was being escorted somewhere.

She moved toward the door, finding a tiny gap. Pressing her face close, she looked out to the woods. Branches waved in the breeze, as if they were bidding her goodbye.

"No…" Kit murmured, raising herself higher. She knew Iomhar and his family had to be out there. The plan had been for them to wait for her return. Hoping that they would still be nearby, Kit pressed her face to the door and bellowed a name.

"Iomhar!" Her voice shook with the effort to scream so loudly.

The horses beside her were immediately spooked by the noise.

"She's awake," Graham Fraser muttered.

"Then make her hold her tongue," Lord Ruskin snapped.

The carriage came to a stop and the door was thrust open. Kit scampered back, heading for the other side. Fraser was climbing in, carrying more rope in his hands.

Kit looked over his shoulder for any sign of Iomhar and his siblings. There was nothing but the empty trees. Running forward, Kit tried to push past Graham Fraser, but he grabbed her around the waist and thrust her back. He moved a strip of cloth to her face, trying to gag her. She continued to scream as Fraser placed a hand over her mouth, muffling the sound.

"Quiet!" he ordered and bound the gag tight. He threaded a second rope around her hands, so her fingers could not move at all, then he left her, jumping down from the cart.

Shakily, Kit scrambled to her knees, but the doors were closed again, and the harsh jolt of the carriage sent her to the floor. Biting at the gag, she tried to release herself from it, but it did no good. The gag and ropes were stuck fast, and Iomhar had clearly been too far away to hear her.

Kit didn't know how long the carriage ride was, for she spent all of it trying to get the gag off her mouth and free her hands without success. She soon grew aware that the carriage seemed to be climbing some sort of hill, for she was tipped backward, and their pace slowed.

When it came to a stop, Kit froze, breathing heavily around the gag and watching as the doors opened. Bright light bled through, revealing Lord Ruskin, now disguised in a poor man's cloak and a short cap. Beside him was Graham Fraser. A third figure was behind them, seeing to their horses.

"How do we do this?" Fraser asked.

"It must look like an accident," Lord Ruskin explained. "She'll go over the cliff with a horse. With any luck, it will seem like the horse lost its footing on the cliff edge."

Kit scurried back at the words, but her ankle was grabbed by Lord Ruskin. She was dragged until she fell out of the cart.

"We'll have to untie her ropes," Fraser began slowly.

"Do it. I'll hold her." Lord Ruskin took Kit's arms and jerked her to her feet, hauling her across the earth. She stumbled over clods of soil and frost-covered grass.

Turning her head back and forth, Kit searched the area around her. They were in the hills, overlooking a sheer cliff drop. A path to their left revealed how they had come up a steep incline. The nearest town was far away from the cliff, some miles away. Even if Kit screamed, they would not hear her. Her voice would be lost on the wind.

"Do it now," Lord Ruskin ordered, turning Kit to face Fraser and holding back both of her arms. "Then, we throw her."

Kit buried her feet into the ground, knowing that she couldn't let Lord Ruskin take her anywhere near the cliff edge. Fraser started with the ties around her wrists, loosening them from her fingers and then dropping the rope completely. Kit tried to lash out at Fraser when her hands were free, reaching for a weapon, but her arms were thrust behind her by Lord Ruskin, so far that she was in danger of having a bone broken.

"Your injuries won't be noticeable after your fall," he warned, holding her still. "Take the gag off now."

Fraser nodded and reached for the gag. Once the fabric fell away from Kit's face, she spat at Fraser, making the man flinch backward.

"Ergh!" He wiped his face, disgusted, then patted his fine clothes, as if she had tainted him. He kept backing up, apparently unable to get far enough away from her.

Lord Ruskin tried to drag Kit toward the cliff edge, but she dug her heels in. The sudden movement startled him, for he had to jerk again to release her from her position.

"This is for my wife, Miss Scarlett. The woman ye watched die," he whispered harshly in her ear.

He was too strong, and kept drawing Kit closer to the edge, even as she fought against him. The wind whistled up the cliff side, buffeting her hair. Her hat was gone. She assumed it had been dropped somewhere in the cart, along with her weapons, for she had nothing else on her.

Pressing her toes against a rock on the cliff edge, refusing to meet the precipice, Kit pushed herself into Lord Ruskin, forcing him back a step.

"Your wife killed herself. I merely watched it happen," Kit reminded him. "I did not deal the blow."

"Ye are the reason she is dead. Ye are a killer. As if ye had wielded the knife yourself." Lord Ruskin's words reminded Kit of the moment she had killed to save her own life. If she could have done it again in that moment, she would have, but she had no weapon to fight Lord Ruskin, and he was too strong for her to change their positions.

"I'm no killer," Kit pleaded, knowing that Lord Ruskin was barely listening to her.

"Ruskin! Ruskin!" Fraser began to shout.

"Not now, ye fool!" Lord Ruskin roared back.

Kit could hear horses' hooves, though she couldn't turn to see where they were coming from.

"Farewell, Miss Scarlett," Lord Ruskin said in her ear. Kit looked down, sensing one opportunity only to escape. His foot was beside her own.

She lifted her foot, knowing it meant he could push her closer to the cliff edge, but it gave her just enough time to slam down hard on his toe with the heel of her boot.

"Argh!" he grunted, loosening his hold, though he did not let go. It was enough for Kit to kick out at the rock in front of her, pushing him onto his back so that she fell on top of him, winding him.

Rolling off him, she hurriedly crawled away, then the sounds of the horses' hooves grew close.

"Kit!" Iomhar's voice rang out.

Kit struggled onto her knees and looked up. Iomhar was at the top of the cliff on his horse with Niall at his side, and the earl rode behind him with Rhona. Fraser stepped in front of Iomhar's and Niall's horses, bearing a pistol in his hand. Iomhar and Niall climbed down from their horses as Fraser took a shot.

The shot clipped one of the horses, making the animal buck and rear, but the bullet did not find its target.

"Kit!" Iomhar called over the horse, looking for her. In his hand he had a rope. He seemed to be threading it around a tree behind him.

Kit moved to her feet, determined to get away, but she was barely standing when Lord Ruskin grabbed her by the waist, tugging her back again.

"No!" she screeched. She could see Niall tackling Fraser to the ground, fighting over the gun. Iomhar ran round the horses, struggling with his injured leg. He was heading straight for Kit, with the other end of the rope in his hands.

As Lord Ruskin turned, moving her toward the cliff, Kit realised what Iomhar was trying to do. He reached for Lord Ruskin's shoulder, thrusting him back, but by that time Kit was over the edge. As Lord Ruskin let go, the ground fell away from beneath her.

A scream erupted from somewhere. Kit half thought it was Rhona's voice, but it could have been her own. She fell through the air, reaching upward as her hands found the rope that Iomhar had tossed to her.

Holding on tight, Kit came to a sharp stop on the cliff, her body colliding with the stone and making her hands loosen momentarily. She slipped a little way down the rope, then managed to cling on again.

She looked down with terror, taking in the distance between her and the bottom of the cliff. It was vast, with a great number of rocks jutting out on the way; she knew she couldn't survive such a drop. She clung to the rope all the harder, her legs swinging.

"Kit?" Iomhar called from over the cliff. A grunt followed, suggesting he had been struck by someone.

"Where is she?" Niall shouted.

"Where do ye think?" Lord Ruskin said with a kind of victory.

"Iomhar?" Kit called, showing she was still alive.

"The rope … the damn rope." Lord Ruskin must have tried to grab the rope, for she felt a pull on the end and then there were the sounds of a scuffle.

Unsure what was happening, all Kit could do was listen to the pained noises and cling to the rope, praying she was not going to fall.

"Rhona!" the earl was shouting at his sister. "The gun. Get that gun!" There seemed to be a fight over Fraser's gun, but beyond that, Kit could make out no more.

Swallowing at the sight of the drop beneath her, Kit felt dizzy. Breathing deeply, she lifted her eyes, determined not to look down again. Slowly, she began to climb. It was hard work, with her muscles straining so much that her arms began to shake. She knew she could not do it for long.

"Kit! He's cutting the rope!" shouted Iomhar.

Kit looked between the rope and the cliff top. She was a good climber, but she had never scaled a cliff of this size before. Unsure what other chance she had, she reached out for the cliff, trying to take hold of it. At first, she couldn't reach it. Turning as she swung there, she reached out again. This time, her fingers just managed to claw at the edge of the stone.

Kit took hold of the rocks embedded in the cliff and manoeuvred herself to the rockface, away from the rope. As she released it, the rope grew heavy and dropped from her hands.

Kit flattened herself against the cliff, watching with her mouth open as the rope fell like a snake, curling up on itself. It whipped at rocks on its way down before landing on the ground, kicking up dust and dirt around it.

"No!" someone roared from overhead. Kit wasn't sure whose voice it was this time, but the sounds of a fight followed.

Straining, she began to climb. Now, she could use her feet as well as her hands, and the ascent became easier. She traversed up the rock, imagining she was climbing one of the timber-beamed houses in London or a dockyard wall — something short and easy, something that she had climbed a hundred times before. Her arms still shook, and her palms were so sweaty that one of her hands slipped off a rock, but she caught another one quickly.

Rocks turned to grass, and Kit found the precipice of the cliff. Levering herself up, she was half over the cliff edge, with her legs still down on the stones when she could at last see what was happening.

Niall was tussling with Graham Fraser, but it was a fight with their hands now. Behind them was another of Lord Ruskin's men, fighting with the earl. Rhona was nearby, picking up a gun that someone must have dropped and shakily checking it was loaded.

Closest to Kit was Lord Ruskin and Iomhar. The two were locked in battle, both bearing swords. When Lord Ruskin reached out and cut Iomhar's cheek, Iomhar backed up, making his opponent smile as he circled his weapon in the air.

"Now ye have a pair," he said, gesturing to the scar on Iomhar's other cheek.

Kit moved forward, wanting to help him. The moment a rock crunched beneath her hand, Lord Ruskin's eyes shot to her. All trace of humour vanished as he saw she was still alive. He ran forward, heading straight for her.

"Iomhar!" Kit barked.

Iomhar launched forward before Lord Ruskin could get far and knocked the sword from his opponent's hand. He elbowed Lord Ruskin in the nose, sending the man backward, clutching his face. With his feet dangerously near the edge of the cliff, Lord Ruskin was at risk of going over.

Kit could see Iomhar had the opportunity he'd wanted — to punish Lord Ruskin for what he had done to his father. She tried to move up again, but one of the rocks gave way beneath her feet.

"Iomhar!" she called as she began to slip. The grass slid between her sweating fingers and one of her feet dangled as her weight tipped back.

Iomhar snapped his head away from Lord Ruskin and ran to her. He reached out and grabbed Kit's hand, stopping her from falling. Her feet still dangled. She looked down once more at the distance she could have fallen.

"Kit? I need ye to reach up now!" Iomhar's voice urged her to look up. He was flat on his stomach, holding onto her with just one hand. Reaching up with her other hand, she held onto his shoulder, allowing him to lever her upward, gritting his teeth as he did so. Kit clambered onto the top of the cliff, kicking the rocks.

"Nay. Come back! Rhona, give me that gun!" Niall was shouting as he snatched the weapon from Rhona's hand.

Kit looked up to see the fight was at an end. The man the earl had fought was wounded but already fleeing on his horse. Fraser was too, having left Niall with a bruise on his cheek. Behind them both, Lord Ruskin was holding a third horse.

"He's leaving," Iomhar said from beside Kit, his dark tone betraying his anger.

Lord Ruskin looked at them both as he pulled himself into the saddle. His face was also red with anger, having failed to kill Kit once again.

Niall hurried forward with the weapon and fired. Lord Ruskin barely dodged the bullet as he rode away, chasing his men down the hill. Niall cursed when the weapon wouldn't fire a second time. With no gun or bullets in his own weapons belt, he cursed loudly and threw the gun to the ground.

"He's gone. So easily, he has gone?" Rhona murmured, moving to stand beside the earl, who was struggling to stay upright, rubbing a sore spot on his ribs.

"That was not easy," Iomhar said. He and Kit were both dangerously close to the cliff edge, their arms locked together. "Kit, ye are shaking," he whispered.

She nodded, knowing how close she had been to death. "Thank you," she breathed. Iomhar clung harder onto her arms, showing he had no intention of letting her go. "You heard me shouting? At Chartley?"

"Aye, I did," he said slowly. "Ye save me, I save ye. That's how we are, is it not?" His words made her smile, the relief breaking through. "I got ye, Kit. Ye are safe now." Her fingers curled tighter around his arms, reluctant to release him.

"That bastard! He's free? We came this close and he's free!" Niall was pacing as he ranted, lost to his ire.

Kit could not summon any words. She was only aware of Iomhar pulling her further away from the cliff edge before she grew weak, unable to go much further. When she moved to her knees, Iomhar wrapped an arm around her. Kit leaned into him, still holding onto one of his arms.

"Kit? Ye are alive," Rhona gushed in relief, rushing toward her.

Kit nodded. "But he's not going to stop trying," she said quietly, looking at Iomhar. "Fraser and some soldiers tried to catch me on the road, on my way to Scotland. He's not going to stop."

"Aye, then we need to get ye out of here. Before Lord Ruskin comes back with any more of his men. It won't take him long to realise we must be staying nearby. He will search every coaching inn within an hour's ride." Iomhar lifted his chin and looked at Niall. "Niall?"

"What?" Niall barked.

"Be content. We may not have got Lord Ruskin today, but Kit's alive."

"Kit?" Niall hurried forward. His anger was dissipating as he moved closer to them.

"Kit?" Iomhar said quietly as he drew her to her feet. "We need to get ye back to London and far away from here."

"There is more you need to know yet," she replied. "I need to tell you what happened at Chartley Castle."

CHAPTER 24

"We need to go. Now!" Iomhar roared once he'd burst through the door of the coaching inn.

Kit struggled to follow. She was weak, and in her mind's eye, she could not stop seeing herself going over that cliff. The feeling of the rope beneath her hands was scorched into her mind. She looked down at her palms as she moved into the house, staring at the grazes.

"What has happened?" Moira appeared on the inn stairs, already with a bag in her hand. Abigail was close behind her.

"We'll explain as we go," Niall called to her. "Och, we must leave now, before Lord Ruskin can send his men after us."

"Ye think he would?" Rhona asked, stopping at Kit's side, her own lip trembling. Abigail took Rhona's hand, standing on her sister's other side.

"Aye, I do not doubt he would," said Iomhar.

His words urged the earl into action. He burst back through the door, shouting for their carriage and horses to be brought at once.

"Niall, we can't go back to Scotland," Iomhar went on.

Silence fell. Faces turned to one another, questioningly.

"It is our home, Iomhar," Moira said. As she reached the bottom step, Niall took the bag out of her hand and urged her forward.

"For now, to protect ourselves, we cannot go home." Iomhar looked at Kit, almost pleadingly.

"Iomhar is right," she said, finding her voice at last. "Lord Ruskin knows where you live. Since all of you saw what happened today, he will want to silence any whispers that may spread. He already tried to see the end of you once, Iomhar. He will not hesitate to do it again."

"It's the same for ye," Iomhar pointed out, stepping toward her.

"Katherine, what happened to ye?" Moira asked, reaching for Kit. She looked at the grazes on her hands and the bruises on her cheeks.

"He tried to kill her," Iomhar said succinctly.

"I beg your pardon?" Moira flinched, twisting her head in his direction.

"We go. Now," Iomhar reiterated.

"Ye do not have to say it again," Niall agreed with a quick nod. "Rhona, Abigail, the carriage."

"Aye," they said together, hurrying out.

"If we are not going to Scotland, where are we going?" Moira asked, hastened to the door by Kit and Iomhar either side of her.

"For now, London." Iomhar's eyes found Kit's over his mother's head. "Not forever, Ma, but for now, we must go."

Moira didn't argue. She went to the carriage, though she reached back toward Kit more than once, checking her injuries. "Are ye sure ye are all right?"

"I am fine, I promise you," Kit replied, before Moira stepped into the carriage. The moment she was inside, the earl instructed the driver to take the road out of Uttoxeter and head to London.

"Ye two!" Niall called to Kit and Iomhar. "Get to your horses. We'll guard the carriage en route."

They hurried to the horses they had left minutes ago. Before Kit could pull herself up into the saddle, she was turned back. Iomhar was in front of her, tilting her chin up, the better to look at the cuts on the side of her face.

"Now my mother has gone, ye can tell me the truth. How badly are ye hurt?" he whispered.

"Iomhar? What is taking so long?" the earl barked from further down the road, already on his horse, but Iomhar ignored him, not looking away from Kit.

"I am sore, and..." Kit swallowed. "I'm still scared. Yet I am fine." She breathed deeply. "These wounds will heal." She held up her hands, showing the grazes on her palms.

"Och, that will take time."

"Iomhar!"

"We are coming! Go ahead, and we'll be there in a minute," Iomhar called to his brother, so firmly that the earl didn't argue again. He rode ahead with Niall, catching up to the carriage.

Once they had turned away, Iomhar reached into one of the bags attached to his horse's saddle and pulled out a linen shirt. He tore the sleeves into strips.

"Ye need to protect these wounds." Iomhar wrapped the strips around Kit's palms, stopping any more blood beading to the surface.

"Thank you," she whispered, barely watching as he worked. She was busy glancing over her shoulder, looking in the direction they had come from. There was no sign of Lord Ruskin, nor Graham Fraser, nor anyone bearing a unicorn tattoo. "Iomhar?"

"Aye?" Iomhar said.

"Thank you for what you did on the cliff top. I could have died had you not ... you know."

"Aye, and I could have died in that dungeon," Iomhar said. "I reckon we have a habit of doing this, do we not?"

"Stepping into danger for each other?" Kit laughed. "I think Walsingham would call us fools."

"Aye, maybe we are." Iomhar gestured to the saddle behind her, then offered a hand to help her up. Ordinarily, Kit would have ignored it and climbed up alone, but today, she took his hand, grimacing at the pain that shot through her grazed palms. "I am happy being a fool, Kit." He held her hand as he said the words, then released it and headed for his horse.

Kit stared after him. At some point over the last couple of years, he had become her dearest friend. He was the one who mattered to her more than anyone else, to the point where she had crossed the country and risked Walsingham's wrath just to see he was safe.

She thought of Iomhar's offer for her to come home to Scotland with him when he decided to return. Turning in the saddle to look at the road ahead, she began to wonder if it was just possible that she could say yes. She needed time to think about what it all meant, but after seeing Iomhar again after so long, she had a feeling it would be hard to say goodbye to him if it ever came to it.

"Ye ready?" Iomhar called, urging his horse away.

"Yes." She rode with him, the two of them galloping until they caught up with the carriage and slowed to a trot behind it. The earl and Niall flanked the coach on either side and Kit and Iomhar rode at the back, constantly looking over their shoulders.

"Kit?"

"Yes?"

"What happened with Mary Stuart?" Iomhar's face was tense. "What did she make of the queen's letter?"

"She tossed it down with disregard," Kit said slowly. "She had no intention of responding to it. She called the queen's offer of an olive branch the act of a child, not the act of a true queen."

Iomhar cursed and looked away. "She talks of acting like a child, when she is the petulant one."

"I know," Kit murmured. "She's made her feelings known. Once we return to London, I must see the queen and Walsingham at once. The queen must be told what Mary Stuart's response was."

"Mary Stuart was happy to see you dead, Kit, wasn't she? She did not care whether such a reply would be delivered."

"That she was. She told Lord Ruskin to take me and do the deed far away from the castle. There was something else, though."

"What?" Iomhar asked. He steered his horse closer to Kit's, the better to hear her.

"She looked at me as your mother looks at me."

"How do ye mean?"

"As if ... they have seen me somewhere before." Kit didn't need to see the expression on Iomhar's face to know it was a mad thought. She had never seen either woman before this trip, yet they had both acted as if they had recognised something in her face. "It doesn't matter. Regardless of whether Mary Stuart wanted her message delivered or not, I will deliver it. The queen should know that her enemy intends to stay on the other side of their battlefield."

CHAPTER 25

Two days later, Kit was once again before the queen, along with Walsingham. They were standing at the bottom of the garden at Richmond Palace, and Kit had just finished relaying Mary Stuart's message.

"That is what she said?" the queen asked. Snow was falling, and she had wrapped herself in a fur-lined cloak to fight the chill. She had refused to go inside, no matter how many times Walsingham had suggested she did. Standing as still as a statue, she looked out across the gardens, her back to Kit. Beside her, Walsingham bent forward, suffering with his usual aching back. His dark eyes were wide.

"You have recounted what happened faithfully, have you not, Kit?" he asked, with a tremor to his voice.

"Every word." Kit nodded, holding Walsingham's gaze to show her sincerity.

She could see from the way he was staring at her that he was scared. His eyes kept dancing over her hands, which were too bandaged to fit into gloves, and he stared at the bruising on her face as if a bird of prey had landed there and pecked at her skin. Kit knew how awful she looked. During the journey from Chartley Castle to London, the bruising had got worse. It looked rather like ink had been spilled beneath her skin, leaking around her eye and the top of her cheek.

"What happened to you, Kit?" Walsingham whispered.

At his words, the queen turned. The wisps of her wig were caught in the wind and curved back over the rim of her hat as her eyes landed on Kit. "This was no easy task I set you, was it?" she asked, before Kit could answer. "Did my cousin do this to you?"

"No, Your Majesty," Kit assured her. "I do not believe your cousin has much taste for drawing blood herself. She orders others to do it. She believes in *sacrifices* for her cause." Kit repeated the words that had been uttered to her with scorn.

"You were to be a sacrifice?" the queen asked, stepping forward. Kit backed up until the queen glared at her, showing she should stand still. She stopped moving, allowing the queen to close the distance between them.

"No. I was to die for two different reasons. I believe the first was for you to know your message had failed, Your Majesty, and that your messenger would not return." Kit held the queen's gaze as she spoke, wanting her to know the dangerous mind of Mary Stuart. "The second reason was more personal. The queen's most loyal servant, Lord Ruskin, wishes to see me dead."

The queen tapped Kit's chin and lifted it higher, the better to examine the wound on her face. Kit stayed very still, aware of the lavish gloves the queen wore. The gold-stained leather was soft on her skin.

"You survived," the queen murmured, her lips flickering into the smallest of smiles. "I hope my cousin knows she failed in that regard." She released Kit's chin slowly, just as Walsingham stepped forward.

Kit could never remember seeing such fear in his face before. He glanced between her and the queen, his lips opening and closing.

"How hurt are you?" he asked eventually.

Kit was startled by the question, but she answered it as honestly as she could. "Wounded, but I will heal. I have another to thank for my still being here." She would soon tell Walsingham that Iomhar was safe, but for now, he had asked her not to.

Iomhar had never trusted the spymaster completely, and after his time in the dungeon, he seemed even less inclined to do so. He wanted time to decide how he was going to approach Walsingham again. Kit had agreed to keep it a secret, even if the idea of keeping things from Walsingham sat uneasily in her breast. It seemed she was keeping more and more secrets from a man she thought she trusted.

"There is one thing I need to say," Kit said, clearing her throat. "When I left London, I was followed. Someone knew I was to leave, and this someone told Lord Ruskin. We three were the only ones in our meeting."

The queen turned an amused smile on Walsingham. "I think your intelligencer is accusing you of betrayal, Walsingham. How interesting."

"Kit!" Walsingham snapped.

"That is not what I am saying." A burning fear sat deep within her stomach. She knew someone on the queen's privy council was a betrayer and was loyal to Mary Stuart. Lady Ruskin had told Kit as much before she had died, and the assassin she had caught in Northumberland had known the spy's codename: the Rose. "Did you tell anyone, Walsingham, of where I was going? Or when I was to leave?"

"No." Yet even as Walsingham uttered the words, he looked away from her.

"Then the only other thing I can conclude is that someone was listening here in these gardens." Kit's words made the queen and Walsingham look at each other.

"What wonderful news you bring to my door, Miss Scarlett," the queen replied wryly. "Someone I think of as a friend, enough for them to be welcome in my grounds, is loyal to my cousin. Is that what you are saying?"

"It is a possibility only. For the moment, the one thing I can tell you with certainty is that your cousin rejected your offer of a new friendship. She knows what she wants, Your Majesty. She believes in her right to rule, and she intends to make that happen."

Queen Elizabeth stepped back. She lifted a gloved hand that shook a little and rubbed one of her eyes before she turned away. Once more, Kit was reminded of a child. Rarely had she seen the queen so scared that the image of the ruler, bedecked like a jewelled statue, would crack to reveal the person beneath.

"She intends to make it happen through any means necessary, does she not? Even my death?" The queen reached out. Walsingham took her hand and patted it, an attempt at comfort. "Walsingham, tell me, my friend. You have never shied away from ill news, and this is some of the gravest I have heard. No one wishes to hear their cousin will see them dead, but it seems I must accept the threat against me. You are my advisor, so I insist you advise me now. What do we do?"

Walsingham looked between Kit and the queen, breathing deeply, before he patted the queen's hand again. "As you know, I will always be honest with you." His voice was gravelly and deep. "The path ahead will not be an easy one now that Mary Stuart has made her intentions plain. Therefore, to protect your kingdom, we must be prepared for death."

"Whose death, Walsingham?" the queen asked.

"Any man's death." Walsingham looked at Kit, his fear palpable. She could see it in the way he looked at the wounds on her face and her bandaged hands. "Most particularly, we must accept that to see you safe, Your Majesty, the threat against you may have to die. Mary Stuart may have to die."

The queen reeled, tottering backward. The reaction was but momentary before she managed to still herself. She said nothing yet froze like the snowy marble statues that could be spied around Richmond Palace Garden.

Kit's own mouth had turned dry. She had witnessed too much death to think of another's easily, even a woman's such as Mary Stuart. She briefly thought of the captain of the guards' face and his eyes that had stared up at the clouds above him, not blinking or twitching again. The mere memory had her bandaged hands resting on the belt that gathered her cloak around her waist.

"We shall see what has to be done, Walsingham," the queen said eventually. "We shall see."

There was something in the queen's reaction that didn't convince Kit the woman wanted to see her cousin dead.

Kit strode toward the house in the street. Her meeting with Walsingham and the queen had left her restless and picking at the bandages around her hands, fraying the linen. By the door, she heard sounds spilling from inside.

Where Iomhar's house had once been silent and empty, except for hers and Elspeth's light footsteps, a cacophony of noise now fell from the windows. Kit glanced up to the window above, certain she could hear Abigail and Rhona arguing between them, perhaps fighting over who would have the finer bedchamber.

Kit had to knock more than once to be heard above the sound. Eventually, the door opened. Rather than Elspeth being the one to greet her, as the cook so often had, there was the face she had prayed would be there for the last year.

Iomhar looked less tired now, but he clearly had still not had enough sleep, for there were shadows under his eyes. He'd been in his chamber sleeping that morning when Kit had left to see the queen. He smiled instantly when he saw her and beckoned her inside away from the falling snow.

"You need more sleep." She nodded at his face as she stepped past him.

"As do ye." He closed the door behind her then reached for her bandaged hands. She tried to pull them away when he held up one of her wrists. "Ye're supposed to keep these on, Kit."

"They're sort of on."

He set about fixing the bandages as Kit looked toward the staircase.

"What happened?" Iomhar asked eventually.

"I'm not entirely sure." Kit chewed her lip and lowered her voice. Glancing over her shoulder, she checked no one else in the family was around before she shared her thoughts. "The queen is frightened; I know that much."

"And Walsingham? What does he think?"

The last words the spymaster had said had left Kit with a resounding chill that had little to do with the snow beyond the windows.

"He talked of how the time may come to see Mary Stuart die. He spoke of her death, as if he yearned for it, with hunger." Her words had Iomhar pausing with the bandages, his expression stilling.

"Is that what ye think he will go after now? A warrant for her death?"

"I do not know, but if that is what he wants, I do not imagine her friend Lord Ruskin will stand back and let it happen." She took her hands away from Iomhar as footsteps could be heard on the stairs. His family were about to disturb them.

"Something tells me we may see Lord Ruskin again. Aye, very soon indeed."

A NOTE TO THE READER

Dear Reader,

Thank you to all those readers out there who have been following Kit's tales. Since the publication of *The Gentlewoman Spy*, the support from readers has been wonderful, and I'm thrilled so many of you are enjoying reading Kit's adventures, as much as I'm enjoying writing them.

Reviews by readers these days are integral to a book's success, so if you enjoyed Kit's tale I would be very grateful if you could spare a minute to post a review on **Amazon** and **Goodreads**. I love hearing from readers, and you can talk with me through **my website** or **on Twitter** and follow my author page **on Facebook**.

I hope we'll meet again on Kit's next adventure.

Adele Jordan

Sapere Books is an exciting new publisher of brilliant fiction and popular history.

To find out more about our latest releases and our monthly bargain books visit our website:
saperebooks.com